THE VILLA

THE VILLA

M. Warnasuriya

Library of Congress Control Number:		2019921246
ISBN:	Hardcover	978-1-7960-8063-6
	Softcover	978-1-7960-8064-3
	eBook	978-1-7960-8087-2

To order additional copies of this book, contact:
Xlibris
1-888-795-4274
www.Xlibris.com
Orders@Xlibris.com
806893

For my grandparents, Dorothy and Leo Bertrand Fernando.
May your good works be a light to those who follow.

PREFACE

I don't know what to make of all that is detailed in this account of *The Villa* and the events that occurred after a very nice couple bought the place and moved into the property. Enthralled by its outward beauty, the couple stepped into the villa, not knowing what was in store for them, within and without its walls, a horrid past that had never been put to rest. Despite unexplainable and tragic circumstances, they insisted on remaining there in the hopes of making the best of things. Sometimes when the best was not what occurred in the past, it may come to haunt those who believe that they could change it. How is it that generations of people who have died still influence those who are living today? The legacies (good or bad) left behind impact the present and the future. Knowing this, it is imperative that one carefully chooses what examples he or she imitates or passes down to generations that follow, for our actions can affect those around us like the ripple effects of a pebble that is cast into the water. Hopefully, the ripple effects that we create during our lives are for the betterment of others and not as horrific as what the couple in this book had to endure during their very short stay. So brace yourself.

1

"Wake up, Jason! It's morning already!" exclaimed Susan as she nudged her still slumbering husband in excitement.

"Okay, okay," he cried, attempting to hide his head under the pillow.

"The movers will be here in an hour," she said, getting up and rushing into the bathroom. "I know, Susan, you've been telling me since last night," he uttered as he yawned and peered out through the window. It was a bright and sunny summer morning. They were moving into their dream home in the mountains that overlook the beach. "I guess you're going to have to wake up too, Penny," he said, looking at the gray cat who was comfortably sleeping on the bed and purring by his feet.

"Isn't it beautiful?" asked Susan while brushing her teeth. "I can't wait to move our things there and begin settling in."

"You know that's not going to happen overnight, right? I mean that place is humongous! Ten rooms," he said, getting up from the bed and opening the window.

"And they're all furnished," remarked Susan as she spat the toothpaste into the sink.

"I know, I know. Don't remind me. I paid the bill. The house and the furniture cost me a fortune!" said Jason while entering the bathroom.

"Well, I hope you're not regretting buying me my dream home," she said, caressing his head.

"No, dear, of course not," he assured her as he squeezed toothpaste onto his toothbrush.

"Okay, just making sure. It's better than this crummy apartment we've been living in for the past two years. I can't believe it! Just think. In a few hours, we will be in our new home." She walked out of the bathroom and began dancing around the room.

Jason looked at his wife and smiled. "If you're happy, I'm happy, dear."

"I am happy," she agreed. "You can be assured that I'm very, very happy."

A moment later, Susan was rummaging through one of the cardboard boxes labeled "Clothes," in search of a shirt and a pair of pants to wear for the day. She found something suitable and got into it. As Jason walked out, he saw his wife putting on her makeup.

"How do I look for move-in day?" she asked gazing at him through the mirror.

"Fine, dear," he responded. "Now where did you put my clothes? This place is full of boxes. I can't find anything."

"In that one right there," she replied, pointing to the box that was adjacent to hers. The room had cardboard boxes scattered all over. She had labeled them to designate the contents. Susan was very organized and paid meticulous attention to detail. She had been planning this move ever since they had bought the villa a few months ago.

Susan and her husband Jason had been married for almost two years. He was a very successful cardiologist in the local hospital and was well on the way to developing his practice. She was a homemaker and had dreams of becoming a writer.

Her mother was an accomplished author, and Susan desired to follow in her footsteps. They had been trying to have a family but had been unsuccessful up to now. Jason believed that his wife needed a change from the small apartment in the city and the cooped-up life. The hustle and bustle which included the late-night sirens from fire brigades, sounds of cars, and trains were stressing her out. Therefore, he purchased the villa in the mountains to help his wife relax and begin to enjoy the start of what she hoped to be a successful writing career and a wonderful family life. Undoubtedly Susan was thrilled when he surprised her with the news of the move. She instantly fell in love with the villa on her first visit—its extravagant interior, the furniture, the huge yard, the surrounding property, and most of all, the ocean that overlooked it. Jason could see that Susan was elated and looked forward to their new life in the beautiful new home.

"What do you think?" he asked as he pulled out a pair of shorts and a plain white T-shirt from the box.

"For our first day? Isn't it a little too casual, honey?" she retorted with a slight grin on her face.

"Well, it's summer and we're moving, so I want to be comfortable. I'm going to sweat in them anyway," he argued.

"Fine," she conceded. "I don't want to go back and forth on this. You look great no matter what you wear."

"Well, thank you," he said, feeling a bit flattered. Jason was, in fact, the tall, dark, and handsome type. He had hazel eyes. This was the first trait that Susan found attractive about her husband. His kind mannerism and caring personality were bonuses. Susan was a brunette with short hair and dark eyes who didn't pay much attention to looks. She, however, was desirable in her unique way. Jason had found her regard for detail and perfectionism to be quite appealing. Through the challenges she had faced as a child—losing her father at a young age and having to sacrifice her college education to work to support her mother who had been ill at the time—Susan had emerged to become a strong woman who knew exactly what she wanted in life. One of her dreams was to go back to school and earn her college degree, which Jason wholeheartedly supported. Susan enjoyed writing as well because this allowed her to be in control of the world that she created through her stories.

A few moments later, they heard a knock on the front door.

"It's them!" she gasped in excitement as she headed toward the door.

"Relax, honey," insisted Jason trailing behind her. "We haven't even had coffee or breakfast yet."

"Okay. You make breakfast, and I'll deal with the movers," she ordered, opening the front door. "Be sure to put some cat food in Penny's bowl."

Penny ambled behind Jason and jumped onto the kitchen counter. Two heavily built men dressed in blue jumpsuits were standing outside.

"Good morning, ma'am," said one of them. "Are you Susan Smith?"

"Yes, I am."

"We're from the moving company. Do you have the address of the place to transport your things?" asked the man.

"Yes, certainly," replied Susan as she hastily walked toward the purse she had kept on the sofa. Pulling out a piece of paper, she went up to the man and handed it to him.

"Thank you, ma'am," the man replied.

Jason was standing by the dining room table, watching everything. He acknowledged both men with a slight wave of his hand.

"Okay, then let's get started," uttered the man. With that, the two men stepped inside the house and looked around.

"As you can see, everything is packed in boxes," explained Susan, pointing to the different sized cardboard boxes that were piled up all over.

"Move all the boxes first, and then the furniture, I guess," she said, "or however you want to do it."

"I guess we could go with that," concurred the man.

Both men hastily began picking up boxes and loading them into the large van parked out on the front yard of the apartment. Jason was making coffee and toast in the kitchen, as Susan came behind him and gave him a joyful embrace.

"Oh, I can't wait!" she exclaimed. Jason glanced at her with a smile. "Just finish making breakfast so I can pack those in," she said, referring to the toaster and remaining mugs and plates. She kissed him, walked back to the living room, and began observing the men. She had marked each box with its contents and whether they were fragile or not. The men followed these instructions because they were aware that Susan was paying close attention.

"Don't worry, honey. They know what they're doing," assured Jason. "Here, have your coffee," he said, handing her a mug.

"Did you feed Penny?" she asked, peering into the kitchen.

"Yes, she's happily eating over there." Penny was in the kitchen gobbling up her food.

About an hour elapsed. The movers had hauled all the boxes to the truck. "It's time for the furniture," said one of them coming in.

"Alright. So we have the sofa, the coffee table, the dining table, and the bedroom furniture," said Susan.

"That's it?" asked the man.

"Yep!"

"Okay. We'll start with the bedroom," he uttered, heading inside. Before long, the apartment was empty.

"I guess that's it, then," said Susan with one last glance. "Did we forget anything?"

"No, I don't think so," replied Jason, as he made a final round, carrying Penny in his hands.

"Did you put the toaster and the mugs in the box?" she asked, stepping into the kitchen again.

"Yes, honey," replied Jason. They just took it into the van.

"Okay, then, I guess, we're ready to go," she said with a flash of excitement.

2

Susan and Jason got into their car. Penny jumped into the back seat and settled herself comfortably on the leather surface. The movers had already left a few minutes ago.

"It's better that they went before us," remarked Jason as he buckled up his seat belt. "It'll make it a more relaxing drive for us." Susan was beaming with excitement. "Boy, if I would've known you'd be this excited, I would've bought that place sooner," he said, gazing at her.

"Are you sure we didn't forget anything?" she asked.

"Yes, I'm sure."

"Did you turn in the keys to the manager?" she asked, peering at the apartment manager's office, which was right across them.

"Yes, last night. He said he'll miss us."

"That's nice," commented Susan. "I'll miss him too. He's a good man."

Jason pulled out of the driveway onto the street. Even though it was a Saturday, the traffic was relentless.

"I'm sure glad I'm not going to be in this traffic mess ever again," she remarked with an expression of relief. "Where are all these people going on a Saturday? Don't they have families to be with?" she questioned in indignation.

"Maybe that's where they're going," replied Jason. A few minutes later, he merged onto the highway.

"Do you see the moving truck?" she asked, surveying the surroundings.

"No, I think they eluded the traffic."

The morning was warm and sunny. People were already out on the streets and in shops. The warm air that came through the open car window rubbed on Susan's face, which she enjoyed.

The villa was up in the mountains and was a bit far from the city. As they continued on the drive, the traffic gradually subsided and the mountainous terrain came into view.

"I love this area," she remarked, gazing at the mountains.

"I know. So do I," agreed Jason. The road became narrower and gave way to a single lane.

"There's hardly any traffic around anymore," commented Susan. "Are we the only people going to the mountains?"

"No, the movers are behind us," responded Jason.

"What? You're kidding!" She immediately turned around and realized that her husband was right. The moving van was behind them. "How in the world did that happen?"

"They probably got stuck in traffic back there," replied Jason while peering through the rearview mirror.

A couple of hours later, the ocean appeared in front of them. The water glistened as it reflected the sunlight. It was as if millions of crystals were floating on the surface.

"Oh, how beautiful!" gasped Susan. "I can't believe we'll be living here."

Jason glanced at her and smiled. "As I said, if you're happy, I'm happy, honey."

Jason made a few turns here and there and, finally, ended up on a narrow road headed toward the mountains. As he continued to drive up, tall trees and bushes appeared on either side. The surroundings were quiet and tranquil. From the corner of her eye, Susan could see the moving truck trailing behind them. A few minutes later, they arrived at a very tall black gate and Jason stopped the car.

"Give me the keys," he said.

Susan immediately opened her purse and took out a rather large set of keys and handed it to him. They were for the new house. Jason approached the gate and unlocked it. As he opened it, the gate creaked loudly. Going back to the car, he handed Susan the keys and continued the drive up. The movers followed.

"The realtor said that there is a caretaker for this place," he said abruptly. "So he better close the gate."

"What? You never told me there was a caretaker," voiced Susan in surprise.

"Oops, I'm sorry, dear. I guess with all the hospital business and surgeries I had to handle, it must've slipped my mind. He's a combination of a caretaker and butler."

"Well, have you met him?" Susan was agitated.

"Yes I have. Apparently, he's been here for years."

"So he lives in the house?" she asked, glaring at him.

"Honey, relax. He's just a harmless old man, and yes, he lives there but purely for our help."

"Well, I don't want anyone in our new home beside us, and I never asked for help," she snapped.

"Don't worry about this now. We'll deal with it later, okay?"

As they continued the drive, the villa and the mountains that surrounded it gradually came into view. The villa itself was a sight to behold. It was a brown brick building with the appearance of a four-story mini castle. A majestic door and tall windows could be seen on the first floor. The second and third floors had several windows each. On the fourth floor was what seemed to be a tower with a colorful circular stained glass window. An elegant water fountain stood across from the front entrance. A cherub was at its center spouting out water from the top. The old brick driveway went around this fountain. A neatly mowed lawn with bright green grass encircled the driveway. Rose bushes were planted in front and by the windows. These seem to continue onto the backyard as well. Jason parked the car at the front entrance and stood still for a moment to marvel at the view.

"This takes my breath away!" gasped Susan as a surge of exhilaration welled up inside her.

"See, that's why we need the caretaker," uttered Jason. "Look how nicely he's maintaining the garden."

"Oh, it's so lovely!" declared Susan while getting out of the car. Penny sprang out from the back seat and began exploring the yard. "I guess you're right. But the discussion is tabled for later."

The moving truck parked behind them. The two men got out and took in the view. "This is some place, Mrs. Smith!"

"Thank you," she said, acknowledging the compliment. "I'll open the door for you. Just put the boxes in the main living room for now. Our furniture can go in the garage. The house comes with furniture."

She unlocked the front door. The two men began unloading. They started to move everything into the house, a short while later. In the meantime, Jason and Susan took a stroll in the garden. As they headed toward the back, the ocean appeared. Few boats were floating on the distant waters. The cool breeze was soothing and the skies were clear. It was silent all around except for the billowing of the occasional surging waves. They walked to the edge of the yard. In addition to the ocean, the surrounding city could be seen for miles out. Beachgoers were already out enjoying the sand and the waves. "This view is spectacular!" voiced Susan in wonder.

"Yes, it's perfect!" added Jason. Several tall trees bordered the backyard, and their leaves rustled against the wind. One, however, stood right at the center. An old swing hung down from one of its branches and it also swayed in response to the wind. "Thank you, darling," she said looking at her husband. He placed his arms around her and embraced her. "This is all for you," he said giving her a passionate kiss.

3

Susan couldn't get enough of the backyard scenery. The ocean enchanted her. "I never want to leave here," she exclaimed, inhaling the fresh crisp air.

"Well, we're going to have to, or the movers will think we've disappeared," said Jason.

"Yeah, I guess. The only thing missing around here is some fancy outdoor furniture. We have a lot of friends to entertain, remember? And I want Mom to come and visit us right away."

"Already?" sighed Jason.

"Yes, already! Now don't complain about it. You know Mom adores you, her handsome surgeon son-in-law." They both began heading toward the front.

"Sure," retorted Jason with a bit of sarcasm.

"She'll be so happy to see that you're taking such good care of me. And I'll bet you, she'll be more impressed when she sees this house. Where's Penny by the way?" she asked, scanning the premises.

"She's probably out, trying to catch a little bird, somewhere. Don't worry, she knows her way into the house," assured Jason.

The movers were still getting the boxes hauled in when Susan and Jason entered the house. The entry room was as beautiful as ever. A lovely vase of red roses stood on the round wooden table that was at the center.

"These were picked especially for you," said Jason.

"What?" She beamed with joy. "But how? You said you weren't coming here until moving day."

"It was a surprise I had planned with the realtor. He took care of it for me."

Susan pounced on him in an ecstatic embrace. "Thank you!" she cried in joy. She walked toward the vase and began inhaling the scent of the roses. "This is the best day of my life!"

The movers approached them. "We're almost done, ma'am," said one.

"Wonderful!" responded Susan while walking into the living room.

Everything had the luster of elegance and good taste. The dark wood floors were polished to a shine. A red rug was at the center of the room and four sofas stood on it. A coffee table was in the midst of them. The furnishings were of fine mahogany and had a vintage appearance. The rustic color of the walls complimented them, and the walls themselves were adorned with framed paintings of sceneries and flowers. The windows had burgundy curtains, which in turn enhanced the room's opulence. A humungous crystal chandelier hung from the painted ceiling. It shimmered as Susan drew the curtains open from the sides.

"This must look spectacular at night! "Is this all mine?" she asked marveling.

"Yes, according to the bill I paid. I think so," assured Jason. "Honey, you saw the place a while ago. Why are you acting so surprised?"

"That was a few months ago. I had forgotten. I still can't believe you could afford all this!"

"Well, all my savings and earnings so far have been invested here. Maybe we can sell the place in a couple of years and double the profit," he suggested.

"Okay, slow down, turbo. We can talk about selling later," she said, surveying everything around her in admiration.

The movers had neatly piled up the cardboard boxes in one corner of the room. As Susan turned around, she saw the two men bringing in their old sofa. "Where should we put this?"

"All our furniture needs to go in the garage," she replied.

"Yes, ma'am," said the man and moved the sofa back out with his partner.

As the afternoon drew near, the movers finished their job. Jason paid them for the day and added a handsome tip besides, which made the men quite happy.

"That's it," he uttered, approaching her. "Now comes the hard part."

"What?"

"Getting acquainted with this place. It'll take days," he said, heading inside.

A few steps separated the living room from the open space next to it. There was a circular red carpet in this space. Two staircases stood on either side of this area and led to the second floor. These stairs continued to the third and fourth floors and were covered with vintage red carpet. They walked into the dining room. It was just as extravagant as the living room. A long wooden table stood at the center. It was adorned with a beautiful red table cloth with embroidery on the edges. Twelve red cushioned chairs were neatly tucked in around the table. A large flower vase was placed at the center. Another crystal chandelier loomed over this vase, not secondary in extravagance to the one in the living room. A giant china cabinet was in the corner. Susan walked up to it to examine all her new chinaware. Teacups, plates, wine glasses, and other items were neatly showcased inside.

"Mom would love these," remarked Susan, looking through the glass.

The study was to the right of the dining room and the den was to the left. "We can check those out later," said Jason. "I'm hungry. Let's see what's cooking."

The kitchen was straight ahead and was a sight to behold as well. Entering in, they saw another small dining table on the side with six chairs around it. A fruit bowl was placed at the center. The walls were a crème color, which enhanced the room's appearance. An island stood at the center of the kitchen with marble counters and wall cupboards surrounding it on one side. The floors were of hardwood and were polished to a shine. Jason approached the fridge and opened it in search of something to eat. Susan grabbed one of the apples from the fruit bowl and took a bite.

"Great!" he blurted.

"What?" she asked, turning around.

"Shepherd's pie!" He took a bite out of it with a fork from the nearby drawer.

"Who made it?" she asked, going toward him. "It smells good!"

"Probably the caretaker," he responded. "Here, have a piece. It's tasty."

"Are you sure it's for us?"

"Well, the last I checked, this is our house, and therefore, whatever is in the fridge belongs to us too."

"Okay. If you say so," she responded accepting a piece. "Yum! It is good."

Susan opened the fridge and peered inside. She grabbed a can of milk, took a glass from one of the wall cabinets, and poured some. Putting the can back in the fridge, she walked into the room straight ahead with the glass in hand. It was another big pantry area except this one was for storage. Baskets of fruits, vegetables, and gallons of water stood on the sides. Straight ahead was a humongous glass door that faced the backyard. She could see the trees and green grass through the square glass panels. The ocean was visible from the side. The swing, which was swaying back and forth, could be seen straight ahead. Susan unlatched the door and opened it. A draft of cold air immediately rushed inside.

"This fresh air is so wonderful," she uttered to herself.

"Come on, honey!" urged Jason. "Finish the pie. It's too big for me."

She turned around and approached him when they suddenly heard a noise from upstairs. "What was that?" asked Susan in alarm. At that moment, Penny came into the kitchen from the back door.

"There you are," cried Susan.

"I don't know, but it sounded like a door being slammed up there," replied Jason, walking up to the base of the staircase and peering up.

"Is anyone else here besides us?" asked Susan, trailing him.

"No, I don't think so," he replied and began climbing up the steps. "Oh, maybe it's the caretaker."

"Wait! Don't go by yourself."

"Why not?" asked Jason, turning around. He was still licking the pie off the fork.

"What if someone's up there?"

"Well, if someone is, I sure want to know who's in my house," demanded Jason. "Come with me," he urged her.

At that very moment, an old man walked up to the base of the staircase and took them by surprise.

4

Susan was startled. Jason immediately climbed back down and approached him.

"Are you the caretaker?" he asked bluntly.

"Yes. Pardon me if I alarmed you. My name is Norton," he replied in a coarse and cryptic voice.

Susan scrutinized the man from head to toe. He was quite tall and dressed in a black suit. From the looks of it, he seemed to be in his sixties or seventies and had gray hair. His face was wrinkled, yet his dark eyes were sharp and compelling.

"You are the new owners, I assume," he rasped, offering his hand to Jason.

"Yes. I'm Dr. Jason Smith and this is my wife, Susan."

"You must be wanting to check out the premises," uttered Norton. "Would you like me to show you around?"

Susan turned to her husband for affirmation. "Well, we're not done with lunch yet. We heard a noise upstairs and were on our way to check it out. From which direction did you come in, Norton?" asked Jason.

"Well, sir, I came from the back door just a moment ago. I went shopping for some groceries for dinner," he replied. "What is that thing?" he inquired in a disturbed tone of voice.

Jason and Susan turned around to see Penny walking up to them. She began rubbing herself on Susan's leg.

"Oh, this is just our cat, Penny," said Susan, picking her up. "Don't worry. She won't bite."

"I see," uttered Norton, eerily glancing at the cat. "I'm not much of a pet lover, madam."

"Don't worry. Penny is not a pet. She's more like family," said Susan, rubbing Penny on the side.

"Back to the subject at hand," interjected Jason. "Is anyone else in the house beside us?"

"No, sir, and don't be distressed. You see, sometimes, I keep the windows open in the rooms up there to let fresh air in. It helps the circulation in a big house like this. The wind probably closed one of the windows," he said.

"That makes sense," concurred Susan.

"I see you're enjoying the shepherd's pie I made this morning," he said pleasantly.

"Oh, yes, thank you. It's delicious," commented Susan.

"Do you live here too, Norton?" asked Jason.

"Yes, of course, sir," he replied. "My family has lived in this villa for two generations."

"Oh, really?" asked Susan.

"You see, Mrs. Smith, my grandfather was the first caretaker to the family that lived here. My father assumed duties afterward. And when he died years ago, I took on the responsibility to care for the place. The previous owner made sure that we were well provided for. I've lived in this villa for most of my life. It's my home and will be until the day I die," he asserted.

Susan listened to him intently.

"I see," responded Jason, chewing the last bit of his shepherd's pie. "What happened to the family that your grandfather worked for?"

"The original family members have died. They had one son who also died at a young age. It was quite unfortunate."

"Really?" asked Susan. "How did he die?"

"He was quite ill for a while. There was nothing that those medicine men could do for him," he observed somberly.

"That's awful!" cried Susan sympathetically.

"They're still here though," sighed Norton, pondering.

"What do you mean?" asked Jason.

"Oh, nothing," replied Norton, as if suddenly nudged from a deep slumber. "What I meant to say is they're still in my heart. They'll never leave."

"Oh, okay," said Jason, glancing at his wife. "Well, I deeply sympathize with your loss."

"Thank you, sir. I see you have your boxes piled up. Would you like me to help you get settled in?" he asked, peering into the living room.

"No, Norton, thank you. I think my wife and I can manage with the boxes. We just came in and would like to relax a bit and enjoy the place before unpacking."

"Of course. How about a tour then?" asked Norton.

"What do you think, dear?" inquired Jason, gazing at his wife.

"That would be lovely," Susan conceded.

"So I assume you're familiar with the ground floor?"

"Yes, we are," replied Susan.

"Let's walk up then." Susan and Jason accompanied him. "As I'm sure you already know, the second and third floors have five bedrooms each. The fourth is what I sort of call an attic. There's nothing much in it but old furniture and things. I rarely go up there because it's so musty and filled with dust. I cannot clean because my bad back won't allow it."

"Oh, we understand," said Susan. "We can get it cleaned up later."

When they came to the second floor, Susan put Penny on the ground. The cat immediately dashed downstairs. Rooms were on either side, three on one side and two on the other. Susan went into them and looked out through the windows. The front yard was visible in the rooms that were on the left and the backyard could be seen through the windows in the rooms on the opposite side. The staircase continued to extend upward on either end.

"As you can see every room is furnished. The master bedroom is right in here," he said, walking into it.

"I know. I've seen it before when the realtor brought us over," interjected Susan.

Norton led them inside. Susan had forgotten how fabulous the room was, as her first visit to the villa was approximately two months ago when Jason had barely met the realtor. The room had brightly painted walls. A king-sized bed stood at the center. It was made of mahogany with four carved poles on each corner. A red bedspread was neatly laid on it. The sheets and pillowcases complemented the spread with their shade of lighter red. White curtains hung from the two enormous windows that were on either side of the bed. Hardwood floors were polished to a shine.

"Norton, I was curious as to who does the cleaning here," Jason inquired, inspecting the floors. "Not a spot of dirt!"

"Well, I do it myself, sir," he answered.

"Now that we own the villa, would you like us to get someone to help you with the cleaning?"

"Absolutely not, sir!" voiced Norton sternly, as if taking offense at the comment.

"I didn't mean to offend you in any way, Norton. It's just that I wanted to make your life a bit easier."

"No offense is taken, sir. Thank you for the kind offer, but I can take care of things here myself. I have been for the past sixty years," he added.

"No worries then," interjected Susan.

"Let's continue, shall we?" said Norton. "Each room in this villa has a bed. If you want the furniture moved, please let me know. I will make those arrangements for you. As you can see, only the larger rooms have their baths," he said, entering into some of the bigger rooms. "It is the same pattern in the five rooms upstairs as well."

"Where's your room?" asked Susan.

"I live in the master bedroom on the third floor," he replied, pointing upstairs. "My father and grandfather also lived in that room. If you'd like me to move elsewhere, I would be more than happy to do so."

"We insist that you remain there, right, dear?" Jason uttered, looking at Susan.

"Yes, Norton. Since you'll be living with us, we want you to be comfortable and think that this is just as much your home as it is ours," insisted Susan.

"Thank you, madam. Let's go to the third floor then."

Norton headed back to the stairway at the end of the hall. The third-floor rooms looked similar to the ones below. The master bedroom was on the same location as the one beneath, yet this one was closed.

"I like my privacy," remarked Norton. "I hope you don't mind. But I could show you my room if you'd like."

"It's alright, Norton. We trust you," assured Susan.

Jason, however, glanced at her with inquisitive eyes. He walked into each room and inspected every corner. "Didn't you say that you left some of the windows open?" he blurted out, looking at Norton. "Well, none of the windows in these rooms or the ones downstairs are open."

Norton was lost for words for a moment. "Oh, sir, my deepest apologies. I must've mistaken then. You know, at my age, I tend to forget things now and then. Just the minor details though," he said apologetically.

"Well, if the windows weren't open, what was that noise we heard a while ago?" continued Jason.

"I wouldn't worry, sir. This is a very big house. The noise comes with the territory," he assured. "Now that you've seen everything, I'd like to get dinner started. I'm sure you have a bit of settling in to do."

"Wait! What about the fourth floor?" asked Susan.

"Oh, madam, it's very dusty up there. I wouldn't want to open the attic. The moment I breathe in the dust, I get an incessant cough. Perhaps another time," he suggested.

"Perhaps," said Jason. The staircase on their end reached up to the fourth floor. "We can check up there later, dear. There's all the time in the world for it."

Susan agreed and all three of them began coming down.

"Dinner will be served promptly at six in the evening in the dining room," said Norton.

"Thank you. We'll be on time," assured Susan.

Norton headed toward the kitchen. Jason and Susan went into the living room.

5

"That was interesting," whispered Susan to her husband. As they came into the living room, Penny was seated comfortably on one of the sofas. "Napping?" asked Susan, looking at the cat. She sat by her and rubbed the cat's head. "Hope Norton doesn't mind you."

"It's our house, Susan. Who cares if he minds or not?" retorted Jason, walking up to the boxes in the living room. "I don't know if I want to empty all these today. Let's just get the ones that have our clothes and take them upstairs," he suggested.

"Okay. You take yours and I'll take mine," suggested Susan, getting up and approaching him. She hung on his neck and kissed him. Jason reciprocated her affections. Then Susan began searching for a box with her clothes. "If I can find at least one, I'm good," she assured. "Got it!" she blurted out, locating one at the far corner of the mound of boxes. "Alright. I'm going up with this."

"Sure. Go ahead. When I find mine, I'll catch up to you."

Susan turned around and headed toward the staircase with the box in hand. She climbed up the steps and reached the second floor. Coming into the master bedroom, she placed the box on the bed. Then walking toward the window, she moved the white curtains aside and opened the shutter. The fresh cool breeze instantly swept across the room. Then she walked back toward the bed, opened the box, and dumped all her clothes out. The room had a massive wall closet. She opened it and peered inside. It was very spacious.

"Great! We both can use this."

Empty hangers hung from the metal bars. She took her clothes and began hanging them up one by one when suddenly she heard a loud bang from upstairs. Running toward the door, she called out to her husband.

"Jason, is that you?" She walked up to the base of the staircase and peered up to the third floor. "Jason, are you up there?" she asked again.

"Up where?" Susan immediately turned around to see Jason approaching her with the box in his hands.

"Wait. Were you upstairs just now?" she inquired, agitated.

"No, I just came from down. What's the matter?"

"Well, I heard a loud sound," she said. "Was it Penny?"

"No. Penny can't make loud noises, honey. She's a cat. We can't even hear her footsteps."

"Well, then what was it?" she asked, troubled.

"Let's go check it out," suggested Jason, placing the box on the floor. They immediately climbed up the stairs to the third floor and began inspecting the rooms one by one. "Nothing," said Jason.

"What about Norton's room?" asked Susan.

"We can't go in there, honey. It wouldn't be proper. Besides, the door is closed. I don't think anyone's in there. Didn't he say he was cooking?"

"Yes. What about the fourth floor then?" she asked.

"Might as well check it out," suggested Jason, going up the narrow stairs to the uppermost floor. "You know, I've never been here. The realtor didn't tell me about it during my first visit. I guess we both were preoccupied with paperwork."

"Well, you should've looked, dear. You've got to fully inspect the property before you sign documents to purchase it. That's the first rule of buying and selling real estate," pointed Susan.

"Thanks for the tip, dear," retorted Jason.

The fourth floor was quite dark and had a dingy odor. "Oh, we need to put windows up here," uttered Susan. "It needs ventilation."

Only a single large door could be seen at the center. This door was equidistant from both staircases. Jason edged toward it and turned the knob.

"Shucks! It's locked," he uttered in frustration. "Do you have the key?"

"No, the keys are downstairs, in my purse," replied Susan.

"Shall I just break it down?" asked Jason jovially.

"On our first day in the house?" cried Susan. "Tell you what. Since we're not in any imminent danger at the moment, let's get out of here."

"You do realize that we can break it down if we want to right?" asked Jason, jerking the lock in different directions.

"Relax, my high and mighty husband. We'll come back with the key later," she insisted, pulling him away.

<u>6</u>

Susan proceeded into the bedroom. Jason picked up the box he had laid on the ground earlier and followed her in. He placed the box on top of the bed and scrutinized the room. "Where am I supposed to put my stuff?"

"Right here," answered Susan, walking up to the wall closet. "My clothes go on this side, and yours on the other," she said, pointing to the section she wanted her husband to hang his clothes in.

"Great!" he exclaimed and began emptying the box. "I see you made a mess on the bed," he commented, looking at all the clothes that were scattered.

"Well, as I said, I was going to put things away, until I heard that damn noise," she exclaimed irritated.

"No need to get hot-blooded now. Let's just finish what we started."

"Fine," snapped Susan as she continued to hang her clothes.

They finally finished putting everything away. Susan stepped back and admired both sections of the closet. "Nicely done!" She went up to the vanity table and began opening the drawers. Many of them were empty. One, however, had a silver hairbrush and a framed silver mirror. She examined them. The name "Eleanor" was carved gracefully at the back of each.

"Who is Eleanor?" she asked, waving the brush.

"I don't know," replied Jason, turning around.

"Well, what do I do with them?" she asked, showing him the brush and mirror.

"Throw them away," replied Jason.

"What if they're heirlooms? Maybe they were of some value to this Eleanor person."

"Then keep them," said Jason nonchalantly.

"I'll think about it." Susan put the brush and mirror inside one of the bottom drawers. "I have to bring my makeup case and combs to put in here."

"Do it later. Let's just rest a bit," he said, jumping onto the bed. "Wow, this is comfortable! Want to try it?" he asked, looking at Susan eagerly.

"Sure, why not?" Susan jumped onto the bed beside him. "Oh, I love how the mattress feels." She fixed her eyes upon her husband, embraced him, and kissed him. "I love this place, honey!"

"I'm glad. For a minute, I was thinking of moving back to our old apartment," he snapped jovially.

"Not a chance, mister!" retaliated Susan.

They both lay on the bed and gazed at the ceiling. A chandelier with elegant dangling crystals loomed over them.

"Where did all this stuff come from? I mean who bought these?" she asked in amazement.

"Probably the people Norton worked for."

"They must've been rich. Look how luxurious all this stuff is. There's so much history attached to these things. If they had eyes and ears, imagine the stories they could tell. Maybe I should write a book about that."

"I'd rather not know what they have to say," said Jason, yawning. "Sometimes things in the past are best kept where they belong, in the past."

"I guess. But I was wondering who will become the caretaker after Norton dies? He didn't mention having any children of his own," said Susan.

"He didn't. Want me to ask him about that?"

"No. Maybe once we get to know him better," replied Susan. Jason turned toward her and began showing affection. "Is he going to be doing the grocery shopping?" she asked.

"Yep. I just need to give him the money and make a household budget for all the expenses around here," replied Jason as he began kissing his wife on the neck.

"I can take care of that. He also needs to know what you and I like to eat and how we want the meals cooked," suggested Susan.

"Tell him. I can't think of anyone else who could make such important decisions for us than you, dear," he said, smiling and clutching her close.

"Speaking of food, let me go down and see if he needs any help with dinner," she suggested, endeavoring to get up. Jason, however, pulled her back to him.

"Oh, leave him alone, honey. He can manage. Besides, I need you here more than he does," he uttered with desire in his eyes.

"Oh, stop. You're making me blush! We have all the time in the world here. Besides, I'm too excited to just stay in bed today. Penny needs to be fed too. She's probably hungry."

"Alright then. Have fun with your cat," retorted Jason, turning around and covering himself with the bedspread. A few moments later, Susan could hear him snore.

"My snoring knight in shining armor," she uttered to herself as she walked out of the room.

The house was calm and quiet. Entering the living room, she sat on the sofa. Her purse was on the opposite side. "There it is." Leaning back on the sofa, she took a deep breath. Gazing at the exquisite room filled her with a surge of excitement. She still couldn't believe that Jason had bought her this beautiful dream home.

A few moments later, she headed toward the kitchen. Norton was hurriedly moving back and forth, incessantly opening and closing the kitchen cupboards. Susan stopped to glance at him. Norton, however, was too preoccupied to notice her. He seemed to be mumbling to himself in anger.

"What, what, what. . ." she could hear him say. "I didn't tell them to come here. Honest. What do we do?" he continued. He seemed to be getting more agitated. Susan felt a bit awkward. Suddenly, she noticed Penny coming in from the pantry area at the back.

"Penny!" she cried. Norton immediately turned around. Susan walked up to the cat and picked her up. "You must be hungry," she said caressing her gently.

"Here, let me get you some food. Oh, hello Norton."

"Hello, madam. Do you have food for the cat?" he asked bluntly.

"Yes, I do. They're all packed up in one of the boxes in the front. I wanted to know if you need my help here with dinner?"

"No, madam. I have things under control," he rasped. "We will be having steak, potatoes, and vegetables tonight. Is that agreeable to you?"

"Yes, it sounds delicious," replied Susan. "Where are the bowls? I need one for Penny."

"Right here, madam," he said, walking toward one of the wall cabinets. He opened it, took a white ceramic bowl, and handed it to her.

"Thank you," she uttered and placed the bowl on the counter.

Putting Penny beside the bowl, she scampered to the living room to get a can of cat food. Norton looked at Penny with disdain. A few minutes later, Susan came back.

"Here you are," she said emptying the can into the bowl. Penny instantly began gulping all of it.

"I love this kitchen," commented Susan.

"Yes, I agree," responded Norton. "It's centuries old. There was only one owner."

"Really!" remarked Susan. "Too bad he had no heirs."

"As I said before, his heir died," replied Norton bluntly as he headed toward the stove.

He had two pots on it and steam was seen coming out of them. Susan walked up to the stove and saw that potatoes were being boiled in one and fresh vegetables were being steamed in the other. "The steak is roasting in the oven, madam," uttered Norton.

"It smells good," remarked Susan. "What do you glaze it with?"

"A mixture of salt, pepper, butter, and herbs," he responded while stirring the potatoes.

"My method exactly," said Susan in a complementing tone.

"Would you like a cup of tea, madam?" he asked.

"That would be nice," replied Susan, petting Penny. "I'll make it, Norton. You've got your hands full."

"Of course," he said. "The coffee and tea are right here," he continued pointing to the ceramic canisters, which were kept on the far side of the counter beneath the wall cabinets.

Susan took a teacup, walked over to the canister, and put a tea bag in. She saw Norton placing the kettle on the stove.

"It'll just take a few minutes for the water to boil, madam."

"That's fine. I'll keep you company if you don't mind."

"So what kind of a doctor is your husband?" he rasped inquisitively.

"My husband is a very talented cardiologist," she replied airily. "He is one of the few good ones around. Now that we live here, he might have to consider moving to a closer hospital or just opening up his practice. He did family medicine too for some years."

"It's nice to have a doctor in the house. I need one from time to time for this aging body of mine," remarked Norton.

"I'm sure he can help you there," assured Susan.

A few minutes later, the water began to boil. Susan grasped the kettle and poured the hot water into her teacup. Placing the kettle back, she stirred the tea. Then she went to the table by the counter, pulled out a chair, sat, and began sipping it.

"So, Norton, you said you've been living here since childhood, right?"

"Yes, madam," he replied.

"Do you have children of your own?" she asked bluntly.

"No, madam. I never had a wife."

"That must get lonely."

"Not really. This house keeps me busy."

"You must feel that we're encroaching on what has been your home all this time."

"Well, although I've lived here, madam, I don't own the place. Never had my own money to buy it," he stated, checking the meat in the oven.

"I want you to know that, even though we're living here now, you don't need to feel as if you're an outsider."

"Thank you for that, madam," he said gratefully. "I appreciate your kind words."

"Alright then. Since you seem to have dinner under control, I'll get back to my cardboard boxes out there. We have a lot to unpack."

Getting up, Susan approached the sink and washed the teacup. Taking the dishcloth that hung from the oven, she wiped the cup and placed it back inside the wall cupboard. Penny had already finished eating and had scurried out of the kitchen unnoticed. Susan took the cat's bowl and rinsed it as well and placed it on the ground by the counter.

"Remember, dinner will be ready at six sharp," he reminded her.

"Thank you, Norton. We'll be here," she said before walking out.

7

Susan came into the bedroom holding the box which contained all her makeup and other personal items and placed it on the bed. Jason was fast asleep. Now and then, he would toss and turn as if disturbed. Susan approached him and kissed him on the forehead. Then she went back to the box and began taking the contents out. She had a case filled with lipstick, blush, and other makeup items. Opening the center drawer of the vanity table, she neatly placed each item inside. Next, she took her hairbrush and comb and placed them in the adjacent drawer. Her hairdryer went in another. Once she had arranged everything, she gazed at herself in the mirror. She couldn't help but notice what an elegant piece of furniture the vanity table was. The mirror was encased inside a stunningly carved oval-shaped wooden frame. Carvings were exquisitely detailed. The drawers complemented these with their designs. As she was admiring them, she could see through the mirror that the chandelier on the ceiling was slightly swaying back and forth. Immediately turning around, she walked toward it. "What in the world?" Looking at the open window, she realized that the swaying wasn't caused by any breeze coming into the room, as the curtains remained perfectly still. Suddenly, she felt light-headed and tired. Sitting on the bed, she took a deep breath. A moment later, the chandelier stopped moving.

"Jason, wake up!" she gasped. He, however, was still snoring. "Ah, forget it," she uttered to herself. "Maybe my mind is playing tricks on me." Taking a deep breath, she lay down by her husband and dozed off a few moments later.

"Time for dinner, honey," came a voice from the side. Susan woke up from a deep slumber. "Boy, you must've been really tired there," uttered Jason, sitting on the bed beside her.

"What time is it?" she asked, rubbing her eyes.

"Almost six. Norton must be waiting for us. Come on," he urged.

Susan sprang out of bed, put her slippers on, and walked out of the room with her husband. The evening had set in. The house was a bit dark and still. As they came downstairs, they could see that the dining room chandelier was on and the table had been set. Norton was walking back and forth from the kitchen, bringing food up to the table. The steak was already laid out on a ceramic plate, and the aroma of the roast made their mouths water. Mashed potatoes and other vegetables were also served onto bowls. A bottle of wine and two wine glasses were kept on the side. A moment later, Norton brought a jug of water.

"This is lovely, Norton. Thank you," commented Susan, taking delight in what she saw.

"Would you like to have a seat, madam?" he asked, pulling out a chair for her.

"Yes." She sat gracefully. Jason was across her. "This is delicious!" she commented while taking a bite of the stake.

"Thank you, madam," said Norton, who stood beside her.

Jason opened the bottle of wine and poured some into both glasses. They toasted their new home.

"It's been in the cellar for many years," commented Norton. "I thought this was the perfect occasion to open it."

"Perfect indeed," concurred Jason.

"When do you eat, Norton?" asked Susan.

"I'll have dinner when you're done, madam," he replied.

"Can you kindly give something for Penny then?"

"Yes, madam. Where is the cat?"

"She should've been here already. Penny can smell food ten miles away," commented Susan, surveying the vicinity.

After dinner, Susan went into the kitchen in search of Penny. She kept calling her, but the cat was nowhere to be seen.

"She's here," cried Jason abruptly from the living room.

Susan headed back. At that very moment, Penny dashed toward her. "There you are. Where have you been?" she asked. "Did you get lost in our big house?"

"Let me take her, madam," offered Norton, coming from behind. "I'll give her some leftover steak."

"Perfect," said Susan, handing him the cat. Penny, however, jumped down from the man's hand and ran into the kitchen almost scraping him.

"Oh!" he cried in indignation.

"I'm sorry she did that," said Susan apologetically. "It takes time for her to get comfortable around strangers."

Norton, however, walked sulkily back into the kitchen.

It was dark outside. The moment Jason flipped the chandelier switch, the room dazzled.

"Wow! This place looks even better in the night!" he exclaimed. The two light poles in the front yard lit up automatically. "They're timed to turn on at seven in the evening," declared Jason.

"I can see that," commented Susan, glancing outside through the front windows. "This may sound strange, but do chandeliers move on their own?"

"What?" asked Jason as if he was perplexed.

"Well, that chandelier in our room moved," she said.

"Must be the wind, dear."

"There was no wind. The window curtains were still."

"Then there can be another perfectly logical explanation," he assured when his cell phone rang abruptly. "It's the hospital," he said, recognizing the number.

"Hello. . . Yes, this is Dr. Jason Smith. Okay, I will be there in an hour."

Susan looked at him with her eyes rolling. "You're kidding! You have to go tonight?"

"Yes, honey. I'm an on-call doctor, remember?" he said, heading upstairs.

"But it's our first night in our new home," she protested in disappointment.

"I know, but I have to do surgery in a couple of hours. They're prepping the patient," he said, going up the stairs. Susan followed her husband into the bedroom.

"Well, when will you be back?"

"I don't know. This particular surgery is about eight hours. And then I have to check up on him in recovery for a few hours, so probably tomorrow morning," he speculated, grabbing his coat and scrubs from the closet. He hurriedly changed as Susan sat on the bed watching him.

"I can't sleep alone in this room," she complained in a sulky tone.

"You're going to have to get used to it. Bring Penny. She'll keep you company till I come."

"I guess," she sighed. "Are you going to look for a job closer to home?"

"I don't know. I love the team I'm working with. They're one in a million. If it's the drive, I can handle it," assured Jason. "Okay, I've got to go." He kissed Susan and rushed down.

Susan trailed behind him. She opened the front door and walked him to the car. "I'm going to park in the garage when I come." He embraced Susan and gave her another kiss goodbye.

"I hope all goes well with your surgery," she said.

"Yeah, I do the best I can. It's a triple bypass. And this one is tough too. So many other health complications."

"I'll see you tomorrow then," she said, waving at him.

"See you, darling." He smiled and drove off.

The evening air was cool and comforting. The trees swayed slightly as the gentle breeze rocked them back and forth. The roses were in full bloom. She went up to a nearby bush and inhaled the scent of the red roses. Although it was dark, she decided to take a stroll. She went to the furthest edge of the front yard, turned around, and observed the villa. The house was a sight for sore eyes, and she marveled at it. The brick walls shimmered in response to the light emanating from the poles. She could faintly see the second-floor hallway light through the window. As she strolled toward the backyard, Penny suddenly jumped in front of her from a nearby bush.

"Oh! Penny! You scared me!" she cried picking up the cat. "Where have you been?" she asked rubbing her back. "Is your belly full? Did Norton feed you?" The cat purred and conveyed her satisfaction.

She came to the backyard. The sea breeze brought a slight chill to the air. "Isn't it nice here?" she asked, gazing at the cat. "Look at the ocean, Penny. Do you know what I want to do? I want to buy a boat and take a little trip out to the sea. I'll bet you this place looks fantastic from out there," she remarked. Penny kept on purring. "So you do agree." The cat looked up at her and let out a gentle cry.

"Want to sit on the swing?" she asked. "Okay. Let's go." Susan went up to the swing and sat down. Penny settled comfortably on her lap. The kitchen lights had been switched off. This was a sure sign that Norton had finished his duties and had retired for the evening. Susan looked up at the second and third floors. Her bedroom light was noticeable from the backyard. Norton's room faced the backyard as well as it was directly above their room. A lamplight could be seen through his window. She could faintly see the profile of someone walking up and down in the room. A moment later, he switched off the light and the room became dark.

"I don't know what to make of him, Penny. Do you?" she asked, gazing at the cat. Then looking up, she suddenly noticed someone move in the farthest room on the third floor. She was startled as that wasn't Norton's room. "Who was that?" she uttered in alarm. She instinctively got up and her heart began beating fast. "Is someone else in the house?"

It couldn't have been Norton because he cannot be in two places at one time. Maybe Jason came back, she thought.

Rushing to the kitchen door, she tried to open it. The door was locked however. "Oh, I hope he didn't lock the front door." Susan put Penny down and ran around the house to the front yard. She came up to the door. To her relief, it was the way she had left it. She came into the house. The living room chandelier was still on. She quickly climbed up the stairs to the second floor and went to her room to find it empty.

"Jason?" she called. "Are you here?" It was silent. Then she went up to the third floor. Norton's door was shut. She peered in the direction of the room where she saw the movement and edged towards it. The door was open, and it was dark and empty except for the furniture. "What in the world?" Susan was baffled. Racing to Norton's room, she knocked on the door. A moment later, he opened it. Norton stood at the threshold wearing his night attire.

"What is it, madam? Is everything alright?" he rasped.

"I'm not sure. I was just outside, and I saw someone in the opposite room."

"Which room, madam?" he asked stepping out.

"That room down the hallway," she replied, pointing at it. "Were you there?"

"Why, no, madam. I came to my room a little while ago and was getting ready for bed."

"I know. I saw your light from the yard. But the minute you turned it off, the light in the other room turned on and someone was moving in there," she insisted.

"What? You must be mistaken, madam. If Dr. Smith left the house, you and I are the only ones here. What about your cat?"

"Penny was with me," responded Susan, who was becoming agitated.

"Well, I don't know what to say, madam, but I assure you, I was here the whole time," insisted Norton. "Is that all?"

"Yes, I guess," replied Susan still quite perplexed. Suddenly feeling something rubbing on her leg she became startled. It was Penny. "Oh, Penny! Don't do that!" she cried.

"If there's nothing else, I bid you good night, madam."

"Yes. Good night, Norton," said Susan.

He went back inside and closed the door. Susan picked up Penny and returned to the room in question. She entered in and scrutinized every corner. Nothing was out of the ordinary. Then she went inside the other rooms and surveyed them as well.

"Nobody's here, Penny," she cried. "What's going on? Am I losing it?" she asked. "You saw the person too, right?" she asked the cat. "Let's go to bed. I think I need a good night's sleep."

Susan went downstairs, locked the front door, and switched off all lights and lamps. Then she came back upstairs to her room and shut the door. Putting Penny on the bed, she took her nightgown and went into the bathroom. Coming out changed, she switched the chandelier off and got under the covers. Penny was by her feet.

"I miss Jason," she sighed. "Well, you're the next best thing, Penny," she said. A few minutes later, she closed her eyes.

<u>8</u>

A week went by. Susan had mentioned the incident with the third-floor room to Jason. Without dismissing his wife's story, Jason checked all corners of the villa to make sure that everything was in place. He was concerned about her and wanted to make certain that she felt safe in their new home. The cardboard boxes in the living room had been emptied. Any items that weren't needed were placed in the garage. Jason was constantly on call at the hospital. It seemed as if he had been assigned extra responsibilities ever since they had moved.

"What's going on at the hospital?" asked Susan on a Sunday afternoon. "You've been on call this whole week. I hardly see you."

"I know," replied Jason. They were in the study, checking out the furniture and books. "This is the ideal place for you to write, honey," he commented, examining the enormous writing desk at the center. The room had tall shelves replete with books of all sorts. They were neatly arranged in alphabetical order, according to the title. Susan perused the books to determine if they were useful to her in any way.

"We can share this desk. It's big enough for the both of us," remarked Jason as he opened the drawers. Old notepads and pens were neatly placed inside. "I am a doctor, and it is about time I had a home office."

"That's nice, honey, but you haven't answered my question," continued Susan as she walked toward the window to open the drapes. The window glass looked elegant with thin wooden bars that crisscrossed each other creating a diamond-shaped design.

"I wanted to surprise you tonight with dinner and tell you the news." A blazing smile flashed across his face.

"What's the surprise?" asked Susan.

"Here goes. I've been promoted at the hospital!"

"What?" exclaimed Susan ecstatically. "Congratulations, honey! That's wonderful!" She dashed toward her husband, hugged him tightly, and kissed him on the lips. "I knew you could do it. I'm so proud of you!"

"I know. Me too," he said, kissing her back.

"What's the position?" she asked.

"I'm the head of the cardiology department now," he replied.

"Wow! I can't believe this! But how, honey? You just started two years ago. Don't you have to be there like forever to get a position like that?"

"Well, the top guns in the hospital like me. Remember the surgery I did a week ago?"

"You mean the one that you were called to the first night here?"

"Yes. It was a great success. I guess someone over there was impressed. The next thing I know, the CEO comes to my office and blurts out the news. And here's the biggest bombshell. My salary has been doubled!" he exclaimed.

"Wow! That's awesome! We have to celebrate!" voiced Susan while pacing in front of him and pondering.

"We'll have a cozy dinner tonight," suggested Jason.

"No. I mean a big party, like with all our friends!" she exclaimed.

"Do we need to? I don't want to brag and jinx everything."

"Don't be crazy. You deserve it. We'll invite everyone we know. I just spoke to Zoe this morning and told her about the house. She's excited to see it. How about next weekend? Is that okay with you?"

"I'm not sure. You know I'm on call for a while right? Now that I'm the head of the department, I have to handle all the problems with the other doctors. I have to conduct meetings, advise them, head the research department, and everything. I'll be practically living in the hospital," he said.

Susan took a deep breath. "That's okay for now. I'll plan it for next Saturday and keep my fingers crossed that you'll be free at least for a few hours. I know you can be here," she assured him. "I'll put together the guest list tonight and start calling all our friends," she said, jumping up. "Oh, this is so exciting!"

"Calm down, honey," urged Jason.

"Isn't this study the perfect place for my writing? I have space to relax and think. I'll make you proud. I'm going to write a story that'll become a bestseller," she cried.

"I have no doubt you will, dear," commented Jason.

"I'm going to make you a nice dinner tonight," said Susan, pondering. "I'll ask Norton to get everything ready for me. But I'm going to do all the cooking."

"Wonderful!" remarked Jason.

Dinner went according to plan that evening. Susan had prepared spaghetti and meatballs with salad and wine on the side. This was her husband's favorite meal. She had also baked a chocolate cake for dessert which made his mouth water. Although the meal was simple, Susan had gone to great lengths to make it extra special for her husband. Norton had also been helpful with the preparations. She, however, didn't divulge any information about Jason's promotion to him, as she did not feel any obligation toward him with regards to personal matters.

Dinner was ready at six o'clock as usual. Jason and Susan toasted the evening with sweet red wine.

"This is finger-licking good, honey," remarked Jason as he stuffed his mouth with spaghetti.

"Thank you. Save some room for dessert."

"These meatballs are excellent. I have never eaten anything like this," he commented.

"That's quite a compliment." Her face lightened with a smile. At that moment, his cell phone rang. "It's the hospital. I have to take this," he uttered brusquely, getting up and taking the call. Susan felt a bit on edge. "Okay, prep him. I'll be there in an hour."

"Got to go, honey," he said, attempting to devour as much of his meal as possible.

"But you haven't even finished dinner," she protested in disappointment.

"Save it for me. I'll finish when I get back," he said, hastily approaching her and kissing her. Susan, however, was pouting. "You're going to have to get used to this. I'm the head of the department now."

"I know, dear. Please drive safely. I love you," she sighed.

"Love you too," he said, rushing toward the living room.

"What about your keys?" she cried.

"Got them in my pocket," he replied while walking out the door. Penny came into the dining room and rubbed on her leg.

"I guess it's just you and me," she sighed picking up the cat. "Norton!" she called.

"Yes, madam," he replied, walking up to her a moment later.

"Has Penny eaten?"

"No, madam. Shall I prepare a plate for her?"

"Yes, please. Put a few meatballs into her bowl. She loves those."

"Right away, madam. Where is Dr. Smith?" he asked, surveying the premises.

"He got called to the hospital again," she replied.

"Shall I take his plate and keep it for him?"

"Yes, please," she said. Norton took Jason's plate and headed toward the kitchen. "Go on, Penny. Follow him."

Susan finished her meal and began clearing the table. She took her plate and glass to the kitchen. Norton was cleaning up and putting things away.

"Did you eat, Norton?" she asked.

"Yes, madam," he rasped. "If you don't need anything else, I shall retire for the day."

"Go ahead. I'm fine. Good night," she responded.

"Good night, madam." With that being said, he left the kitchen.

Susan poured some water in the kettle and placed it on the stove to make some tea. Looking through the glass door straight ahead, she could see that it was dark outside. She opened one of the counter drawers and took a notepad and a pencil in hopes of making the guest list for the party. Instantly Penny jumped up to the counter. "Oh, Penny! You keep on scaring me. Don't do that!" The cat was gazing at her with her big black button eyes. "Don't give me that look. The next time you scare me, you're going to be on a timeout."

As the water began to boil, the kettle gave out a hissing sound. Susan turned off the stove, took a cup from the cabinet, and poured hot water into it. Then she grabbed a tea bag from the canister and put it inside.

"So who shall we invite?" she asked, directing her gaze at Penny. She took a sip of the tea and let out a deep relaxing breath. "Let's see. We'll start with Mom, Zoe and Andrew, Rosie, Charlie and his wife." She began jotting down names on the notepad. "It's going to be great! I'm going to get caterers." After writing the initial names down, she suddenly became alarmed when Penny let out a cry. Her hairs stood on edge, and she shrieked in fear. Susan looked up, attempting to see what scared the cat. The moment she did, she saw someone sitting on the swing outside. From what she could see, he wore a black hood and cape. His grayish face and black eyes seemed to glare at her. She screamed in alarm and dropped the teacup. The cup broke into pieces, and the hot tea spilled on her foot and the ground. She cried out in pain. Susan instantly felt dizzy and began losing her balance. Holding onto the counter, she started to gasp for air.

"What's happening to me?" she uttered. Looking up again a moment later, she noticed that the swing was empty. She became frightened. Gradually, her breathing became normal and she regained her composure. Taking out her phone from the pocket, she dialed Jason's number.

"Oh, pick up, pick up, please!" There was no answer however. "Where is he when I need him? There's someone out there," she cried, looking at Penny, who was still rattled. Then she dialed the local police. The line, however, was engaged. "Great! I'm stuck alone here with an old man and a cat!" she uttered in frustration. "No offense, Penny." Marshaling her courage, she grabbed a knife from the counter. "Alright, let's take care of this the old fashioned way," she resolved. Edging slowly toward the back door, her foot throbbing in pain, she stepped out. It was dark, but the backyard light post allowed her to see at a few feet radius.

"Who's out there?" she shouted. "Come out now. I've got a knife, and I've called the police." She walked to the side. Nobody was there. Then she turned back and walked in the opposite direction. Penny had stepped out of the house as well. "Do you see anyone?" she asked.

Penny was silent. Susan peered in all directions. Seeing no one around, she quickly picked up the cat, stepped inside, and locked the door. Hastily going upstairs, she knocked on Norton's door. A few moments later, he opened it.

"What's the matter, madam?" he asked. He was wearing his night robe and pajamas.

"There's someone outside," she cried.

"Who?" asked Norton in surprise.

"He was dressed in black. I don't know who it was, but Penny saw him too."

"What do you want me to do, madam? Should I call the police?" he asked nonchalantly.

"I tried, but the line is engaged," she replied, dialing the number again from her cell phone. The line was still busy. "My back is bothering me tonight, madam. Otherwise, I would go outside and check," said Norton, placing his hand on his back.

"It's okay. You may go back to bed," said Susan. She called Jason again. He, however, still didn't answer. "He must be in surgery," she uttered.

After dialing the police again, she finally got someone on the line and explained the situation. Since the villa was a bit far from town, she was told that it would take the police at least a half hour to get there. "Great!" she remarked in annoyance. Susan looked at her foot. It was red, and she was feeling a stinging pain. She took some ice from the fridge, sat at the kitchen table, and placed it on her foot. A few minutes later, she opened the cabinet under the sink, took the first-aid kit, and put some ointment on. Penny rubbed herself on Susan's leg.

"It's okay. The police are coming. We'll just wait for them." After putting medicine, she walked toward the living room. Penny silently trailed behind her.

About an hour elapsed. Susan could finally see a car pull up to the front yard. She immediately opened the door. Two officers entered the house. They were dressed in black and had badges. Both men were tall, handsome, and well built for their job.

"What's the trouble, ma'am?" asked one of them.

"I saw someone outside," she replied.

"Where exactly?" asked the officer.

"In the backyard. He was dressed in black and was sitting on the swing, and then the next minute, he was gone," she uttered in frustration.

Susan led the police through the kitchen to the backyard. They walked out and patrolled the premises for a few minutes with their flashlights. She waited patiently inside the kitchen with Penny in her arms. A short while later, the two officers came in and locked the back door.

"Well, ma'am, we couldn't find anyone. Your yard is very big. He could've gotten away from any direction by now. Just keep the doors and windows locked. If you see anything else, just give us a call," he said, handing out his business card.

"But it took you guys an hour to get here. The first time I called, the line was engaged too," snapped Susan.

"We're trying our best, ma'am. There are so many crises situations we have to respond to, and we're currently short of staff. I apologize for the inconvenience," he said.

"Thank you," said Susan somberly as she walked them out from the front.

"Remember to keep the doors and windows locked," advised the officer as he got into the car.

Susan watched them go around the fountain and drive off. She peered in all directions, came inside and locked the door. Switching off the chandelier, she walked upstairs to bed in hopes of getting some sleep.

9

Jason didn't return home until the following evening. The minute he got in, she relayed to him all the events of the previous night. He apologized to her over and over again for not being able to answer the phone in the middle of surgery. He was also surprised to hear of Norton's indifferent attitude toward the incident.

"He's old, honey. Maybe he can't fight off an intruder. That's probably why he acted that way," he observed.

"I don't know what to think about that man anymore. Whoever was out there scared poor Penny too. He was dressed in black. His head was covered in some kind of a black hood. I was only able to get a glimpse of him before I almost passed out," she said in distress. "One second, he was there, and the other, it's like he vanished into thin air."

Jason sat by her in the living room and listened intently. "Do you want me to go out and check?"

"No. You look wiped out. Just stay with me. Besides, the police surveyed the area. I'm sure he's gone by now."

"How's the foot?" he asked examining it.

"Better."

"What were you doing in the kitchen?" he asked, yawning.

"I was making the guest list for your party."

"Who are you inviting?"

"Just Mom and our closest friends. Since your parents are out of the country, they can visit later."

"That's fine," he said, lying on the couch. "I will invite a couple of my colleagues from the hospital too." He put his feet up on her lap, and she began massaging them. A moment later, she could hear him snore. She slowly got up and placed his feet on the couch then headed upstairs to get a blanket to cover him. As she reached the second floor, she heard a voice coming from above. Automatically assuming that it was Norton, she went to the third floor and noticed that his door was open halfway. She cautiously edged closer and peered in. Norton was pacing back and forth as if distraught. He was babbling out loud. She stood by the door and listened.

"What do you want me to do?" he snapped in anger. "I can't tell them to leave. This is their house now. It doesn't belong to you or your son. You better tell him that." He grew increasingly agitated. "I told the master to stop acting up. He doesn't listen to me and I can't control him. This will only end up in disaster for him and you."

A cold chill went through Susan's body as she heard these words. She edged closer to the opening to get a better view of who he was supposedly talking to. The room was dark and dingy with gray walls. A king-sized bed was at the center and was covered with a black sheet. Norton was standing next to the bed, but his face was turned in the opposite direction. Peeping in, Susan saw that he was staring at a gold-tinted urn. "What in the world?" It was placed at the center of a wooden cabinet that stood against the wall. Directly above this wall hung a humungous portrait of an old man with a fierce-looking expression. The man had a white beard, a long pointy nose, and sharp eyes. Only his face and upper part of the chest were depicted in the portrait. Norton gazed at it and remained still for a moment.

"You tell me what I should do," he demanded. "This is not going to end well. He's going to take me to the grave," continued Norton in exasperation.

Susan cautiously stepped away from the door. Then she took a deep breath and mustered her courage. Walking back up to the door, she knocked. A moment of silence ensued. Suddenly, Norton stood at the threshold with an angry expression on his face.

"Norton, who are you talking to?" she demanded.

"That is my affair, madam," he replied bluntly. His voice was hoarse.

"I heard you from downstairs and came up to see if you were in any kind of trouble."

"Well, as you can see, madam, I'm perfectly fine," he retorted.

"If you don't mind me asking, who is in that picture?" Norton was silent.

"Well, Norton, who is it?"

"It's the original owner of this villa," he replied.

"Is that him in the urn too?"

"That's not your concern, madam," snapped Norton again in anger.

"Yes, it is my concern. If it's in my house, it is my concern!" she shouted.

At that moment, he went into the room and slammed the door. Susan was shocked. She immediately turned around and walked back down to the living room. Jason was still fast asleep. Although she endeavored to wake him, he turned around as if he didn't want to be interrupted.

"Oh, what do I do?"

That night, Norton didn't come down to prepare dinner. Susan, therefore, took it upon herself to cook. She made pasta and a salad on the side. While she was cooking, Jason walked into the kitchen.

"How long did I sleep?" He was rubbing his eyes.

"A long time, honey," replied Susan, who was distracted. Jason came to her and grabbed her from behind.

"Are you alright, darling?" he asked, gently kissing her neck.

"No, I'm not alright," she answered in indignation and attempted to avoid his advances.

"What's the matter?"

"It's Norton," she snapped.

"What's wrong with him now? And by the way, where is he? Shouldn't he be cooking? That's what I pay him for, right?"

"He won't be coming down. He's too busy up there talking to a dead old man."

"What?"

"Yes. He's talking to the original owner of this place. He's got a picture of him in his room and probably the man's ashes up there too. It's freaking me out. When I asked him about it, he slammed the door on my face."

"Let me go up there and set him straight," resolved Jason.

"Honey, please be careful. I don't trust him, and I don't want him living here anymore," she uttered.

"Okay, I'll talk to him," he assured as he walked out of the kitchen.

Penny came running from inside the dining room. "Hungry?" Susan asked. The cat jumped on to the counter. Susan grabbed a can of cat food, put it in its bowl, and placed it in front of her. Penny began eating ravenously. "Boy, you're really hungry!" A few minutes later, Jason returned. "What happened?" she asked curiously.

"He won't open the door."

"I told you. The stubborn old ox," she snapped.

"We'll get him when he calms down a little. Just be patient, dear," sighed Jason.

Dinner was quiet. "I'm glad you're not going to the hospital tonight. I've been missing you all week. Are you ever going to get a day off?"

"No. There's no such thing as an off day for me. It's just the time in between. Depends if it's long or short." After dinner, Jason helped his wife with the dishes. When the kitchen chores were complete, Susan put on a pot of coffee.

"How much are you paying Norton?" she whispered.

"A thousand dollars a month," he replied.

"Okay. I just wanted to know. Maybe we can find him a nice home and keep on giving him that amount as an allowance," she suggested.

"Let me think about that."

"Here. Take your coffee. I want to go outside for a walk. Want to join me?" she asked with a gleam in her eyes.

"Yes, I'd love to get some fresh ocean air into my system after all this brouhaha," responded Jason.

The two of them stepped out the back door with their coffee cups in hand. The evening was cool and tranquil and the sun was setting over the horizon, painting the sky with a combination of orange and purple. The cadence of the waves that surged assuaged their vexation. Several beachgoers were seen enjoying the waves.

"The evenings are so beautiful here," commented Susan as she inhaled the ocean breeze. "I want to explore the property a bit. Maybe it'll give me some inspiration for my writing."

"Have you started writing?" asked Jason.

"No, not yet. I've been thinking about it though. Maybe I'll start tomorrow."

"I've been thinking too," interjected Jason.

"About what, my handsome husband?" asked Susan gazing at him.

"When I'm at work, you must feel awful lonely in this big house. We need more life here."

"What do you mean?"

"I mean don't you think it's time we tried for a baby again? We can have one and then another and maybe one more," he declared.

A spark of joy flashed across her countenance. "I do get lonely. It's just me and Penny here. Maybe it's time," she agreed with a smile on her face. Jason placed his coffee cup on the ground, embraced her, and placed a kiss on her forehead.

"So you want to try?" he asked again.

"Yes, I do. I'm thrilled. But wait, who's going to help me when the baby comes? You're never home."

"Maybe you can get your mother to come and stay with us for a while to help. There's plenty of space here for her," he suggested.

"Okay. I'll hint on the idea when I speak to her tomorrow. Now that you brought it up, remind me to call our friends and invite them to the party on Saturday. I haven't even planned anything yet. I have to call the caterer, get some decorations and everything," she uttered, pacing back and forth.

"I'll remind you, honey. He's probably asleep."

"Who?" asked Susan. Jason had his eyes perched on the third floor. "The old man up there," he replied. Norton's room was dark.

"Yeah, probably. You should've seen how upset he was, raving like a madman."

Before they knew it, night had fallen and it was getting windy. The trees around were swaying back and forth, enhancing the chill.

"Let's check the property out a bit," suggested Jason.

"Now? But it's too dark."

"Oh, come on. That's the fun part, walking in the middle of the night. I'll never get to see this place otherwise," he said, grabbing her hand.

"Okay. Do you have a knife or something with you?"

"For what?"

"Well, if someone jumps at us, we need to defend ourselves."

"Don't worry. Nobody is going to attack us. All this land is ours, remember? I was told that the only dangers here are deer and foxes."

With that said, the two of them ventured out. The land in the front and back stretched out a few acres in all directions. Except for the driveway, everything else was covered in vegetation. Tall trees studded the land from everywhere.

"Do we need a flashlight?" asked Susan.

"No. The house is right behind us. There is absolutely no way that we can get lost," assured Jason confidently.

"Okay, honey, if you say so," conceded Susan as they trudged along the grassy and shrubby terrain. They continued for a while. "Where does our property end?" she asked.

"When you start seeing the mountains," he replied. "At least, that's what the realtor said. The surrounding area belongs to the city. He called me a couple of days ago, by the way. I forgot to tell you."

"Really?"

"Yes. He asked me how things were going here. I told him that you love the place so far."

"Well, I do," said Susan, except for Norton and the strange things that happened.

They trudged on for a while. Susan was feeling a bit on edge. "Do you know where you're going, honey?" she asked, clutching to her husband's arm.

"Sure, darling. As I said, the house is right behind us." Susan turned around, but all she could see were tall trees. "No, it's not."

"I wouldn't worry. We'll turn around in a bit," he assured.

"It's very wooded out here," commented Susan, looking around. They had been walking for a while. "I should've worn a coat. It's cold," she complained, clutching onto Jason. "And you're wearing shorts."

"I'm not that cold. I guess my body is used to it, being in those frigid surgery rooms all day," replied Jason.

"Let's turn back," urged Susan. "It's too dark to go any further. We're going to get lost."

"Alright." Suddenly, Susan spotted someone abruptly moving among the trees a few yards ahead. "Someone's out there," she voiced in alarm.

Jason peered in the general direction she was pointing at. As he looked, he could see a white figure moving. "Who's out there?" he shouted. "This is private property, and you're trespassing."

Silence ensued. The white figure then appeared in between the two trees a few feet in front of them. Susan was overcome with terror. "Jason, who is that?" she cried, hanging onto him. A second later, the figure vanished.

"What? Where is it? It was just there a minute ago!" she exclaimed, her eyes examining the terrain ahead. She could feel her knees knocking together.

"Alright. Let's get out of here. I'm going to call the police," said Jason.

At that very moment, the figure appeared right in front of them. It was a woman dressed in a white lace gown. She was holding what looked like a newborn baby in her hands. She had long dark hair and had a dejected yet terrifying appearance. Her eyes were jet black. Tears were rolling down from them. She stared at Susan, as if she was about to devour her, and then looked down at the newborn she held. The child wasn't moving. Susan was stone cold and suddenly became paralyzed. Jason was in shock as well. Despite his fear, he looked at the woman.

"Who are you? What do you want?" he asked.

The woman turned her gaze at him. She opened her mouth and was about to say something but vanished at that very instant. Susan fell to the ground. Jason stooped down and called to her, but she was unconscious.

10

Susan opened her eyes and realized that she was in bed. Jason was pacing back and forth in the room, speaking to someone on his cell phone. Daylight crept into her bedside through the window curtains. She took a deep breath. "Jason, honey," she uttered.

"Oh, you're awake!" he exclaimed, approaching her. "I'll call you back," he said to whoever was on the phone.

"What happened?" she asked in confusion.

"Well, I had to carry you back to the house last night because you passed out." Susan suddenly recalled the events of the previous night and sat up on the bed agitated.

"Relax, honey. Relax," insisted Jason as he placed both hands on her shoulders to placate her.

"So last night was real?"

"Yes, it was," he sighed. "I called the police. They're outside all over the property."

"Did you tell them what we saw?"

"Well, I told them we saw a woman walking in the middle of the night in our property and that she suddenly vanished in front of our eyes. I don't know how many of them believed that last part."

"Who was that?" she asked. Jason could sense his wife's fear.

"I don't know, honey, but I will get to the bottom of this somehow. Let's wait and see what the police have to say first before jumping into any conclusions."

"I want to go and get some coffee." Susan got out of bed.

"Are you alright? How do you feel?" he asked.

"I'm fine, honey," she said, putting on her shoes. "I'll never go out to those woods again in the middle of the night," she declared.

"Don't say that. You can't be frightened of your own home," he protested.

"I know, but until we find out who that is and get rid of her, I'm not going exploring."

As they came into the kitchen, they could see police officers swarming the backyard. Norton was making coffee.

"Good morning, madam," he said, looking at Susan.

"Hello, Norton," she responded.

"Did you sleep well?" he asked.

"Apparently like a baby. I wasn't even aware that I was in bed," she replied.

"I've already made coffee for you, and breakfast is underway," he said, pointing to the bacon and eggs cooking on the stove.

"Thank you," said Susan, taking the coffee. Norton handed Jason a cup as well.

"Norton, I want to ask you about the previous night. Who were you speaking to in your room?" asked Susan sternly.

"I'm afraid I don't know what you mean," he rasped.

"Well, remember when I came to your room and asked you who was on the painting and who you were speaking to?"

"No, madam. I don't remember," replied Norton as if puzzled. He was in surprisingly good spirits.

"What?" voiced Susan. "You slammed the door on my face!"

"Oh my goodness, madam! I would never do that. You must be mistaken."

Susan took a deep breath and turned to Jason, who was confused himself. "Oh forget it," she finally said. "I don't understand anything around here." The frustration in her face was quite poignant.

One of the police officers came into the kitchen a short while later. Susan and Jason were already having breakfast. They stopped momentarily as he approached them. Susan noticed that this was the same officer she had spoken with previously. He was tall and quite handsome with dark eyes and sharp features.

"Well, sir, there's nobody out there," he said in a rough voice.

"What?" exclaimed Jason. "But we saw a woman with a child last night."

"I don't know what to say, sir. We can't find anyone. My officers looked at every square inch of your property. It's clear. You're in no danger."

Jason looked at his wife who was as disappointed as he was.

"What do we do now?" she asked the policeman.

"The same thing I told you before, madam. Lock the doors and windows at night and don't go walking outdoors in the dark. If someone was there, they're gone now. I will let the detective know about this matter as well. He might contact you."

"Thank you, Officer," said Jason as he walked him out. Susan could hear the police cars leaving. Jason came back to her a few moments later. "Well, that's that I guess," he said, getting back to his breakfast.

"What about Norton?" she whispered cautiously.

"Don't worry. He's not here. You don't have to whisper."

"Where is he?"

"I sent him to bring groceries. He won't be here for a while."

"Do you believe what I said about him?" she asked, glaring at her husband.

"Of course, honey. I believe you. Maybe he just forgot."

"You know what, I want to go to his room and see what he's hiding in there," she said getting up.

"Honey, don't!" insisted Jason.

"Why not?" snapped Susan.

"Well, the man does have the right to some privacy."

"Not in my house, he doesn't" cried Susan, storming out of the kitchen. She began climbing the stairs. Jason followed her to the third floor.

"We need to fill these rooms with kids. It's too quiet up here," he commented. The third-floor hallway was dark.

Susan opened the curtains on the side window. A bit of sunlight slanted through. "We'll talk about kids later," she said going up to Norton's door. She turned the knob, but to her disappointment, it was locked.

"He locks his room?" she asked, looking at Jason. "Let me get my keys," she said, going down the stairs. In addition to the front and back doors, each room in the villa had its lock. Susan was under the impression that she had Norton's room key somewhere in her keyring. A minute later, she came up with the keys and began inserting each inside the keyhole to no avail. Finally, she was left with the last one. That, however, was not a fit either. "I don't believe it," she said in indignation. "He has the key to this room and I don't."

"Calm down, darling. Let the man be," he appeased her.

Susan followed him to the living room. Jason sat on the sofa and placed his feet on the table nearby. "If he tries to hurt you, I'll throw him out."

"Oh, alright," conceded Susan as she sat by her husband.

"I have to go to the hospital in a bit. Are you going to be alright?"

"I guess so. I have to call everyone today. And by the way, you were supposed to remind me of that.

"Sorry, honey. My mind is preoccupied right now. When you're done with that, take a drive out to town," he suggested. "You haven't been out since we moved here. Go get some fresh town air."

"How? You're taking the car."

"Call a cab. There's an excellent cab service here. I'll get you a car next week."

Susan thought for a moment. "Maybe I will." Then she kissed and embraced him.

11

It was the day of the party. Things seemed to be calm in the villa. Susan had been up since five in the morning, getting things ready. Cleaning and decorating the house was no easy task. She had ordered fresh flowers to be brought for the vases the previous day. Roses of different colors adorned the house. Jason had bought outdoor furniture for the backyard. Tables and chairs were neatly placed out back by the delivery men. The catering company was supposed to come at ten in the morning, as the guests would be arriving a little after. Fried chicken, roast beef, vegetables, fruits, and various types of desserts were on the menu. Norton had helped a bit with the cleaning and other preparations the previous day, but he suddenly complained about his back problem and consequently retired to his room. Susan didn't mind, as she wanted to handle matters herself without having to listen to anyone's opinion about things. Jason had endeavored to get the day off upon his wife's request. The hospital had complied conditionally with the understanding that he would still be on call for the day if needed. Some of his colleagues from the hospital were also on the guest list. All their good friends were invited. Susan was very excited.

It was seven in the morning. Jason was still asleep. Susan came into the bedroom to check if he was awake. The moment she entered, a chill went through her body. The window had been left open all night, and the room was cold. Although it was early fall, the ocean made the nights frigid. Jason was tossing and turning, as if disturbed by a bad dream. Susan approached him and sat on the bed beside him.

"What's the matter, darling?" she asked gently, rubbing his chest. Jason immediately opened his eyes.

"Oh, thank goodness it's you," he uttered.

"Why did you say that?" she asked, caressing his head.

"I had a nightmare."

"I know. I could tell."

"It was that woman we saw the other night. She showed up in my dream."

"Oh, you had to bring that up! I'm still getting goosebumps thinking about her," she snapped. "Come down and help me with the party stuff. That'll help you get rid of that unpleasantness. I've put on a nice pot of hot coffee too."

"Alright," he uttered, getting up and heading toward the bathroom. A minute later, he came out with a T-shirt and a pair of shorts, ready for the morning. Susan sat on the bed, peering out through the window. "Are you okay? You seem upset," he said.

"Mom can't make it," she responded.

"That's too bad. Why?"

"She's a bit under the weather and isn't up for the drive."

"That's okay, honey. She can come for a visit when she's better. I tell you what. We'll go and pick her up when she's ready to come."

"I guess," she sighed.

"Alright. Come on. I need coffee if you want my help," he urged her.

Penny was asleep on Susan's side of the bed. "Oh, I hardly even notice her now," she commented, looking at the cat. "I've been so busy lately, and most of the time, she's nowhere to be seen. Wonder what she's up to."

"Cat business probably. Let her sleep," said Jason as they walked out of the room.

Jason poured coffee for both of them. "I know this is your second one," he said, handing her a cup.

"Thanks. I need it," she uttered, sitting at the table. "I called Zoe yesterday," she said.

"Really? How is she?" Zoe was Susan's best friend since high school.

"She's doing well. So is Andrew. And by the way, she's pregnant."

"Oh wow! Didn't they just get married a few months ago?" asked Jason, listening intently.

"Yep. Six months to be exact and two or three months pregnant. She's saying she can't wait to see our new home."

"I'll bet you can't wait to see her too, right?"

"Yes. I haven't seen her for so long with their world tour and everything. Andrew is really into traveling. Ever since she got married, it's as if I've lost my best friend," she uttered.

"Well, honey, that's what happens when you get hitched. Priorities change. At least, you're going to have a chance to catch up today. Maybe they can stay the night too and go tomorrow. Andrew and I can enjoy a drink in the night if I'm here. Oops!" he exclaimed.

"What?" asked Susan in alarm.

"I can't drink while I'm on call."

"Good! You don't need to drink to have a good time, honey. I'll ask them if they can stay the night though," said Susan, sipping on her coffee.

"You're going to have your baby too just as soon as we get a chance to spend some quality time together," assured Jason.

"Sure. I wonder when that's going to happen," said Susan sarcastically.

"Well, it can happen now if you want, but I see you're preoccupied. So we'll wait until the atmosphere is more agreeable," said Jason as he finished his coffee. "Who else is coming?"

"Everyone on my list said they'll be here. A total of about thirty people will be buzzing around today, Dr. Smith."

"Alright. What is it that you want me to do for this party?" asked Jason, washing his coffee cup.

"I need you to clean the restrooms and see if they have an ample supply of soap, towels, and other necessary items."

"Great! I see my many years of medical school training have finally paid off! Washing restrooms has been my dream, darling," he said with sarcasm.

"It will be good for you. Just make sure you scrub up good before the next surgery."

"And what will you be doing, wife?" he asked.

"Everything else," she replied.

A few moments later, they went in separate directions to complete the cleaning tasks. After scrubbing two bathrooms, Jason began to complain.

"Why can't we pay someone to do this? My back hurts," he whined as he saw his wife past by him in the hall.

"There's no time for that. Just do the best you can. I doubt that all the restrooms will be needed," she speculated. "I just want the guests to be comfortable and feel like home."

It was almost ten in the morning. Susan was dressed in a lovely red gown for the occasion. She wore some of her elegant jewelry.

"You look radiant, darling," uttered Jason, coming up to her from behind and kissing her neck. He wore a nice shirt and pants.

"You look very debonair, Dr. Smith," said Susan, giving him an embrace and a kiss.

The catering company arrived shortly after. Susan welcomed them from the front door. Fresh fruits, vegetables, desserts, and the main course were brought in in elegant silver pots and pans. These were placed on the kitchen counters and tables. Susan had ordered the best wines. Jason had ordered whiskey and other drinks as well.

"The ladies can have wine, and the men can have the strong stuff," suggested Jason.

"You know, if Zoe wasn't pregnant, she'd beg to differ," protested Susan. "And I'll bet you, before you know it, some of my other lady friends will finish your whiskey too."

"Fine, I take it back. We can share," he conceded as he laid the glasses out for the alcohol.

Five caterers stayed behind to help with the serving. They were professionally dressed and began preparing hors d'oeuvres.

Suddenly the front doorbell rang, and Norton went to answer it. As he did, Zoe and Andrew walked in. Susan went hastily toward her.

"Oh, Zoe and Andrew, welcome!" she exclaimed. She raced up to her friend and embraced her.

"Thank you, darling," said Zoe.

Jason walked up to them as well and shook Andrew's hand. "Nice to see you again, man," he said to him.

"Your home is beautiful!" exclaimed Zoe, looking around with a bright smile on her face.

"Come in. Come in. Sit down," urged Susan as she walked her friend over to the sofa. "I see that congratulations are in order for the mom-to-be," she said, touching Zoe's belly.

"Thank you, so much. We just found out a couple of weeks ago," said Zoe, sitting down. She was a tall redhead who was quite attractive. Her baby bump was slightly visible through the thin crème-colored dress she had on. Andrew was also very handsome with short brown hair, dark eyes, and sharp features. He wore a deep blue suit for the occasion. He, however, paled in comparison to Jason, who had stunning good looks regardless of what he wore.

"I hear that you got promoted to head of the department of cardiology, Jason," said Zoe, smiling at him.

"Who told you that?" he asked.

"My friend here told me about it yesterday. So you're the guest of honor," she remarked, kissing him on the cheek.

"Well, I don't know about that, but since it is a party, we can celebrate,' said Jason, giving her an embrace. "Come on, Andrew. Let's you and I get a drink. You can have a shot of whiskey while I drink some soda," he said, getting up.

"What's up with the soda, buddy?" asked Andrew perplexed. "You need something stronger."

"Can't. I'm on call," replied Jason with a slight frown.

"Fair enough," said Andrew, placing his arm on Jason's shoulder as they headed inside.

Susan looked at them and laughed. "Oh, those husbands of ours," she observed.

"Yeah. Where would they be without us, right?" commented Zoe.

"Exactly. I'm the brains behind his body," said Susan laughing.

"So, darling, this house is stunning!" uttered Zoe, clasping her hand. "I'm so happy for you."

"Thank you. He surprised me with it. I didn't know until the end," added Susan. "Enough about me. Look at you! A world-tour honeymoon and now a baby on the way. When are you due?"

"In June," replied Zoe as she gently rubbed her belly. "I can't wait! I've already started to get the nursery ready."

"So when are you going to be a mom?" asked Zoe.

"Oh, I don't know. Jason and I talked about it. I want to have a child, so I won't feel lonely in this big house."

"What does Jason say?"

"He's ready to be a father. In fact, he's the one who brought it up," said Susan, recalling the conversation from a few days ago. "We've been trying for a while. I don't know," she sighed.

"Maybe the house will do the trick," remarked Zoe. "It's a very beautiful and peaceful place. That's what's needed sometimes."

"I hope so," conceded Susan.

"Well, I'm excited for you." Zoe reached out and held her hands again. "Oh, boy! Where has the time gone? It feels like just last week we were in high school, and now, look at us."

The doorbell rang again, and Norton walked out to get it.

"Who is he?" asked Zoe directing her eyes toward Norton.

"That's the caretaker," answered Susan. "He came with the house."

At that moment, she saw something moving on the side by the sofa. She instinctively turned around to see that it was Penny. The fur on her back was standing straight, and she looked terrified.

"Penny! What's the matter, baby?" cried Susan, picking her up.

"Oh, she looks afraid," remarked Zoe.

"I know. What's the matter, Penny? Did something scare you?" she asked, stroking her back.

As Norton opened the door, several other guests walked into the house. Susan stood up and went toward them to welcome them. Some of her friends embraced her and presented her with gifts. They all walked into the living room and sat.

"This is a beautiful home, Susan!" remarked her friend Alexandra. She was a tall blonde dressed in lavish attire. "Congratulations!"

"Oh, thank you," she said. smiling at her friends.

Jason and Andrew came to the room with their respective drinks in hand. "Welcome everyone!" said Jason pleasantly. "Please make yourselves at home."

The caterers brought the hors d'oeuvres and wine to the front. The guests began enjoying the treats. While she was engaged with her guests, Susan noticed that Penny had the overwhelming urge to jump down. Without ado, she put her on the ground. She instantly ran out.

"Penny!" she called. "Oh, that cat. I haven't the slightest clue what's gotten into her," she said, turning toward Zoe.

"Animals are like that. They've got mood swings like us," remarked Zoe.

As the afternoon drew near, more guests began arriving. Wines, cocktails, and appetizers were brought to the living room. Then Susan called all her guests to the dining area for a grand buffet-style lunch. All the food platters were neatly placed on the table. A line formed instantly. The caterers served the guests as they went from one platter to the next. Susan was going to and fro, attending to their needs as well. She made sure that everyone was enjoying themselves. Deserts were served in the kitchen. Fresh fruit salad, cakes, pies, ice cream, and other sweet treats were placed on the kitchen counter. Jason's friends and colleagues from the hospital were out at the backyard, eating with him and having a good time. She went out and interrupted their party now and then to make sure that they were eating well.

"We're fine, honey," uttered Jason.

"Alright," she said. "I just want to make sure that nobody gets overly buzzed around here."

"There's no danger of that," cried Andrew, who was laughing uncontrollably with an empty bottle of whiskey in his hand. "Hey, Susan, just make sure that my pregnant wife doesn't drink, alright?"

"Sure," replied Susan rolling her eyes. "You two can spend the night here because you're too stoned to drive."

"No problem. I hear you've got like fifteen rooms up in this place," he uttered, as if he were about to drop. Susan looked at Jason in anger and pulled him out of his seat.

"Darling, why did you give him the bottle of whiskey? Now I won't hear the end of it from Zoe. You know how she is with Andrew and his drinking."

"Okay, don't worry. I'll keep an eye on him," he assured.

12

As evening drew near, the party was still in full swing. All the guests had come out to the backyard to enjoy the cool sea breeze. They were socializing, laughing, and enjoying the food that was still being catered. Some occupied the outdoor furniture while others were seated on the grass. One of Susan's friends was riding the swing. Zoe stepped out to the backyard. She immediately inhaled the fresh air. Susan walked right behind her to make sure she didn't trip on anything.

"Oh, this place is so beautiful! The beach is awesome in the evening," she uttered. The trees swayed now and then, and the horizon remained serene and still.

"I know. It relaxes me," agreed Susan.

"Look at my drunk husband over there," she said, pointing to Andrew, who was a bit inebriated. "He promised me he would control himself." She looked disappointed. "It's been like this ever since we were dating. I don't know what to do to get him to stop drinking."

"Don't worry. Stay the night with us. He'll be well by morning," suggested Susan.

Zoe was the sister that Susan never had. They were high school friends at first. But then as the years went by, their friendship grew stronger. Zoe helped Susan through some rough times in her life. They strolled to the edge of the yard.

"How's the magazine work going?" asked Susan.

"Good. I have to get back to work next week. Being an editor is mighty demanding," replied Zoe.

"I could just imagine," sighed Susan.

"Are you happy here?" asked Zoe.

"Yes, I am. It's my dream home," replied Susan. She looked out to the ocean and took a deep breath. "Things are finally looking up for Jason and me."

"Good. If you're happy, then I'm happy for you both," said Zoe, holding onto her.

"Thank you, friend. You know I love you, right?"

"Yes, I do. And I love you too," said Zoe, embracing Susan. A minute later, she pulled out a camera from her purse and took a picture of the sunset. "I want to remember this house and every part of it, beginning with the sunset," she commented.

"Why?" asked Susan laughing.

"Because Andrew is going to buy me one just like it," she responded.

"Good for you, darling," said Susan.

"Or, maybe I could feature this place in my next month's issue," she uttered pondering.

"Oh, how wonderful!" remarked Susan with a gleam in her eye.

"Do you mind if I go around the yard, taking some more photos?" she asked.

"The photographer in you is coming out?" asked Susan.

"Yes. I want to put an album together first."

"Sure. But don't venture out too far," cautioned Susan.

"No worries," said Zoe.

"I need to attend to the caterers. They're preparing to leave. See you in a bit," said Susan as she headed back into the house.

"Alright, darling," said Zoe as she strolled to the other side of the yard with the camera on hand.

Night had fallen. The guests were still socializing. After a while though, one by one they began to leave. Each thanked Susan and Jason profusely for the invitation and showered them with compliments about the villa. By eleven o'clock in the night, almost all the guests had left. Susan and Jason were busy waving goodbye to them out in the front yard. One by one, they drove off until, finally, the house was quiet. They closed the front door and came into the living room. Norton was walking up and down attempting to clean up the living room and dining areas.

"Norton," she called.

"Yes, madam," he replied.

"Don't worry about cleaning now. Go to bed. You're tired. We'll finish all the chores in the morning," she suggested.

"Oh, thank you, madam. I am a bit tired. It's been a long day for me. Good night then," he said and took his leave.

"Good night, Norton," said Susan and Jason. "And thank you for the help."

"Oh, I'm tired too," remarked Susan stretching out on the sofa.

"Let's lock up the kitchen door and hit the sack," suggested Jason.

They went into the kitchen. The back door was wide open. Jason went outside to do a final check of the premises. Turning to the side he noticed Andrew, who had fallen asleep on one of the lawn chairs and snoring away.

Jason went toward him and called. "Andrew, wake up!" He, however, had a difficult time opening his eyes. Susan came outside as well.

"What's going on?" she asked, looking at her husband.

"It's Andrew. He's fast asleep, honey. I think we're going to have to take him into the bedroom so he can sleep it off."

"Well, I'm not going to carry him. You are," she uttered in indignation. "Wait! If he's here, where's Zoe?" she asked, looking around.

"I don't know. All this time, I thought they had left," replied Jason.

Susan began calling out to her friend and walking around the yard. There was no response however.

"Honey, go check in the front. Maybe she's talking to someone out there," suggested Susan.

Jason ran out to the front. All the cars had left and the driveway was empty. Susan began nudging at Andrew.

"Andrew, wake up! Where's Zoe?" she asked.

Andrew finally opened his eyes and looked at her. "What?"

"Where's your wife?" she shouted.

"I don't know. And don't be so loud," he said as if half dazed. "What did I drink?"

"Whiskey, Andrew. A whole few bottles for that matter," replied Susan in exasperation. "Now where is Zoe?"

"I don't know. The last I saw, she was with you," he uttered, attempting to get up.

Jason came back. "She's not there. The front yard is empty. She's probably inside the house, sleeping in one of the rooms."

"Maybe you're right," said Susan in a bit of relief.

"Come on, buddy. Let's get you inside," uttered Jason, taking hold of Andrew. "You go and check the rooms."

Susan came into the kitchen. She went to the dining room and looked around. Then she went into the den. Beer cans, wine glasses, and paper plates were everywhere. "She's not here," she uttered and went into the study. It was empty as well. "Okay, she's not in the living room because Jason and I were just there."

"What was that, honey?"

Susan turned around and saw Jason walking inside with Andrew, who was still quite drunk. "Put him in one of the guest rooms," she ordered and climbed the stairs hastily up to the second floor. She checked their bedroom. It was empty. Walking along the hallway, she turned the lights on in each of the other rooms. "Zoe!" she called out. All the rooms were empty. She checked in the restrooms as well. Zoe was nowhere to be seen. Anxiety gripped her.

"Any luck?" asked Jason, who had already come up to the hallway with Andrew.

"She's not in any of the rooms here or the restrooms. I'm going to check upstairs. Maybe she went exploring," suggested Susan as she made her way hastily to the stairs. She walked down the hallway, turning on the lights in each of the rooms on the third floor. There was no sign of her friend. Her heart began to pound. "Where are you, Zoe?"

Did she go up to the attic? she thought to herself. The idea of climbing the stairs to the fourth floor brought her goosebumps. "You'd better not be up there, Zoe. Even I can't stand that floor," she cried.

The fourth floor was very dark and as still as a tomb. She walked to the attic door and tried to open it. "Oh, my keys are down," she said to herself in frustration. "Zoe, are you in there?" she shouted, pounding on the door. There was no answer, however. *Well, if the door was locked from day one, she couldn't have possibly gone in there,* she thought. As she came down the stairs, Norton stepped out of his room. "What's the racket, madam?" he asked.

"Zoe is missing. Have you seen her?"

"Who is Zoe, madam?"

"She's the lady who had the red hair. And she's pregnant."

"No, I didn't see her," assured Norton. "Would you like me to help you look?"

"Yes, please," said Susan as she went downstairs. The moment she came to the second floor, she saw Jason. "Did you find her?" he asked.

"No. She's not in any of the rooms. Where's Andrew?"

"He's in the restroom throwing up."

"Never mind him! I'm really worried," remarked Susan. "The last time I saw her, she was outside in the backyard taking photos. I told her not to venture out to the property. Do you think she's lost out there?"

"I don't know, honey, but I'm calling the police," said Jason, dialing the number.

"Did you find my wife?" asked Andrew coming out.

"No. She's not in the house. Jason is calling the police," she replied.

"Oh my gosh! I hope she's not outside in the dark. What time is it?" asked Andrew.

"It's eleven thirty," said Susan, looking at her watch.

"I'm going out. Do you have a flashlight?" he asked.

"Yes. Come with me," ordered Susan as she walked downstairs. She came into the kitchen, opened a counter drawer, and pulled out two flashlights. "Here," she said, handing one to Andrew.

Jason entered the kitchen as well. "The police are on their way," he said. "Andrew, we'll go together. I don't want you to get lost out there in the dark. Believe me it can get scary in the woods. Susan, you stay here. When the police come, explain to them what happened."

"Alright, honey," she said, kissing him.

Jason took the other flashlight from Susan. "Are you okay to walk, buddy?"

"Yes, I'm fine. I just want my wife," he said in distress.

"Let's go find her, then" urged Jason.

The two men stepped out into the backyard. Susan watched them as they walked on into the night.

13

The police arrived half an hour later. Two cars were parked in the front. Susan could see that their red lights were flashing. She let the officers in and explained the situation to them. The head of the squadron instructed two of his officers to search the house thoroughly for Zoe. The others were instructed to scout the outside area. Norton was disturbed by the noise. He came down and was surprised to see so many police cars and officers. Now that the police were on the search, Susan asked Norton to retire for the evening. He was happy to comply.

Jason and Andrew had already gone far out into the property. They used their flashlights to look around and constantly called out to Zoe. She, however, was nowhere to be seen. Andrew was becoming frantic.

"Do you think something happened to her?" he asked in agitation.

"I hope not. Susan and I don't like to take walks in these woods at night."

"Is something wrong? What are you not telling me?" asked Andrew as he trudged along.

"We've seen someone roaming around in the night."

"Who?"

"A woman dressed in white. She was holding a baby in her hands."

"What?" asked Andrew in disbelief. "Well, where did she come from?"

"I don't know, buddy. Susan was terrified when she saw her the other night. She passed out and I had to carry her back to the house."

As they walked on, they heard noises from behind. Turning around, they saw flashlights and officers heading toward them.

"Well, you're going to have to tell the police about that," said Andrew.

"We already did. I don't think they believe us," said Jason.

At that moment, the policemen came up to them and asked them questions about Zoe.

"We're going to take over," said one of the officers.

Andrew and Jason watched them spread out in all directions.

"You know what? I don't care, I'm not going to stop until I find my wife," insisted Andrew.

The search went on for several hours and more officers were called in with their search dogs. Jason and Andrew accompanied the officers.

"Your property is so big," uttered Andrew. "How are we going to find her? Who knows where she went?"

Jason could see that Andrew was delirious with worry. "We'll find her. I'm sure of it," he uttered in a placating voice. A few moments later, they saw one of the police officers walking hastily toward them.

"Which one of you is the husband?" he asked.

"I am," replied Andrew. "What's the matter?"

"We've located your wife," he said gravely.

"Where is she?" asked Andrew agitated. "Let me go to her," he said, attempting to run.

The officer however held onto him. "Sir, we have found her body," he said.

"What? Her body? No!" he shouted and began running up. "Zoe!" he cried.

The officers attempted to restrain him, but he fought them off and continued to run toward the general direction where many of the police had already gathered. As he approached them, he could see that they were surrounding someone who was lying flat on the ground. Coming closer, he saw that it was Zoe. She was lying on the ground with her mouth open and arms stretched out. At the sight of his motionless wife, Andrew began to cry hysterically.

"No! No! Zoe!" he cried.

He ran toward her, dropped to the floor, and attempted to revive her. She however didn't move. Two officers went toward Andrew and held him on either side. They tried to get him to leave, but he continued to fight them off. Jason also came running to the scene. Seeing Zoe's motionless body, he became sullen.

"We discovered this camera near her," said one of the officers approaching him. "Apparently she was out here taking pictures," he uttered.

"Maybe you should examine the photos she took," suggested Jason.

14

Susan was growing increasingly impatient as she waited for hours to receive news of her friend. The officers who were searching the house confirmed that Zoe wasn't inside. She kept looking out into the woods to see if Jason, Andrew, or any of the other policemen were coming. A little while later, she could see a flashlight shining in the dark. She walked toward it to see who it was. An officer was coming back. He approached her with a grave expression.

"Ma'am, we found her," he said coming closer.

"Oh, thank goodness!" exclaimed Susan with an overwhelming feeling of relief. The officer, however, came up to her and stopped.

"Ma'am, what I meant to say was that we found her body in the woods."

"What?" cried Susan. "What do you mean body? Please tell me she's okay."

"I'm sorry, ma'am, but your friend is dead," he uttered in a sullen voice. The policemen who were searching the home joined them.

"Go and help with the recovery effort. Just go straight ahead. You'll see them," ordered the officer who was with Susan. The other two hastily followed instructions. Susan couldn't breathe. She didn't know what to do and went into denial.

"No, it can't be. She was with me a few hours ago. How could she be dead? Did you know that she's expecting a baby?" Tears came rolling down her cheeks.

"Yes, ma'am, we know. We found her on the far side of the property in the woods. She had gone there to take pictures with her camera."

"I told Zoe not to go too far. Why didn't she listen to me? How could this be? She's going to have a baby, and I was going to ask her if I could be the godmother." Susan began to sob. Jason came back to the yard. The moment she saw him, she grabbed a hold of him. "Please tell me it isn't true!" she cried.

Jason held onto her. "I'm sorry, darling. She's gone. They're bringing her here now."

"How is this possible?" asked Susan, gazing at Jason with teary eyes and in disbelief.

"I don't know, but I'm getting a funny feeling about all of this. They found the camera in her hand. The officer in charge is going to get images developed. Hopefully, we can get an idea of what might have happened to her."

It was well into the early morning hours. The police finally brought Zoe's body to the front yard. An ambulance had already arrived with a stretcher. Susan ran up to see her friend, as she was still in disbelief. The body was covered in some sort of black cloth. She went toward her and removed the cover from her head. Zoe's eyes were closed, and she was lifeless. Susan teared up uncontrollably. She kissed her friend on the forehead before one of the officers approached her and asked her to step back. Jason held her from behind.

"Come on, honey," he urged her.

"No. This is not possible!" she exclaimed and continued to sob.

Andrew was by Zoe's side sobbing hysterically. They took the body into the ambulance. Andrew got in with her. A few moments later, it drove off. Some of the police cars remained in the front yard. The detective walked toward Susan and Jason with the camera in his hand.

"I need to ask you, folks, some questions," he said.

They walked into the living room. Jason asked the detective to have a seat. Susan attempted to control her grief. Jason held her hand and urged her to sit with him.

"I'm detective Eric Johnson from the downtown police department. I'm so sorry for your loss, ma'am," he said. He had a very stern voice.

"Thank you," responded Susan as she wiped her tears. The detective was a tall man with a beard and mustache and had inquisitive eyes. He was dressed in a full gray suit and wore a gray coat over it.

"How close were the two of you?" he asked looking at Susan.

"She was my best friend. We were very close." Jason held her hand from the side.

"I have the camera that your friend had." He pulled it out of his pocket and placed it on the coffee table in front of them. "We're going to get the photos developed right away because this is the only evidence we have to go by at the moment." Susan shook her head in agreement.

"I spoke to her husband, Andrew Bellamy," uttered the detective. "He stated that he was drunk here with the two of you. Is that correct?"

"Yes," replied Jason.

"And what were your friend and her husband doing here?" asked the detective.

"We had a party," uttered Susan, wiping her tears. "It was for my husband. He was just promoted. So I wanted it to make it both a housewarming and a congratulations party for him. Zoe and Andrew were our guests."

"I see," said the detective, taking down some notes in his little pocketbook. "And there were others here?"

"Yes. Our friends and Jason's colleagues from the hospital."

"Did they see Zoe here?" asked the detective.

"Yes. You can call them and ask if you'd like. I can give you their information," said Susan somberly.

"Thank you. I have to question them and get statements. But in the meantime, I will get the photos from the camera and be here in the morning," said the detective. "You folks take care." He stood up and began heading toward the front door. Jason accompanied him and opened the door for him. Bidding him farewell, Jason locked the door and came back to Susan who was crying hysterically on the sofa.

"Oh, honey, I'm sorry," he uttered and embraced her.

15

Dawn had set in. Susan lay asleep on the couch when the doorbell rang. She abruptly woke up and saw Jason heading toward the door. "Honey? Jason?" she uttered scratching her eyes and noticing that she had been covered by a warm blanket. A moment later, Jason came into the living room with the detective. Susan got up and immediately recalled the terrible events of the previous night. She was still wearing the red gown from the party.

"Good morning, Mrs. Smith," said the detective.

"Good morning," replied Susan. "What time is it?"

"Ten o'clock,' replied the detective, checking his wristwatch. "I am sorry to bother the two of you, but I needed to see you," he uttered gravely.

"What's the matter?" asked Jason. Susan noticed that he held a large envelope in his hand. Jason approached her and gave her an embrace and a kiss on the forehead.

"Well, we have photos. May I sit?" he asked politely.

"Yes, of course. Would you like some coffee?" asked Jason.

"A little later perhaps," said the detective, sitting down. Susan sat beside him. He opened the envelope and carefully took the photos out and laid them on the table. "I think this is the sequence," he uttered, as he arranged them in order.

Jason and Susan peered closely at them. Susan immediately recognized the snapshot that Zoe had taken of the sunset. It was in the middle. There were some photos at the beginning of the sequence of Andrew and her. Susan's eyes welled up with tears. "I am sorry if these images are troubling, but I have no choice but to show them to you."

"So what are we looking at?" Jason asked.

"Well, as you can see, she was taking pictures of your property. She must've loved it to go out by herself in the middle of the night like that."

"I don't know if I should take that as a compliment, considering the circumstances," responded Jason.

Susan examined the last few images to determine what Zoe was looking at during her final moments. The last two made her shudder.

"You saw that too, right?" asked the detective, looking at her. Jason glanced at the photos as well.

"Is that what I think it is?" he asked Susan.

"Yes. It's her," affirmed Susan.

"Who?" asked the detective.

The one before the last showed the woman in white walking in between the trees. The final one was a vivid full-blown image of her with her black eyes glaring and her mouth open. Apparently, Zoe had knowingly taken pictures of the apparition.

"We saw her when we first went walking into our property a few days ago at night. It was this woman in white who appeared out of nowhere. She was carrying a child. We didn't know what to make of it at first. Then she suddenly vanished and appeared right in front of us with her child. It was unlike anything we've seen before," explained Jason.

"Did you tell the police?" asked the detective.

"Yes, of course. I had to call the police because my wife fainted at the sight of her."

"Well, in these photos, there's no child," said the detective, pointing to the pictures.

"Do you think Zoe was trying to speak with her?" asked Susan.

"Or maybe she was terrified," stated the detective. "The woman probably attacked her."

Jason and Susan glanced at each other. "When I told the police about what we saw that night, they didn't believe me," said Jason.

"Why wouldn't they believe you?" asked the detective with a quizzical expression on his face.

"I don't know. You're going to have to ask them that," said Jason.

The detective took a deep breath. "I see," he uttered standing up. Susan kept glancing at the last photo. The apparition was horrifying, and a chill overcame her.

"I don't know what to make of all this. I guess we'll find out the cause of death from the coroner's report."

"She was pregnant," uttered Susan, wiping her tears.

"I know. I'm so sorry," said the detective, turning to her.

"Where is Andrew?" inquired Jason.

"We just let him out. We had to question him. He's in the clear except for a bit of alcohol in his system."

"Oh, thank goodness!" uttered Susan.

"What should we do, Detective?" asked Jason.

"Well, folks, this is your property. I heard you paid cash for it," remarked the detective.

"Where did you hear that?" asked Jason with a surprised expression.

"News gets around in a small town like this. Everyone down there is wondering who bought the lonely house up on the hill."

"I didn't realize that we were famous," exclaimed Jason.

"Are you kidding? Do you know how long this house has been on the market? Almost twenty years."

"How come nobody bought it before us?" asked Jason.

"It cost a fortune, and there's a history here. I guess someone like you needs to walk in and take the reins into their hands."

"What history?" asked Susan.

"That's a topic for later, ma'am," replied the detective respectfully.

"Well, I want to find out what's happening in my property and who this woman is," asserted Jason.

"Who's that?" asked the detective, looking behind them.

Susan and Jason turned around to see Norton popping up from the dining area. "Oh, that's the caretaker," replied Susan.

"Do you mind if I ask him some questions?"

"No. Go right ahead," said Jason.

The detective walked toward Norton. Susan saw them talking. Norton seemed to be perturbed. A bit later, the detective approached them.

"Well, I sure can't get anything out of him. He says he has no clue about anything. I'd better get going. Here's my card," he said, as he handed his business card to Jason. "Please call me directly if you have any further information. You take care." With that, he headed toward the front door.

They watched him drive out of the yard. The sun was out and it was warm. Susan looked up to the sky and thought about the friend she had lost. It was as if a piece of her heart was suddenly ripped out.

16

Jason stayed home from work. Susan was in great distress and inconsolable at times. She had to send word about Zoe's death to all the friends who had been at her home the previous day. This was no easy task. She felt drained at the end. Jason asked Norton to make some chicken soup for her.

"I can't eat anything," she cried.

"Honey, you have to. Otherwise, you're going to get sick," said Jason.

"Where's Penny? I need her," said Susan, looking around her. Whenever she was upset, Penny had a way of soothing her. "Penny!" she called out. "Oh, where is she when I need her?"

"I'll find her for you. Just relax on the couch."

A bit later, Norton brought a bowl of chicken soup. "Here, madam," he said, placing the bowl on the coffee table in front of her. "I made you the best. The recipe I used is passed down from my great-grandparents," he remarked.

"Thank you, Norton," said Susan. "But I'm not in the mood to eat anything. I'm sorry. Maybe a little later perhaps."

"It's okay, madam. Just have a sip or two. Believe me it's quite good."

"Have you seen Penny? I need her with me right now."

"No, madam. Actually, I haven't seen that cat anywhere since yesterday."

"Can you look upstairs? And by the way, Norton, I need the keys to the attic and your room. At least a duplicate to your room."

"You already have the keys in your ring, madam. I gave them to the realtor," he insisted.

"Are you sure?"

"Yes, madam. I'm positive."

"Okay, I'll check later."

"Is there anything else I can do for you, madam?" he asked.

"Yes. Just see if you can find Penny alright?"

"Of course, madam. I'll get on it right away," he rasped.

About half an hour had elapsed. Susan was lying on the couch on her pajamas. She couldn't control her tears. Numerous thoughts clouded her mind. She felt responsible for her best friend's death. *Why didn't I stop her from taking those pictures? I should've sensed something. She was pregnant. I should've stayed with her the whole time.* These were the thoughts that plagued her.

"I can't find her anywhere, darling," cried Jason, coming in from the dining area.

"What?"

"Let me look upstairs," he said, climbing the steps.

"Norton is already looking up there," she cried. Jason came back down shortly. "She's not upstairs either." Susan began to worry. She stood up agitated. "Was Norton searching too? Where is he?"

"I didn't see him."

"He said he'll help. Maybe he just went into the room and locked himself up. You know, I don't think he likes Penny at all," commented Susan, putting her slippers on.

"Don't worry about that. When was the last time you saw her?" asked Jason.

"Yesterday when Zoe was here," she replied. "I need to call Andrew too. He must be distraught."

"Okay, relax. I'll call him," said Jason, dialing the number.

While Jason was occupied, Susan went out to the front yard to see if Penny was anywhere around. It was past midday. "Penny! Where are you?" she called out. She walked along the driveway peering in every direction. "Penny!" she cried again, as she went to the furthest edges of the yard. Suddenly, she heard a noise from the side. Immediately turning around, she saw something moving in the bushes. "Penny?" she called. "Is that you?" Susan edged closer to see if the cat was playing tricks on her. Looking down, she noticed something red on the ground. Approaching it, she realized that this was blood. She moved the bushes to get a better look. There on the ground lay Penny. She had been stabbed. The bloody knife lay on the ground next to her. "Oh my goodness! Penny!" she cried. "Jason! Jason!" she shouted in distress. A few moments later, Jason came running out.

"What's the matter?" he asked.

Susan couldn't control herself. She fell on the floor and began screaming out loud. "It's Penny. She's dead. Someone killed her," she cried.

"Where?" asked Jason.

"There," gasped Susan pointing to the puddle of blood that was becoming bigger by the minute. Jason went toward the bushes and looked inside. "Oh no! Oh, Penny!" he voiced.

"Who's done this?" she uttered, bawling.

Jason peered in every direction. "Did you see anyone?"

"No," replied Susan, sobbing.

Jason went to her and helped her up. He embraced her tightly. "I don't know about you, but I think I have an idea," he said in anger. "It's the old man in the house. I'm going to get to the bottom of this right now!" he shouted, racing toward the front door. Jason stormed into the house and began calling Norton. He didn't answer. Going into the kitchen, he noticed Norton taking out a huge pie out of the oven. "Norton!" he shouted. The old man turned around and gazed at him. "Did you not hear me call you?" he shouted.

"Oh, I'm sorry, sir. I didn't hear you. You know at my old age, I'm a bit hard of hearing," he said with a smile.

Jason approached him. "Did you do something to my wife's cat?"

"What do you mean, sir?"

"Well, Penny is dead. She has been stabbed. Did you do that?"

"Absolutely not, sir! I'm shocked that you think that I did something so horrendous," he declared.

"Well then, who did it?" snapped Jason in anger.

"I haven't the slightest clue, sir. As you can see, I've been here cooking lunch for you and the madam."

"Why weren't you looking for Penny when Susan asked you to?"

"I was sir. I, however, had to use the facilities as I haven't been feeling well lately. I'm so sorry to hear about your cat sir, but I assure you, I did not lay a hand on her," he insisted.

Jason glared at Norton for a minute, turned around, and stormed out of the kitchen. As he came into the dining area, he could see Susan coming inside. She was distraught. Jason hastily made his way toward her and held her.

"Am I going crazy?" she asked.

"What do you mean?" asked Jason looking into her eyes.

"Is all of this real, or am I imagining it?"

Susan felt a bit disoriented and fell into Jason's arms. He held onto his wife and walked her to the couch. "Sit, honey."

"I don't know how much of this I can take," she said crying. "First, it's Zoe and now Penny. What's happening? Is someone out there trying to harm us?"

"I don't know, darling. I don't know. The police looked at every inch of the property last night. They couldn't find anything. Let me call Detective Johnson," he said.

"What happened with Norton?" asked Susan. Her eyes were red and her face was swollen from crying.

"He insists he didn't touch Penny. From the looks of it, he seemed sincere, but I'd bet you he's the culprit." A moment later, he got the detective on the phone.

"Hello, Detective Johnson. This is Jason Smith. We need you to come to the villa right away. Something awful has happened. I cannot explain it on the phone," said Jason. "Alright, thank you."

"He'll be here within the hour."

17

When Jason saw the police car pull into the yard, he rushed outside. Susan remained indoors. She was plagued with a throbbing headache as a result of extreme grief and lack of sleep. Detective Johnson stepped out and approached Jason, who explained to him what had occurred. He led the detective to the pool of blood by the bushes and Penny. The detective asked the officer who accompanied him to take pictures of the crime scene. He wanted to question Susan. Jason, however, advised him against it, stating that she was under too much stress and grief. The detective was happy to comply. Jason went to the garage and found a hand shovel. He went to one of the furthest edges of the backyard and began digging a hole. Detective Johnson noticed this and asked the officer to take Penny to the back. The officer put on a pair of gloves, got a trash bag out of the trunk of his car and walked toward Penny. He opened the bag, placed it on the ground, carefully took the cat, and put her inside. Both of them walked toward the backyard where Jason was still digging. As they came closer, the detective noticed that Jason was wiping his tears.

"Are you alright, Dr. Smith?" he asked.

"Yes," he replied. "I'll manage. It's my wife I'm worried about."

The officer placed the bag in the hole that Jason dug. "Are you sure you don't want your wife to be here?" he asked.

"It's okay. She's been through enough," he said. He took some dirt and threw it down. The officer began filling the hole with the shovel. "You know, we had her since the day we got married. Believe it or not, she was a present from my mother-in-law. Susan loves cats."

"I'm so sorry," said the detective. "I hope you find better times soon. I need your help to solve this case though before anything else happens. Please keep me posted about everything."

Jason shook his head in compliance. Detective Johnson and the officer went back to their car and drove off. Jason remained by Penny's grave for some time.

"Rest in peace, Penny," he sighed and headed back to the house.

It was evening. Susan had fallen asleep on the couch. Jason went upstairs, brought a thicker blanket, and covered her. He then went to the kitchen to make himself some coffee. While he was waiting for the coffee to brew, several calls came to him from close friends. They were concerned about Susan and how she was coping with Zoe's death. Jason graciously accepted all condolences on her behalf and explained to the callers that Susan was sleeping. Andrew was also one of them. He was distraught. Jason comforted him and assured that he would come to see him soon.

A few hours elapsed. Jason sat by Susan, who was still asleep. He made a few calls to the hospital, informing them about the day's events. He was advising one of his fellow physicians on procedural matters in the department when, suddenly, he was startled by Susan's screaming. She woke up in terror.

"What's the matter, darling? I'm here," exclaimed Jason holding her.

"Oh, it's a nightmare! It was awful. I was falling, and I had nothing to hold onto. I was falling into a big black hole. I was calling for you, but you weren't there," she uttered.

"I'm here. I've always been here and I always will," he said, embracing her.

"Where's Penny?" she asked with tears still flooding her eyes.

"I buried her in the backyard," he replied.

"Why didn't you call me?" she asked, wiping her tears.

"I thought you had been through enough. Detective Johnson and his officer were there with me. I'll fetch you some dinner. You haven't eaten anything all day," he said, standing up. "I've put on a pot of coffee too if you'd like some."

"Alright, I'll have some," she said.

"Come with me," he urged her.

Susan got up and followed her husband into the kitchen. It was dark outside. "What time is it?" she asked, pulling in the blanket.

"Eleven," he replied looking at his watch.

"Have you heard from Andrew?" she asked.

"Yes, while you were sleeping. He called me."

"How is he?"

"Bad. He's so upset. I'm worried about him."

Susan was silent yet couldn't control her tears. Jason went up to her and hugged her. She began to cry on his shoulder. "I told him I would go and see him as soon as I get the chance," said Jason. "Listen. Do you want me to stay home tomorrow as well?"

"No, honey. You can't miss work. I'm sure they need you. Go ahead. I'll be fine," she assured wiping her tears.

"Are you sure? I can stay another day if you want me to."

"No. I'll be fine. I'm going to call Mom and ask her to come here and stay with me for a while."

"That's a great idea," said Jason in relief, as he handed her the coffee. "There's some shepherd's pie in the fridge. I'll warm up a piece for you," he said, opening the refrigerator. He took the pie, cut a piece, put it on a plate, and placed it inside the microwave.

"Where's Norton?" she asked looking around.

"I don't know and, frankly, I don't care. I haven't seen him since I exchanged words with him this afternoon. He's probably locked up in his room," speculated Jason.

They sat at the dining table and began eating. "It's so dull without her," she observed.

"I know, darling. I feel the same way. I'll get you a puppy."

"Oh, I don't know. I don't want to replace her yet."

"Call Zoe's mother tomorrow," said Jason.

"I don't know if I can. I feel responsible," she said, wiping her tears. "It's not one person but two, her and the baby."

"It's not your fault, honey," assured Jason.

"At least I told her I loved her," said Susan.

"What do you mean?"

"Those were the last words we said to each other, I love you."

Jason smiled. "How wonderful!" he declared.

"I should've been with her. She was pregnant. What type of a friend am I?" she asked in indignation.

"But she's a grown woman, honey. You can't tell her what to do or be with her all the time," he protested. "Come on. Let's go to bed. We're both exhausted." Jason took the dishes to the sink and washed them. Then he checked to see if the kitchen door was locked. Susan went out to the living room to do the same. The house was still. Turning off the kitchen lights Jason joined his wife. "Locked everything?"

"Yes," sighed Susan.

The two of them came into the bedroom. Jason closed the door. He pulled out his pajamas from the closet and walked into the bathroom. Susan took out her nightgown and quickly changed into it. She opened the window by her bedside. The cool air rushed inside and soothed her. Then she got into bed and pulled the covers over her. The bed was warm and comforting. Jason came out of the bathroom in his pajamas, turned off the lamp by his side, and got into bed as well. He edged closer to his wife and kissed her. "How are you feeling?" he asked.

"I don't know," she sighed.

"Maybe I can help you relax a bit," he uttered kissing her.

Although she was grief-stricken, the fact that he was there made her feel safe. Susan looked deep into his eyes.

"I love you," she said.

"I love you, too," he said.

They made passionate love, which made Susan forgot her troubles for at least a short while. Afterward, Susan turned the other way. Jason moved toward her and encircled her from behind. This lulled her to sleep.

It was late into the night. Susan suddenly woke up, as she felt someone caressing her from behind. Instinctively assuming that it was Jason, she turned toward him to cuddle with him. Jason, however, was sleeping on his belly and was snoring away. A strange sensation overtook her body, and she began to perspire. She glanced at the clock by her bed table. It was one o'clock in the morning. Getting up from bed, she walked toward the open window to take in some fresh air. It was dark and quiet outside. She peered down at the lawn when, instantly, the hooded black figure appeared. It stood on the grass, lifted its head, and glared directly at her as if in anger. Its black eyes were piercing. Susan was petrified and became as stiff as a statue. Suddenly, she heard a sound from behind. As she slowly turned around, she noticed the ceiling chandelier swaying back and forth. There was no strong gust of wind coming into the room however. Turning back to the garden, she noted that the black figure was gone.

"What?" she uttered to herself. It was nowhere in sight. "Jason!" she called. He, however, was slumbering away. Susan sat on the bed. Her heart was racing and a lump of fear built up inside her stomach. This was the same black figure that appeared in the backyard weeks before. Marshaling her courage, she got up, opened the bedroom door, and walked out. The hallway was dark. She went down the stairs, headed toward the dining room, and switched on the chandelier. Going into the kitchen, she grabbed a knife from the counter and made her way toward the living room. She switched on the main chandelier there and paused for a moment.

Taking a deep breath, she uttered out loud, "I can do this. This is my house, and I'm not going to put up with this anymore!"

She advanced toward the front door and opened it. The cool air instantly brushed against her body, but an eerie feeling came over her. Most of the front yard was visible from the light that came from the light post. She stepped out with the knife in hand and scrutinized the surroundings.

"Where are you?" she shouted. "Show yourself, you coward!" She made her way to the lawn area that directly faced her bedroom. Nobody was there. "Did you kill my cat?" she shouted in anger. "You leave my property alone whoever or whatever you are! Do you hear me?"

She walked back to the front yard. It was as still as before. "Alright, I tried," she uttered to herself and walked into the house. Closing the door, she leaned against it and let out another deep breath. "That was good, Susan," she complimented herself. "You're some woman!"

18

It was ten o'clock in the morning when Susan opened her eyes. She turned around and saw that Jason wasn't in bed. A note lay on the side. It read,

> *I had to go to the hospital for a couple of hours. Didn't want to wake you. Coffee is on downstairs.*
> *Love,*
> *Jason*

Susan sat up on the bed. Morning sunlight trickled into the room from both windows. A moment later, she remembered what had happened during the night. She sprung out of bed and went toward the window. Looking down, she saw Norton on the far edge of the yard. She promptly changed her clothes and headed downstairs. She poured herself a cup of hot coffee and went out to the backyard. Seeing Norton, she hastily made her way toward him.

"Norton!" she called.

He turned around. "Yes, madam."

"What are you doing?" she asked.

He was wearing gloves and a small shovel lay on the ground beside him.

"Oh, I'm trying to plant some tomatoes, madam," he replied. "The sir left about an hour ago. He told me not to wake you."

"Where were you last night?" she asked reproachfully.

"I was sleeping, madam. Why do you ask?"

"Because I saw someone here. I don't even know if it was a person. It just appeared out of nowhere and vanished in front of my eyes. A black figure of some kind."

Norton's face immediately became sour as he turned toward her.

"Norton, what are you hiding?" she demanded. He however was silent.

"You must not ask me questions. It's not your concern, madam," he rasped in an assertive tone of voice.

"What do you mean it's not my concern? This is my house, and I need to know what all this mumbo jumbo is," she demanded.

"You're in danger," he said bluntly.

"If you're trying to scare me, it's not going to work Norton," she declared.

"Believe me, madam, this is beyond your understanding. Please leave it be. I cannot tell you anything," he said and went on digging the ground.

"Norton, did you kill my cat?"

"As I said, I cannot say," he responded bluntly.

"Oh, I don't know what to do with you!" she snapped in anger. "Alright. Fine. I'll get to the bottom of this myself," she shouted and headed in the direction of the kitchen.

On her way, she noticed the freshly covered soil on the other side of the yard and went toward it. Instinctively she realized that this was Penny's grave. When she came to it, she sat on the ground beside it and touched the soil.

"I'm so sorry, Penny. I didn't mean for this to happen," she uttered. Tears flooded her eyes. "Don't worry, I'll find out who did this to you." She placed a kiss on the soil and walked away.

It was afternoon, and Susan waited for Jason. She took out her phone and dialed her mother's number. To her consolation, her mom answered.

"Hello, Mom."

"Yes, darling. How are you?" she responded from the other end.

"Not good. Zoe's gone," said Susan somberly.

"I know. Jason called me and told me everything. How are you holding up?"

"Not good, Mom. When can you come here for a visit? Are you feeling any better?"

"Oh, it was a little flu that I had, but I feel a lot better. In fact, I'm on my way up there, now," she said.

"What? That's so great, Mom! Who's driving you?"

"I don't need anyone to drive me, darling. I'm coming by myself. Jason gave me the address." Susan was thrilled. "How far away are you?"

"Well, darling, can you come out of the front door?"

Susan immediately got up from the couch and ran toward the front. Opening the door, she came out to the yard. A red car pulled up to the driveway. She hung up the phone and walked hastily toward it. The car stopped by the cherub fountain.

"Mom!" she cried with joy.

"Hello, darling," said her mother. Susan ran toward the car. Her mother got out and embraced her.

"Oh, Mom. How nice to see you!" she said, holding onto her.

"It's nice to see you too, darling."

"What a wonderful surprise!" Susan's mother was an older lady. She was well dressed in a white business suit. She had short dark hair and blue eyes. "You look beautiful, Mom," remarked Susan.

"Thank you. You look wonderful yourself. And what a beautiful home!"

"It is, isn't it?"

"Let me get my bags out of the trunk," she said.

"Oh, of course. Let me help you," said Susan, walking toward the car. Her mother opened the trunk and took three bags out and placed them on the ground. "Leave the car here. Jason will park it in the garage when he gets home."

She grabbed two bags from either hand and headed toward the front door. Her mother took the other bag and followed her. Susan noticed her mother gazing around and smiling.

"Oh, darling, this is the most beautiful home I have ever seen!" she exclaimed.

"Thanks, Mom," she responded, smiling. Her mother's eyes gleamed when they entered the living room area. Susan placed the bags by the front table.

"Put them here, Mom. We can take them up to your room later. You must be tired. Come on in and relax on the couch," she said.

"Okay, darling." They went into the living room. "I'm in awe!" gasped her mother glancing in every direction. "This house must be very old. The furniture is so elegant," she remarked.

"Come and sit," insisted Susan.

"Okay, darling. It's a long drive up here from home. But the view is stunning. I enjoyed every bit of it," she said, sitting down. Susan sat next to her mother.

"I am so happy you're here," she said.

"Me too, darling. Where's Jason?"

"He's at the hospital. He'll be back soon."

"Oh, let him take his time. I heard about the promotion. I'm so happy for the two of you."

"Thank you. He's been working very hard the past few weeks since the promotion."

"That's the life of a doctor, dear. You're going to have to get used to the long hours," commented her mother. "How have you been? How are you coping?" She clasped onto her daughter's hand.

"Not so well. Zoe's gone and so is her baby. I feel like it's my fault," she said woefully.

"Oh no! How can you say that? You two have always been such wonderful friends for so many years."

"I know. That's why I feel responsible. I should've been with her," uttered Susan sullenly.

"Well, you can't be there to protect her every moment. She's got to take care of herself."

"That's what Jason told me."

"Well, he's right. How's Andrew?"

"I don't know. I haven't spoken to him. Jason did though."

"He's got a big family. I'm sure, they're helping him in this difficult hour."

"Mom, there's something else."

"What, darling?"

"Penny's dead too."

"Oh my goodness! What happened?"

"We think someone killed her," she replied wiping her tears. "When I was walking out in the front yard yesterday, I found her body."

"Oh, that's terrible! I'm so sorry. She was my wedding present to you."

"Yes, I know. I miss her."

"Darling, is everything okay? I sense that something is troubling you?" she said, looking into Susan's eyes. She was very close to her daughter and could sense distress. Ever since her husband's death, Susan was her only family. She treasured her daughter more than life itself.

"I don't know, Mom. It's just that I'm so thankful for this house. I mean, look at this place! It's so gorgeous! It's my dream home. But at the same time, all these bad things are happening around me. I can't figure out the cause. I feel like I'm losing my mind," she said, holding her head.

"Calm down, darling. Listen to me," she said, clutching Susan's hand. "For as long as I can remember, you've been such a headstrong girl. You were my anchor since your father died. I've always admired your strength. It's brought you to such a wonderful place in your life. Whatever the problem is, I'm sure you can solve it and make things work."

"You think so?" asked Susan, looking at her mother.

"I don't just think so. I know so," she replied resolutely. "So you've got such a big house. When am I going to see some grandchildren around here?"

"Well, Mom, soon hopefully. Jason and I are talking about it. I want to have a baby," she uttered, smiling.

"Wonderful! So the next time I visit, you can give me some good news."

Norton came into the living room. Susan turned toward him. "Norton, this is my mother, Janet Lowry."

Norton walked up to her and shook her hand. "It is a pleasure to make your acquaintance, madam," he rasped in a very respectful tone.

"The same here," uttered Janet "I'm sorry. Who are you exactly?" she asked.

"I am the caretaker here," he rasped.

"Oh, I see. How nice. I didn't realize my daughter needed a caretaker. She never mentioned you to me," she commented, looking at Susan.

"Oh, I apologize, Mom. Yes, Norton came with the property," remarked Susan, feeling a bit awkward.

"Can I get you any refreshments, madam?" he asked.

"Yes. Bring us some coffee," replied Susan.

"Very well," said Norton. He turned around and walked back to the kitchen. Janet looked at Susan.

"I don't like him," she whispered with a sour expression.

"I know. Me neither," uttered Susan, sitting down. "Unfortunately, he lives here too," she whispered.

"What do you mean, unfortunately?"

"Well, we're obliged to keep him because he's lived here for decades"

"Listen to me, darling. This is your house now. You are under no obligation to keep anyone if you don't want to."

"I know, Mom. I don't know what to do."

"Have you spoken to Jason about it?"

"Yes. Jason's got a bigger heart when it comes to matters like this."

"If you're uncomfortable with that man staying in your home, speak to your husband and come to an understanding," whispered Janet.

"Alright," agreed Susan.

Norton brought a tray with coffee and scones. He had used elegant silver chinaware for the occasion.

"Thank you," said Susan.

"You're welcome, madam. Let me know if you need anything else. Lunch will be ready in about an hour."

"Thank you, Norton," said Janet.

19

After lunch, Susan took her mother on a grand tour of the house. She was quite impressed. Then she brought the luggage to the room next to their bedroom.

"Do you like this one, Mom?" she asked.

"This is perfect, darling. "I'm only here for a week."

"That's it? Can't you stay longer? A week is no time at all."

"Well, honey, I have to get back to work. They had to hire a temporary replacement at the front desk until I get back."

"Isn't it time you retired? You've been at the secretary job at the senior center for years."

"Retire and do what? Working gives me purpose. And I've started a new manuscript too. Speaking of which, how's the writing coming along?"

"I haven't even had the chance to put a word on a page yet. The moving in, getting settled, and now all this turmoil has gotten me worked up to the bone."

"I know. I'm sorry. Things will get better," she assured.

Suddenly they heard a noise from downstairs. "Hello! Is anyone home?" came a voice.

"It's Jason!" exclaimed Susan in excitement. "Come on, Mom."

They stepped out of the room and made their way hastily downstairs.

"Hello, Janet," said Jason.

"Hello, Jason. How are you, darling?" she asked, giving him an embrace.

"Fine, just fine. Thanks for coming to see us. Susan has been missing you."

"I know. I'm here for a week, and don't you worry, I'll take care of her for you," she assured.

"Oh, Mom, I'm not a baby. You're embarrassing me!"

"Well, darling that's a mother's prerogative to embarrass her child. Mind you though, it's all out of love," she said. Susan rolled her eyes at that remark.

"So what do you think of the house?" asked Jason.

"It's beautiful! I love it! You've taken very good care of my little girl," she uttered with a big smile.

"Mom. I'm not a little girl anymore," protested Susan in irritation.

"Whatever you say, darling," said her mother, looking at her.

"Have you had lunch yet?" asked Susan, looking at her husband.

"No, not really."

"Norton made some lamb stew. I saved you some."

"Thanks, honey," he said making his way to the kitchen.

"Oh, can you park Mom's car in the garage?"

"Sure. After my meal," he said. "I need to speak with you for a moment," he uttered gazing at her gravely. Susan instinctively felt that something was amiss. She looked at her mother. "Mom, can you excuse us for a moment?"

"Sure, darling. I'll go up to my room and start unpacking," she said and headed towards the stairs. Susan turned to Jason. "What is it?"

"Detective Johnson called me today about Zoe. The coroner's report has come in," he continued sullenly. Susan suddenly got a chilling feeling in her stomach.

"Tell me," she said.

"She died of a heart attack," said Jason. Susan was taken aback.

"How?" she asked.

"I don't know. But when a healthy woman suddenly has a heart attack, something isn't right."

20

The following day, Susan and her mother got ready to go to town on a shopping spree.

"You need to get out more, darling," advised Janet.

"I know. I did go out to town once since we moved here," said Susan in her defense. "Who's going to do the driving? You or me?"

"I think I can handle it," said Janet.

They both came down the stairs and went into the kitchen for some coffee. Norton was busy with breakfast preparations.

"Good morning, Norton," said Susan.

Norton turned around and greeted them as well. "Breakfast is on the stove, madam."

"Smells good," commented Janet. Susan took two plates from the counter and placed them on the table. "Where's Jason?" she asked.

"He got called in for surgery in the middle of the night. I don't know when he'll be back."

Norton laid the scrambled eggs and bacon platters on the table. Susan brought toast and butter. They sat at the table and began to enjoy breakfast.

"The ocean is lovely," remarked Janet. "I can hear the waves."

"That's the best part," added Susan.

"I want to take a walk along the beach," said Janet while chewing into the bacon.

"Sure, Mom. We can do that in the evening."

After breakfast, Susan took the plates to the sink to be washed. "I'll do that for you, madam," insisted Norton.

"Thank you," said Susan.

"Thanks for breakfast, Norton," uttered Janet.

"You're welcome, madam," he said. "Any plans for the day?"

"Yes, we're going out to town," she replied.

"How wonderful! Enjoy your trip."

"I will," she said. Susan realized that Norton's disposition had drastically changed from what it was the previous day. "Norton, are you feeling better today?" Norton glanced at her with a surprised look on his face.

"I don't know what you mean, madam. I'm perfectly fine. Thank you for the concern," he replied.

"Okay then. We'll see you in the afternoon," she said.

The two women stepped out of the villa and came into the garage. It was massive enough to fit three vehicles. In addition to the cars, it housed numerous tools and garden equipment.

"Darling, what's all this stuff?" asked Janet, scrutinizing the surroundings. "Not even your dad had so many tools."

"I don't know, Mom. All of that came with the house. I guess it's ours now. I'm sure Jason can use them for all his home improvement projects."

Janet was dressed in a fancy navy blue dress suit and matching blue pumps. A gold purse hung from her shoulder. Susan, on the other hand, wore a plain white shirt and blue jeans. She had her hair tied in a ponytail. Susan always admired her mother's unique sense of style.

"Mom, you look so nice," she remarked.

"Thank you, darling. I've been wearing this old thing for years," she responded, getting into the driver's seat. Susan got into the passenger seat and buckled up. "Ready?" asked Janet.

"Yep. Let's go," said Susan. "I'll help you back up."

Janet carefully reversed the car. As they were passing the driveway, Norton stood by the front door and waved at them. Susan waved in turn.

The day was sunny, and the air was comfortably cool. The surrounding mountainous terrain was exquisite. They drove out of the driveway and followed the narrow road down. Susan was happy to be out with her mother.

"I can't remember the last time we did this, Mom," said Susan.

"Me neither, darling. You know, I'm not so skilled at taking these turns. Keep an eye out, so I won't run over a boulder or something."

"You're doing fine," assured Susan.

"I don't like him," remarked Janet.

"Who?"

"That Norton."

"You told me that yesterday, Mom. Why don't you like him?"

"Because he's a liar, and he's hiding something. I mean something big," she said gravely.

"How do you do that?"

"Do what, darling?"

"Make assumptions like that," stated Susan, a bit irritated.

"It's not an assumption. It's called a mother's intuition. Usually, I'm right about these things."

"You should've been there at the party. You could have used that intuition to stop Zoe from venturing out by herself."

"Oh, darling, I didn't mean any offense by what I said. It's just that when it comes to you, I get a bit, how should I say?"

"Paranoid?" retorted Susan.

"No. Overprotective is a better word," remarked Janet.

"Mom, I'm a grown woman. I can take care of myself."

"I know that. But when you're mother, no matter how old your children are, you want to shelter them from harm. You're all I've got."

"I know, Mom, and I love you too," sighed Susan.

"What's wrong, darling?"

"Well, Mom, the fact of the matter is, your intuition is right on target. He is hiding something."

Susan continued looking out to the mountains. The wind was caressing her face and she felt sullen on the inside. Her mother looked at her with concern.

"Well, do you have any idea as to what he's hiding?"

"I've seen things in the house and around the property. Things that neither Jason nor I can explain," she answered, still gazing out.

"What kinds of things?"

"Well, over a week ago, we were walking in the property at night, and we saw some kind of an apparition. I got so scared and passed out. Jason called the police, but they didn't believe us. Now Zoe is gone because of it," she said.

"That's strange. What does that have to do with Zoe? I thought she had a fall of some kind," said Janet.

"No, Mom. She was taking pictures of the property in the night. You know how she likes to explore. The last two pictures show this apparition. It's a woman dressed in white. She must've seen it and got scared. The coroner's report says that she had a heart attack."

"Oh, darling! That's awful!"

At that very moment, Susan's cell phone rang. It was Jason. "Hi, honey," she said.

"Where are you?" asked Jason from the other end. He was calling from his hospital office.

"Mom and I are going for a drive."

"Good. You need that. Listen. Andrew called me."

"Okay. What's up?"

"Zoe's funeral is tomorrow at ten in the morning."

"So soon?"

"Yes. He's not in good shape, honey. He's falling apart. I feel so bad. I'm taking the morning off tomorrow, so we can attend the funeral."

"Okay. That's good. Where's it going to be?"

"In the church downtown. Listen, honey, I've got to go. A patient is waiting for me."

"How was the surgery?"

"It went well. He's in recovery. Only time will tell. Got to go. I love you," he said before hanging up the line.

Susan turned off the phone and placed it back inside her purse. "That was Jason calling from the office."

"Yes, I could tell. Is everything alright?"

"Zoe's funeral is tomorrow morning. I want you to come with us, Mom. I don't know if I can get through it," uttered Susan with tears in her eyes.

Janet patted her shoulder. "Sure, darling, I'll be there with you," she assured. "Listen to me," she said sternly. "No matter what's happening in the house, I know you will figure it out. Don't let that old man scare you."

"I know, Mom. I know. I'm going to find out what he's hiding. I wish you could stay with me and help me."

"I can't, darling. Besides, you're a strong woman. If anyone can find answers, it's you," assured Janet.

Before long, they had left the mountainous terrain behind and entered into town. "Where do you want to go?" asked Susan.

"Oh, I don't know, maybe the stores. I do want to do some shopping," she said, scanning the vicinity. People were out and about on the streets. "Perhaps, afterward, we could stop for lunch somewhere."

"That sounds nice," said Susan.

Soon they arrived at a shopping center. Parking the car in the lot, both ladies got out and headed toward a clothes store. They went inside and looked at the merchandise. About half an hour later, they came out with a few shopping bags in their hands.

"That blouse was really lovely on you, darling."

"I know. That's why I bought it," voiced Susan.

They walked into another shop with lovely home décor items. Vases, lampshades, framed art, and chandeliers adorned every square inch of its interior.

"Oh, how lovely!" exclaimed Janet. "This vase would look so nice on my dining table," she remarked.

Before Susan realized it, her mother was purchasing half the store. "Mom, your car is too small for all of this."

"It'll fit," she assured.

The shop workers were thrilled to assist her in taking the items she bought to the car. They helped her place everything in the trunk. Whatever that didn't fit was placed on the back seat. "See, I told you it'll all fit. It's time for lunch. I'm starved," she said. "This fresh ocean air is working up my appetite."

"I think we're going to have to drive a bit more for the restaurants, Mom," said Susan getting into the car.

"Fine. Let's go," she said, pulling out of the parking lot.

They drove around a bit in search of a place to eat. Finally locating what seemed to be a café, they pulled into its parking lot. It was a small yet elegant spot with indoor and outdoor seating. The outdoor tables and chairs had green umbrella-like shades above them. Not many customers were outside.

"This is perfect for the two of us," remarked Janet.

"Lunch is on me. You spent all your money shopping today," said Susan as they walked into the café.

"If you insist, darling, I'd be happy to oblige."

The interior of the café was as elegant as it was outside. Its glass doors were painted with pictures of various treats and soups. The ground was made of hardwood, and the walls were painted in a dark shade of brown. The exquisite stained glass ceiling lights that hung over every table enhanced its overall appearance and warmth. As they walked toward the counter, they could see different types of freshly baked bread, scones, pastries, and other goodies on display. The menu was put on view right above the counter. A waitress walked up to them shortly.

"Good afternoon. What can I get for you, ladies?" she asked.

"Good afternoon," said Susan. They gazed at the menu for a few moments. "I'll have the soup of the day, two pastries, and a cup of coffee," said Susan.

"I'll have the same," said Janet.

"Right away," uttered the waitress, ringing them up at the cashier's desk.

Susan paid the bill and asked if they could be seated out front. The two women walked outside and chose a seat all the way on the side of the café where it was shady and quiet. Sitting down, they hung their purses on the chair.

"This is a beautiful town!" exclaimed Janet.

"Yes, it is. I think that's why Jason chose it. He wants me to be relaxed all the time."

"He really loves you. I can see it."

"Yes, and I love him very much too."

"Your father was like that. He always looked out for my welfare. When he died, I was left alone with you. I had to come out of the cocoon he had created for me. And believe me when I tell you this, the world is a cruel place."

"I know, Mom. You told me so many times," said Susan, looking at her mother.

"I'm sorry. I know what I say can be a bit redundant at times. I just want to make sure you'll be okay after I'm gone."

"Don't worry, Mom. I'll be fine. Jason is very good at planning for the future."

"Well, I'm glad. But I do want you to pursue your writing," she said.

The waitress brought their food.

"Thank you," said Susan.

They continued their conversation over lunch. After the meal, they took a long stroll along the beach. "I can see the house from here," cried Susan, looking up.

The villa was all the way on top of the hill. The backyard and the surrounding trees were also visible. Gazing at her new home Susan wondered what history and secrets it held.

21

As evening drew near Susan and her mother returned to the villa. The garage door was still open and Jason's car was visible.

"He's here," commented Susan with a flash of excitement. "Go into the garage, Mom," said Susan.

Janet parked the car inside as instructed and got out. "This place is more beautiful in the evening than during the day. The weather is perfect!' she exclaimed.

"Do you want to take your bags inside?" asked Susan, looking at her mother.

"No, darling. Let them be in the car. Otherwise, I'm going to have to haul all those things back again when I leave, and that's a bother."

They took a stroll in the front yard. Susan neared the rose bushes and began inhaling their scent. Some of them were a deep red shade.

"Are you ever going to pick those?" asked Janet.

"It never occurred to me," replied Susan.

"Perhaps you should take some for the funeral tomorrow. Make a bouquet for Zoe," she suggested. Susan looked at her mother who was walking toward her. "I'll help you if you'd like," she suggested gently. Susan was sullen. Tears came rolling down her cheeks. "Look, darling. I know you're going through a tough time. But I want you to know that I'm here for you." She held her daughter's hand. Susan turned toward her mother and embraced her and began crying.

"It's okay. Let it all out. It's not your fault. If Zoe were here, she'd tell you that." A moment later, Susan regained her composure, took a deep breath, and smiled. "I'm okay, Mom. Thank you. I'll get some scissors to cut these. Making a bouquet is a great idea," she concurred.

"Alright. Go get the scissors, and maybe a vase to put them in," ordered Janet, who was also tearing up. "I'll wait out here a bit longer to inhale some of this beach air that I don't get at home." Susan opened the front door and went inside. The house was calm and quiet. She headed toward the kitchen. At that very moment, Jason walked out and almost bumped into her. Susan was startled.

"Oh, honey, you scared me!" she exclaimed.

"I'm sorry. I could say the same about you," retorted Jason.

"What time did you get home?" she asked.

Jason gave her a tight embrace and a kiss. "A couple of hours ago," he answered. "I missed you. Where did you go?"

"Mom and I went out shopping."

"That explains it," said Jason jovially.

"Where's your mother?"

"She's out by the rose bushes, waiting for me to bring a pair of scissors. We're going to make a bouquet for Zoe."

"That's nice," said Jason, following his wife to the kitchen. The smell of fresh stew was everywhere. "Oh, it smells good in here. Did you cook?"

"No. Norton made dinner."

Susan opened one of the counter drawers and grabbed a pair of scissors. Then she opened the cabinet under the sink and took a glass vase. "These come in handy when you've got flowers growing in your garden," she said, looking at it. "Want to help me?"

"No. I think I'll wait here. I'm afraid of those thorns," he replied.

"You're such a baby. Well, come on out anyway. Get some fresh air," urged Susan.

"No, honey. I'm tired. I had an exhausting day," he sighed, sitting down at the table and holding his head.

Susan sensed that something was amiss. "What's the matter, darling?"

"I lost a patient today," he sighed.

"Oh no! What happened?"

"Well, the surgery was a success, but a couple of hours later, he just stopped breathing. I tried my best to revive him, but he was gone."

"I'm sorry," said Susan, sitting beside him. "It's hard being a surgeon, isn't it?"

"Isn't that the truth?" he said.

"You can't save them all, darling. All you can do is your best," she said, gently caressing his head.

"Tell that to the patient's family," he sighed.

"Come on outside with me. A little fresh air will do you some good," she suggested, pulling on Jason's hand. He got up and walked out with her.

Susan's mother was standing by the rose bushes. "There you are. I've been waiting for you."

"I bumped into my husband here."

"Hello, Jason," said Janet with a smile.

"Hello, Janet," said Jason.

"You look exhausted, darling. Are you alright?" she inquired.

"Oh, I'm okay. Just a long day at the hospital," he replied.

As it grew dark, the wind began to turn direction. It was very chilly. "I think that's enough," said Susan, looking at the vase. She had picked over a dozen long-stemmed deep red roses.

"Yes, that's enough," concurred Janet picking up the vase and surveying it. "I'll ribbon these up for you."

Susan held Jason's hand as they walked into the house. The garden light poles had already lit up.

After dinner, Jason went straight to bed.

"Is he alright?" asked Janet.

"He lost a patient," replied Susan.

"Oh, I'm sorry. That's the tough part of being a physician."

They sat at the kitchen table with the vase. Susan had found some nice white ribbon.

"Where's Norton?" whispered her mother.

Susan looked around. "I don't know. Maybe he went to bed early."

"Alright. Let's get this started." Janet carefully took the roses out and tied the stems together using a white ribbon. The thorns pricked her a couple of times during the process. Susan looked in the kitchen cupboards for tissue paper. "Here, wrap the bouquet with this."

"Oh, thank you, darling," she said taking the tissue.

Once the bouquet was done, they placed it on the table and examined it.

"Yeah, Zoe would like this," commented Susan.

Her mother gave her an embrace. "Alright, darling, I'm tired. I hope you don't mind if I hit the sack," she said jovially.

"Sure, Mom. Thanks for a lovely day," she said, kissing her mother good night.

Susan remained in the kitchen for a bit, reminiscing on the events of the day. She felt a bit at peace, knowing her mother and husband were with her.

"I wish I could make her stay," she uttered to herself. Then turning off the lights, she went upstairs to her room. Coming in, she saw that Jason was already fast asleep. She went into the restroom, brushed her teeth, put on her nightgown, and climbed onto the bed. Kissing Jason on the cheek, she laid back on the bed. The thought of having to bury her best friend broke her heart.

"I'll see you again someday, Zoe," she sighed and closed her eyes.

Susan was fast asleep. Her body felt relaxed as Jason's hand was massaging her back. He stroked her up and down from her neck to the lower back. "Oh, honey. That feels good!" she uttered, feeling a bit aroused. A warm sensation took over her body. It was one she had never felt before. Suddenly waking up, she turned toward Jason. He, however, was fast asleep. She suddenly became alarmed. Looking up, she could see the chandelier swaying back and forth. At that instant, the black-hooded figure appeared by her bedside. Susan was terrified and her body froze. Although she tried to scream, she couldn't. She was paralyzed. Its face was gray, and its dark eyes glared at her in anger. Then it suddenly vanished from sight. The chandelier stopped swaying. Susan breathed again and fell back on the bed. Her body was covered in sweat and her heart was beating fast. She felt as if she was about to pass out.

"Jason!" she cried. "Jason, help me!" she uttered as everything became a blur.

22

"Susan! Susan! Wake up, honey!" Susan opened her eyes. It was bright. "Honey, are you alright?" She looked around groggily. Jason was getting ready. "Good. You're awake," he uttered, smiling at her.

"What time is it?" she asked.

"About eight fifteen," he responded. "Honey, you look worn out. Are you feeling alright?" he asked, approaching her and sitting by her bedside. He placed her hand on her forehead. "You're burning up with fever," he said in agitation.

Susan immediately recalled what had happened in the middle of the night. "Honey, I saw the dark figure last night in the bedroom. It was the same one I saw a few weeks ago on the swing and a few days ago on the yard."

"Are you sure?" he asked in alarm.

"Yes, positive. I called you in the middle of the night because I felt as if I was having a heart attack. Didn't you hear me?" she asked.

"Oh, I must have crashed so badly. I was dead to the world," he replied, stroking her hair. "Alright, I want you to stay in bed today. I'm going to call Detective Johnson and have him deal with this," said Jason taking his phone.

"Oh no! I have to go to Zoe's funeral," she protested, getting out of bed.

"But you're burning up with fever," he argued.

"I don't care! I'll rest after the funeral," she said walking into the restroom. Turning on the shower, she stepped in. She let the cold water run over her body from head to toe. It calmed and relaxed her. Thoughts of the previous night plagued her though. Having to say goodbye to her best friend and the baby she was carrying brought agony to her mind. Stepping out, she took a deep breath. Jason came into the bathroom. He was dressed in a black suit and looked strikingly handsome.

"How are you feeling?" he asked, placing his hand on her forehead.

"Fine, dear. What needs to be done, needs to be done regardless of how I feel," she asserted, wiping herself. She walked into the room, opened the closet, and pulled out a black dress. "Don't tell my mother anything that I said. She's going to freak out."

Susan quickly put on the dress, dried her, hair, and put on her makeup. Jason sat on the bed and watched her the whole time. Susan gazed at Jason from the mirror. "Alright! Let's go," she ordered, putting on her shoes and grabbing her purse. Jason stood up and walked out of the room with his wife.

"There you are," said Janet, stepping out of her room. "Do we have time for some breakfast?"

"Let's go down and see. Norton must have something prepared," replied Jason.

"Good morning, darling," said Janet, kissing Susan.

"Good morning, Mom. You look lovely," remarked Susan, gazing at her mother.

Janet wore a black dress suit and a very elegant black hat. The hat had on a combination of black- and crème-colored flowers with a pearl trim around the petals. She wore matching black pumps.

Coffee was already brewing, and breakfast was on the table.

"Great!" said Jason, grabbing a plate and serving some bacon and eggs for his wife.

Norton came inside from the back door. "Good morning," he said.

"Good morning, Norton," uttered Janet. Susan, on the other hand, was feeling a bit glum and didn't say anything.

"Okay, if we're going to make it on time, we're going to have to be quick about this," uttered Jason.

"Is there anything else I can get you?" asked Norton looking at everyone.

"We're good here, thank you," replied Jason, who was gobbling up his food.

"Are you feeling alright, darling?" asked Janet looking at Susan. "You look a bit flushed."

"Fine, Mom. It's the funeral and the thought of having to bury my best friend is just overwhelming."

"Eat something, darling," she said.

"I don't have the appetite," snapped Susan.

A few minutes later, Jason got up and asked Norton to clear the table. Susan took the bouquet. "I'll pull out the car," he said as he headed toward the back door. Janet gulped her coffee as fast as she could and grabbed her purse.

"Ready?" she asked, looking at her daughter.

"Let's get this over with," sighed Susan and walked out of the kitchen.

Her mother followed her. They came around the backyard toward the garage. Jason had already pulled the car out and was patiently waiting for them. Susan got into the front passenger seat and Janet got into the back. A moment later, Jason exited the driveway.

Susan kept the bouquet on her lap. As she gazed at the mountains, a myriad of thoughts invaded her mind. She wasn't in the mood for conversation. Jason noticed this and didn't want to impose on her. He placed his hand on her thigh. Susan held onto it.

It was ten minutes before the funeral. Aware of the time, Jason sped up a little. The fact that there was hardly any traffic on the road helped with the situation. Susan, however, was lost in her thoughts to notice much of anything that was going on.

"I think this is it," uttered Jason as they neared what looked like a church.

Susan lifted her head to take a peek. A steeple and cross came into view. People were seen walking into the church. Many of them were dressed in black or dark attire. Jason pulled into the lot at the back and parked the car. They all got out and began heading to the church.

Jason held his wife's hand. A large framed picture of Zoe was placed at the entrance. It was on a stand and two flower rings were placed on either side. Susan stood in front of Zoe's picture and looked into her eyes. Zoe was smiling in this photo. Tears came rolling down her cheeks as she uttered, "I'm so sorry."

Jason stood beside her. "Come on honey, the service is about to begin."

Susan wiped her tears and went in with him. Janet followed them. As they walked down the center aisle, the coffin could be seen straight ahead. Susan held onto Jason's hand tightly. Many mourners were seated on either side of the church. Some of them glanced at them as they walked up. Susan went straight to the coffin. It was half open. Zoe's body lay motionless. She wore a beautiful white dress, her hands covered in gloves and clasped together. Her face looked pale. Susan couldn't contain herself. As she looked at Zoe's face, she broke down in tears. Jason held onto her and helped her walk to a nearby seat. As they passed by the front row, they saw Andrew. Jason and Susan both embraced him before they went to their seats. Another picture of Zoe stood by the coffin. Flower rings surrounded it. Susan surveyed the premises to see who was present. Zoe's entire family was there and so was Andrew's.

"Are they blaming me?" she whispered to Jason.

"No, darling. Please don't think that way. It's nobody's fault," he assured her.

Janet also held onto Susan's hand. Her eyes were flooded with tears as well. A few moments later, the pastor walked to the front of the church and the service began. He was a short gentleman with glasses and wore a white cassock for the service. He spoke about Zoe and the many positive qualities she exemplified throughout her life. The congregation cheered as these were mentioned. Finally, he posed this question, "And what can we learn from Zoe's life today?" He looked around with a stern expression on his face. "It is to live life to the fullest. She died doing what she loved," he asserted.

Susan thought about this and Zoe's final moments. Despite what the pastor had said, she believed that the apparition seen in her property was solely responsible for Zoe's untimely demise. At that moment, she was overcome with anger and was determined to put an end to whatever was haunting her villa.

Zoe's brother gave a touching eulogy. Everyone in the church was moved by his words. When the service was finally over, the coffin was fully closed. Six pallbearers held onto it and walked slowly down the aisle. Andrew and Zoe's mother followed with the rest of their family members. Susan, Jason, and Janet trailed behind. Other friends followed behind them with teary eyes.

The casket was taken to the nearby cemetery where a plot was waiting. Susan quickly placed her bouquet on top of the coffin before it was hauled down to the ground. Friends and family threw flowers in with kisses and final remarks. Susan held onto Jason and watched. Susan's mother stood by her daughter's side. One by one, the mourners began walking out of the cemetery. Some of Susan's friends came up to her and embraced her offering their condolences. Susan hugged them and wept. Jason went up to Andrew who remained by his wife's grave. Andrew gazed at him.

"My wife and child," he cried. "What do I do now?" he asked. "If only I wasn't drunk that night, she would still be here."

"Don't blame yourself," urged Jason. "It's nobody's fault."

"I was supposed to protect her, and I failed," he sobbed.

Jason gave him a tight embrace. Andrew's mother walked up to him and held his hand. She looked at Jason and gave him a faint smile. Jason realized that this was his cue to leave. He turned around and walked back to Susan who was still talking to her friends. He came up to her and greeted those who were speaking to her. They, in turn, acknowledged him. After the conversations and well wishes were exchanged, everyone went in separate directions to their vehicles. Susan and Jason also began walking back to their car. Getting in, Susan took a deep breath.

"It's over, darling," said Jason holding onto her hand. "You did good," he assured.

"That was a lovely service," remarked Janet.

"It sure was," added Jason.

23

A week had passed, and Janet was getting ready to go back home. Susan tried to get her to stay with her for a few more days, but her mother insisted that she had to get back to work at the senior center.

"I'll call you and check up on you. And I promise that when I do retire, I'll come and stay here. By that time, this place will be bubbling with the laughter of little ones," she said with a flashing smile.

"Mom, that's a lot of pressure."

"No pressure at all, darling. It's every mother's dream to have lots of grandchildren."

Susan accompanied her mother to the garage. She helped put her luggage into the car. The merchandise that was purchased a week ago during their shopping spree was still in the trunk. Susan recalled the experience with fondness.

"When I come to visit again, we'll go on another shopping spree," she assured Susan, giving her an embrace.

Susan couldn't control her tears. "I'll miss you, Mom," she said.

"I'll miss you too. It's time you started a family of your own now. And remember what I said. Be strong."

Susan shook her head in agreement. Janet got into the car and pulled out of the garage. She went around the cherub fountain and gave her daughter a blowing kiss. "I love you, darling," she said, smiling.

"I love you, Mom. Drive safely," exclaimed Susan in return. Her mother gave a thumbs up and drove off.

Suddenly it was quiet. Her eyes studied the vicinity. Although it was midday and the sun was bright, she felt dejected on the inside. Jason had left for the hospital early morning. "What do I do now?" she asked herself.

Taking a deep breath, she headed inside. Closing the front door, she proceeded toward the study. Upon entering it, her eyes beheld its grandeur and opulence once more. She hadn't been in there for a few weeks and had forgotten how beautiful and tranquil the room was. This was truly the office of someone of significance in the past who also may have been an avid reader, as demonstrated by the hundreds of books that were encased in its wooden wall shelves. Susan had made it a point to go through these books to determine if she was interested in the same topics as the previous owner.

It was dark in the study, as the drapes had been drawn in. She went toward the window, moved the drapes to the sides, and pushed the windows open. Fresh air swept inside, and a bit of the ocean came into view. Turning around, she headed toward the center table, pulled out the chair, and sat down. Pens and pencils were neatly placed in jars on the side. A couple of writing tablets were also there. Taking one and pulling out a pen, she began writing. Each time she paused, she gazed at the ocean. This helped her maintain focus. She continued to write page after page. Before long it grew dark.

"Goodness! I've got to eat something," she uttered to herself, glancing at the wall clock. She closed the windows and pulled the drapes in. Then with one final look around, she stepped out of the study.

The house was still. Taking out her cell phone, she dialed Jason's number.

"Hi honey," Jason responded from the other end.

"Hello, darling. You're not home yet. What's going on?"

"Well, I have to pull a double shift today. I won't be coming tonight. Maybe early tomorrow morning."

"Oh no! That'll be almost twenty-four hours since you left."

"I'm sorry, darling. I have to go. I'm needed in surgery again," he said and hung up the phone.

"But it's lonely here without you," she complained. There was no response on the other end however. "Hello, hello, Jason," she called. "Great! I got hung up on," she snapped in frustration.

Susan went into the kitchen and foraged for food. There was nothing on the stove. She opened the refrigerator and found no leftovers. "Okay. I guess, he didn't cook today," she uttered, referring to Norton.

She opened one of the wall cabinets and got a hold of a canister of pasta. Taking a pot from the counter, she filled it up with water, poured in the pasta, and placed it on the stove to boil. "Alright. Is there any tomato sauce in the house?" She rummaged through the other wall cabinets. "Oh, good!" Locating one, she placed the can on the counter for later use. Then she opened the fridge again in search of a bag of salad. "No salad, great! I need my greens. That will go on the grocery list for tomorrow."

As she walked back to the stove to check on the pasta, she was startled by a noise coming from the back door. Immediately peering to see what it was, she noticed that Norton was stepping inside through the back door. She was relieved that it wasn't an unwelcome stranger. As Norton came closer, she noted that he wasn't looking at her. Instead, his gaze was fixed on the path ahead. His hair was disheveled and his clothes were dirty.

"Norton!" she called out. "You didn't make any lunch today."

He, however, didn't respond but kept on walking straight. The pupils of his eyes didn't move. He exited the kitchen and headed toward the stairs. She followed him. "Norton!" she cried. "I'm calling you!" He, however, kept going up the stairs without any acknowledgment.

"Oh, that man!" she snapped in anger. "A bit of common courtesy would be nice," she retorted. Susan stormed up to the third floor and saw Norton going into his room and slamming the door shut. Susan banged on the door. "Norton, open up!" she shouted in exasperation.

"Get out!" came a thundering voice from inside.

"What?" cried Susan in alarm.

"Get out of my house!" he bellowed again. "This is my house and you're trespassing," he shouted.

"Norton, what's the matter with you? Did you forget that this is my home now, and you're the one who is trespassing? If you behave this way, I'm going to have to ask you to leave," she declared in anger. "Do you hear me?" There was no response however.

A few moments later, Susan turned around and stormed back down. "That's it! I've had it with that man!" she cried in anger and went back to the kitchen.

The pasta was at the point of burning. She raced toward the stove and turned it off. Then she took the pot and drained whatever little water there was, steaming in anger the whole time. Putting back the pasta in the pot, she turned around to get the tomato sauce. Right behind her stood Norton. His eyes were as white as snow, including the pupils. Susan screamed in alarm.

"Norton!" she cried and attempted to push him away. He stood as still as a statue. Then he began uttering syllables she couldn't understand. "Norton! What's wrong with you?" she cried hastily, moving away from him. Then grabbing her phone, she dialed the police. As the phone rang, she saw Norton turn around. He gazed at her with a surprised expression. His eyes were back to normal.

"Madam. Are you alright?" he asked, approaching her. Susan was still waiting for the police to answer the phone. "Madam, is everything okay? You look frightened."

"Well, of course, I'm frightened. What are you doing acting like that?" she shouted.

"Acting like what, madam?"

"Like some kind of a lunatic, that's what! You were shouting at me a few minutes ago when I was knocking on your door. And your eyes were pure white a few seconds ago. You looked horrific!" she cried.

"Madam, you must be mistaken. I don't have the slightest idea what you're talking about," he declared. "Now have you eaten?" he asked. Susan didn't reply. "Let me make you some dinner. I'm sorry I didn't cook anything for lunch. It's just that I've been busy," he explained, taking the pasta pot and hastily mixing in the sauce.

"Busy doing what?" asked Susan in puzzlement. "Oh, this police department is of no use," she cried, hanging up the phone.

"Now that I think about it, madam, I have no idea what I was doing," he uttered, as if bewildered. An awkward silence ensued. "Here you go, madam," said Norton, putting some pasta on a plate and handing it to her. "Enjoy. Now is there anything else I can get you? Perhaps some coffee with your meal?" he asked.

"No, thank you," replied Susan, feeling quite awkward.

"Alright then. Good evening to you, madam. Do I have your permission to retire for the day?"

"Yes," replied Susan.

With that, Norton exited the kitchen and headed up the stairs. Susan remained in shock.

24

Susan was still shaken up by the events of the evening. She locked all the doors and windows in the house, turned off the lights, and came into her bedroom. Closing the door, she took a deep breath. It was eight o'clock. She attempted to phone Jason again. He didn't answer. Sitting on the bed, she pondered for a while. "Oh, Penny, I miss you." Then she thought about her mother and dialed the number. "She must've gone home by now."

"Hello, Mom," she called.

"Oh hello, darling. It's nice to hear from you," uttered Janet.

"Did you get home alright?"

"Darling, you're breaking up. What was that?"

"Hello, Mother? I can't hear you. Hello?" All she heard was static on the other end. She tried the number again and got static again. "Oh, now what? What's going on here?" she shouted, dashing the phone on the bed in frustration. For the first time since she moved into the villa, she missed the old apartment they used to live in. She didn't even walk up to the window for fear of seeing the black apparition again. Lying on the bed, she gazed up at the ceiling and began musing. Her mind wandered and thoughts of Zoe crept in.

Susan had fallen asleep. She, however, woke up abruptly to footsteps in the hall. The hardwood floor was creaking as a result. It was two o'clock in the morning. "Finally, he's home."

Assuming that it was Jason, she sprang out of bed and edged toward the door. Opening it, she called out to her husband. The hallway was dark and silent. Peering into the corridor, she realized that Jason wasn't home yet. "It's probably that Norton," she uttered, slamming the door. "I can't wait to get rid of that old man!" She felt trapped in her own home.

Suddenly, she was overcome with the urgency to throw up. Running into the restroom, she opened the faucet and began coughing and vomiting. Washing her mouth and face she looked at herself in the mirror. Her eyesight suddenly became a bit blurry.

Regaining her composure a few minutes later, she walked into the room. Jason was changing his clothes by the bed and she was startled.

"Oh, honey, you scared me!" she cried.

"I'm sorry dear," said Jason, looking at her.

"Did you just get in?" she asked curiously.

"Yes, and I am exhausted. Two open heart surgeries back to back," he said, sitting down on the bed.

"Wait. You weren't walking along the hallway about five minutes ago?" she asked.

"No. I just came in. What's the matter with you?"

"It's just that I heard footsteps and thought it was you."

"Well, I'm here. And I sure don't know whose footsteps you're talking about. What are you doing up at two in the morning?"

"I felt sick," she replied, sitting beside him. "I'm sorry you had such a long day," she continued, kissing him on the cheek.

"Yes, well, I need a twenty-four-hour nap now," he retorted, getting under the linens.

"Honey, can I speak with you a moment?" she asked.

"Not now, darling. I can't keep my eyes open," he said, getting underneath the covers. A few moments later, he was snoring.

Susan looked at him with longing eyes. Taking a deep breath, she kissed his forehead. Then switching off the light she cuddled beside him.

25

Susan got up in the morning with the urgency to throw up again. Jason was still fast asleep. She rushed into the bathroom and began coughing and spitting. She was also having severe pains in her stomach. Washing her face and mouth, she came back to the room. Jason was barely waking up. "Good morning, honey," he uttered. "Where have you been?"

"The bathroom," she said groggily. "I'm throwing up my guts."

"What's wrong?" he asked, looking at her.

"I don't know. I'm feeling sick probably with everything that happened yesterday," she said lying back on the bed.

"What happened yesterday?" he asked wide-eyed.

"It's Norton. He was acting like a maniac, shouting at me, and telling me to get out of here. It was quite the experience. I don't know what to make of that man anymore. One minute he's lucid, and the other he's a raving lunatic," she complained.

"He was shouting at you?" asked Jason, sitting on the bed. "Let me give him a good piece of my mind," he voiced, getting up.

"Hold on, honey. There's something seriously wrong somewhere. One minute, he's yelling, and the other minute, he doesn't remember what he did. It's like there are two completely different people inside him or something."

"I don't care. Nobody shouts at my wife!" he declared in anger. "What do you want me to do?" he asked sitting by her side. "Shall I tell him to leave?"

"I think you should. Maybe he's the one who's walking up and down the hall, trying to scare me," snapped Susan.

"Alright, I'll talk to him. You look pale," he said, placing his hand on her forehead. "There's no temperature though."

"Darling, I miss our old apartment," she sighed.

"What?" cried Jason in surprise. "This is our dream home."

"I know, but I'm lonely and it's so big," she complained.

"But I thought this was what you wanted," he said in disappointment.

"Yes, I do love this place. But I feel that something is happening here, and I can't figure out what it is. Did you hear from the detective?"

"I have a couple of missed calls from him. I was so busy yesterday."

"What time do you have to be at the hospital today?"

"I took the day off. Dr. Adams is covering for me since I worked his shift yesterday," he said, lying beside her and caressing her hair.

"I started writing yesterday," she said.

"That's great, honey," responded Jason. "What did you write about?"

"Can't tell you. A writer always keeps his or her work discreet until it's published," she replied.

"Fair enough," conceded Jason. "Come on. I'll make some eggs for you."

"Oh, I'm not sure about that with my stomach like this. I don't know if I'll be able to hold it in."

"Come on. You'll be fine. I'll make you some hot coffee to go along," he said, getting up and grabbing her hand. Susan had no choice but to follow him.

Jason went into the living room and opened all the drapes. It was a beautiful sunny morning. Then he went to the kitchen. Susan was seated at the table with her head down. "Are you alright?" he asked checking up on her.

"Yeah, I guess."

"Where is he?" he inquired, surveying the premises. "Shouldn't he be up cleaning or something? The furniture is so dusty."

He put a pot of coffee to brew. Then opening the fridge, he took out some eggs, the butter, and bread. He put two slices of bread in the toaster. Taking the skillet from the cabinet, he put some butter on it and placed it on top of the hot stove. Then he beat the eggs and poured them into the skillet to cook. Susan approached him and offered some assistance. But before long, she felt nauseous. She raced to the sink, opened the faucet, and began coughing and spitting up.

"Oh, my goodness! What in the world did I eat?" she cried.

Jason patted her back as she coughed. "Hold on a minute," he said and abruptly went out of the kitchen.

A few moments later, he returned with his stethoscope in hand. Susan was still standing by the sink. Seeing that the eggs were about to overcook, she ambled up to the stove and turned it off.

"Alright, let's have you sit down first," he uttered, helping her to the table. "Take a deep breath, honey."

"I'll try," she said.

He inserted the ear tips in his ears and listened to her heartbeat with the chest piece. Then he placed the chest piece on her back and listened. "Keep breathing."

A moment later, he stopped and gazed at his wife. "Well, I can assure you there's definitely something wrong with your heart."

"What?" cried Susan in alarm.

"It's about to explode with love," he replied jovially.

Susan slapped him on the stomach. "Don't tease me. I'm not feeling well."

"Alright. Let me listen to your stomach. For that, you're going to have to lie down." He helped her stand up and escorted her to the living room couch. "Lie down while I listen to your stomach." Susan sat on the couch and laid back. Jason moved the table closer and sat beside her.

"Do cardiologists know how to treat stomach bugs?"

"Yes, of course," he said, listening in with the stethoscope. Susan waited patiently. After he was done, he took a deep breath. "Alright, I might be wrong on this, but I think there's a big chance that you might be pregnant."

"What? Pregnant?" she cried in shock. "Are you sure?"

"Yes, very likely."

"How can you tell?"

"Well, I heard a tiny heartbeat in there," he said, kissing her stomach.

Susan was thrilled. She was laughing out loud. Then a moment later, she ran back to the kitchen sink to throw up. Putting the stethoscope on the couch, he hurried behind her. As she began throwing up, he continued to pat her back. "Alright. You're going to have to stay in bed for a while because you're having terrible morning sickness."

"Do you have something for it?" she asked.

"Well, I think the best medication for you is getting plenty of rest."

"Thank you, Dr. Smith. I'm kind of cramping too."

"As I said, rest takes care of that too."

Jason helped his wife get upstairs back to bed. "You stay here. I'm going to go downstairs and make some tea for you."

"I'm hungry too," complained Susan.

"Alright, some buttered toast will take care of that." He embraced and kissed his wife. Congratulations mom-to-be!" Jason was thrilled.

"Congratulations, dad-to-be!" exclaimed Susan.

"Just stay put alright?" he ordered, looking at her with stern eyes.

"Yes, Doctor," conceded Susan with glee.

26

Jason brought some breakfast for his wife.

"You know, I can get used to this attention," she commented.

"Drink the tea first and then slowly chow down the toast," he said, sitting by her side. "I'm so happy."

Susan could see that he was beaming with joy. "Me too. Wouldn't it be great if we had twins?" she asked.

"Wonderful! The more the merrier," he said watching her eat.

"What about you? Aren't you hungry?" she asked.

"I'll eat later," he said, gazing at her. "Norton's downstairs in the kitchen. He's cooking."

"Did you speak to him?" she asked sipping on her tea.

"No, not yet. I don't want to spoil this moment by getting angry with the man. I'll approach him sometime during the day and break the news to him."

"Alright, honey. Just don't tell him that I'm pregnant. I feel uncomfortable around him."

"I won't," he assured.

After getting some rest, Susan began to feel much better. She took a bath and changed into some fresh clothes. It was almost midday. As she stepped out of the room, Jason approached her and grabbed her hand.

"What's the matter?" she asked in alarm.

"Nothing. Everything is perfect. And what's more, I have a surprise for you," he said, escorting her down. "Oh, by the way, please be careful when you go up and come down these stairs, alright?"

"Yes, honey, I'll be careful," she said. "Now what's going on?"

"Just be patient." They walked through the living room. Norton was there dusting the furniture.

Susan looked at Jason and whispered, "Did you tell him something?"

"Yes. I put him in his place," he assured her.

As they passed by, Susan could see from the corner of her eye that Norton was staring at her. "Where are we going?" she asked with a quizzical expression.

"I told you. It's a surprise," he replied. They came out to the garden. The weather was a bit warm. "Go and sit at the edge of the fountain," he ordered.

"What if I fall in?" she asked, going toward it.

"You won't," he said.

"Did you tell him to leave?" she asked, sitting down and touching the water. It was nice and cool.

"Yes, I told him. He keeps on telling me that he doesn't remember ever shouting at you or anything else for that matter. Maybe he's losing his memory altogether."

"I don't think so because he was giving me angry looks just now," said Susan.

"Don't upset yourself over this. I'll deal with him," he sighed.

Just then, they heard a car pull up to the driveway. Susan stood up and turned around. It was a red convertible. She didn't recognize the person driving it. Another car came behind it driven by someone else. Jason signaled the driver of the red convertible to approach the cherub fountain. The driver followed instructions and stopped the car right in front of them.

He got out of the vehicle, walked up to them, and handed the keys to Susan.

"Congratulations, madam! this is for you!" he exclaimed, smiling.

Susan was dumbfounded. Jason looked at her with gleaming eyes. "Well, say something."

"Wait a minute. This car is mine?" Susan was in disbelief.

"Yes, it is. You know, Mrs. Smith, as I drove into the garage last night, I noticed that we've only got one car. It's time we had two, don't you think?" Jason thanked the driver. He got into the other car, and the two men drove off shortly.

"You mean you bought this?" inquired Susan, touching the shiny new red convertible.

"Yes," he replied.

"When?"

"A few hours ago while you were sleeping upstairs."

"How did you do that?"

"Why so many questions? Just made a few calls," he replied. "Get in."

Susan opened the door and sat on the driver's seat and turned on the ignition. Jason jumped in from the other side. "Alright, just pull into the garage." Susan steered the car around the fountain and drove into the garage.

"I can't believe it!" she said beaming. "My own car," she voiced out in amazement.

"And what's more, it's brand new," added Jason.

"Thank you, darling." Susan gave him a warm embrace and a kiss.

"Now you won't have to be cooped up in the house so much. You can go out shopping or just drive around town if you'd like."

"That would be great!" said Susan, feeling the steering wheel. "Should we go for a drive?"

"I would love to, honey, but are you up to it?" asked Jason, placing his hand on her stomach.

"Well, I feel much better after seeing this. Besides, you can drive just in case I do get sick."

"Okay, then let's go out to lunch," he suggested. "Pull out the car, and I'll switch seats with you."

Susan did as her husband directed and sat on the passenger seat while Jason got behind the wheel.

"The garage is packed," she commented, looking at their old furniture. "Let's haul all the junk up to the attic. I still haven't been up there."

"Alright," agreed Jason as they drove out of the yard.

27

Susan enjoyed the ride in her new car. Jason took her to a nice restaurant where they talked over lunch. She had forgotten all about the morning sickness and devoured her meal.

"It has been weeks since we've been out together," she commented.

"Sorry about my busy schedule, honey, but it can't be helped," responded Jason apologetically.

"Oh, I know, darling. You're a big shark in the hospital now, and I'm so proud of you," she said, attempting to put him at ease. So what do we do after lunch?" she asked as if ready for an adventure.

"Well, I was thinking of stopping at the hospital for a quick checkup," responded Jason as he paid the bill.

"Are you okay?" she asked.

"I'm fine, but you need to get checked out since you're pregnant and everything," he suggested.

"Oh. Do I have to? Those doctors make me nervous," protested Susan in an agitated tone of voice.

"Well, you must get used to regular checkups and doctors now that you're pregnant with twins," said Jason as they walked out of the restaurant.

"Twins? How do you know that?"

"Isn't that what you want?"

"Yes, but who knows? It can be just one baby," she said.

"Doesn't matter. You have to go for a checkup nevertheless," he insisted.

Without further fuss, she complied.

Susan had to wait in the hospital gynecology section to be examined. A nurse came shortly and drew her blood to determine whether she was truly pregnant. Susan hoped that the test would be positive, as the idea of being pregnant for the past few hours had taken her to new heights of excitement. When the results substantiated her hopes, she was delighted and relieved at the same time. She was told that she had conceived a few weeks ago. The doctor came to see her and prescribed her some prenatal vitamins and specified the list of things she has to do to take care of herself and the unborn baby. Jason was by her side and vouched that he would see to it that his wife adhered to all the rules. Once the visit was over, Susan was thrilled to come out of the hospital.

"Oh, thank goodness that's done," she declared.

They got into the car and pulled out of the hospital parking lot and began heading home. The wind rubbed against Susan's face and blew on her hair. This brought in her an overwhelming feeling of exhilaration and joy. For the first time in a while, Susan realized how fortunate she was to have such a loving spouse, a mansion for a home, a beautiful brand-new car, and most of all, a baby on the way. However, the grief over the loss of her best friend and the fears of the apparitions she had seen in and around her home brought a grim reminder of the present battles that were raging.

"Am I a bad person if I'm happy for myself?" she asked abruptly.

Jason glanced at her in puzzlement. "No, honey, you're not. Why are you asking that?"

"Well, because Zoe and her baby died, and Andrew is in utter misery. What's more, all these strange things are happening in our house," she responded somberly.

"I know it's a tough time for both of us with everything that's going on, but it's all going to work out. You have to learn to take things easy now. Otherwise, you'll put the baby at risk," he insisted.

"I'll try," said Susan.

28

It was close to the evening when they finally arrived home. As they pulled up to the driveway, Norton was seen watering the rose bushes by the front windows of the villa. He turned around and waved at them. Susan waved back.

"I thought you were mad at him," commented Jason.

"Oh, what the heck! I'm going to let bygones be bygones and give the man a second chance," she replied with renewed resolve.

"Really?" asked Jason, who was attempting to be supportive.

"Yes, darling. But if things go sour, I'm going to put my foot down and make good on that ultimatum that I gave him yesterday," she declared.

As they drove into the garage, Susan realized that their old furniture had to be hauled out. "I don't want scratches on my new car," she uttered.

"I'll have the movers come in tomorrow and have them take the old stuff up to the attic," said Jason getting out.

"Speaking of which, I want to go up there. Go and ask him for the keys," ordered Susan.

"Why now?" protested Jason, who was hoping to catch a nap.

"Well, you hardly get a day off like this, and I don't want to go up to the attic by myself. I need to know what's in there. After all, it's our stuff now right?"

"Right," assured Jason.

"Hopefully, I can find something useful for the baby's room."

"Like what?"

"A crib maybe. That vintage furniture is the best," she remarked.

"And we've got plenty of it in all the rooms," retorted Jason.

The evening air was soothing. Susan felt a sense of joy, knowing that she was going to become a mother soon. The thought of getting the nursery ready excited her.

As they came to the front, Norton greeted them. "Did you have a nice drive in the car, madam?" he asked.

"Yes, we did. I wanted to know if you have the key to the attic?" inquired Susan.

Norton's countenance immediately changed. He became a bit hostile. "I'm sure you have them in your keyring, madam. I gave it to sir when he bought the place," he snapped.

"No, I don't, Norton. I have the keys to the rooms and the doors downstairs but not the one for the attic," she insisted. "I've tried each key in its respective room and came short of one. It's the one for the attic. I'm sure of it."

"Well, madam, I certainly don't have it," he declared in anger and turned away.

Jason became furious and was about to tell him off. Noticing this, Susan placed a placating hand on him and urged him not to say anything. Jason stormed into the house and headed toward the stairs. Susan scurried behind him. "Where are you going?" she asked.

"Well if he doesn't have the key, there's always one sure way to open a door," he uttered in anger.

"Honey, calm down," cried Susan.

The fourth floor was cold, dark, and uninviting. "This is the floor that gives me the creeps," commented Susan.

"Honey, this is your home now. You can't be afraid of it. As I said before, if you really want, we can remodel this part and get some windows put in."

"Why thank you, husband. I'd like that. Get started on that right away."

They came up to the attic door. It was locked. "Alright, move out of the way," he ordered. Susan did as was told. Jason stepped back and kicked the door as hard as he could. The lock loosened. When he kicked it a second time, part of the door broke off from its hinges and the lock fully gave way.

"Old doors!" he remarked.

Carefully moving the broken door to the side, he edged in. Susan followed. The musty odor which came from the dark interior overwhelmed them.

"Ugh! It smells like old rot!" declared Susan covering her nose. Jason pulled his shirt over his nose. He managed to locate the light switch and flipped it to no avail.

"Great! Nobody bothered to change the bulb," he commented.

They could see the round stained glass window in the distance. Getting there, however, was a challenge due to the many furniture items and other objects that were in the way. Although the attic was massive, it was also packed to capacity.

"Alright, honey, I don't think our old furniture will fit up here," said Jason, squeezing himself through the narrow pathway he could manage.

"I agree," remarked Susan trailing behind him.

"What is all this stuff?" she asked. "And it's covered with a century of dust."

"When did Norton say he cleaned up here?" he asked.

"Never, honey. The man's got a back problem, remember?"

"Right," uttered Jason in a sarcastic tone.

Jason wanted to somehow make his way to the other end and open the one window. Old beds, chairs, tables, and numerous boxes were piled up all over the place. Some of the furniture was stacked on top of each other and stood against the dark and dingy walls. Shelves and cabinets were also seen in the far corners. As Jason slowly ambled through the narrow spaces, he held onto his wife.

"Honey, be careful not to knock onto anything," he cautioned her.

Cardboard boxes were piled up in certain spots. Susan stopped and opened one. Her hands were covered with dust. Wiping them off on her pants, she pulled out what seemed to be framed pictures.

"Look at this," she uttered. "These must be people who lived here."

She glanced at one after the other. Some were of men and others were of very well-dressed ladies. Jason momentarily paused to take a peek at what his wife was showing him.

"Come on, honey," he urged her.

Susan carefully put the pictures back into the box and trailed along. As they gazed up, they could see that the ceiling was made of wood panels. The tower roof was above this. A small, very old, and dusty chandelier loomed from the center of this ceiling. The glimmer of light that came from the round window revealed the hundreds of cobwebs that were entangled in each of its tiny lightbulbs.

Susan was amazed at the amount of clutter in the attic. "What do we do with all of this?" she asked, awe-stricken.

"I don't know. We're going to have to get rid of it," replied Jason.

"But there's so much history in all of this," argued Susan.

"It's not our history, darling. It needs to go. Maybe we can donate all this old furniture to an organization that helps the poor or something."

"Right," she agreed.

They were slowly but steadily approaching the window. The rays of light that filtered through the glass revealed the many other things that cluttered the room. Bookshelves as tall as the ceiling stood like sentinels on the side walls. Hundreds of books were piled up inside them. Susan considered it to be a nearly impossible task to even try to determine what these books contained.

"Well, one thing I can tell you is that, for a family line that had only one heir, they sure had a lot of books," she remarked.

As they edged closer to the window, Susan could see how grimy the glass was. Managing to somehow get to it, Jason unlocked the latch and pushed the window open. He could feel the fresh air rushing in.

"That's better," he uttered, looking at her. He peeked out through the window. The whole front yard and some of the surrounding property came into view. "Look!" he said, pointing out. Susan came up to the window and peeked outside. Her eyes surveyed the surroundings.

"This is beautiful!" she exclaimed. "Maybe we can make this place into some kind of a playroom for our children."

Jason agreed. "We have to first get rid of all this clutter, honey," he said.

As Susan moved to the side, she bumped into what seemed to be a wooden box. Bending down, she took off its lid. Inside were stacks of books. Taking one out, she examined it. The dark brown cover had a leather feel and had embossed gold writing at the center. Susan edged closer to the window to get a better glimpse of the title, "Journal of Eleanor Mortimer." She opened it to reveal the browned up and tarnished pages. The writing, however, was intact. Whoever Eleanor Mortimer was, she had excellent penmanship.

"Look, honey, it's someone's journal."

Jason was too busy peering in the opposite direction. The first entry of the journal had the date April 17, 1867, on the top right-hand side. "Wow, these are ancient!" she remarked.

She took another journal out. It had the same cover characteristics but contained entries from a year later. Susan realized that the journals in the box contained the life story of Eleanor Mortimer who could possibly have been a matriarch or someone of importance to the family and lived in the villa over a hundred years ago. Looking to the right, she noticed a rather large gold-framed portrait of a woman. Susan came near it to get a better view. It was covered with a thick coat of dust as well. From the looks of it, she was very beautiful and strangely familiar. She had dark hair, sharp features, creamy skin, and dark eyes. She wore an elegant dress and her neck was adorned with lavish pearls.

"Is this you?" she uttered. "Honey, look at this," she said.

Jason walked up to her. "What, dear? I'm searching for your crib."

"This is Eleanor Mortimer," she said pointing to the portrait.

"Who's that?" asked Jason confused.

"She's probably the wife of the original owner of this house. Does she look familiar to you?" she asked, scrutinizing the picture.

"Honey, this woman probably died decades before we were born," he replied. "How could she be familiar?"

"These are her journals," she uttered, showing him the books she was holding. "I wonder if the man who is in the picture in Norton's room was her husband."

"Does it matter?" asked Jason.

"Well, darling, I need you to take this box of journals to my room."

"But why? It looks heavy."

"I want to read them and learn about her life. It intrigues me," she voiced.

"Alright," he conceded. He knew from a couple of years of experience that arguing with his wife especially when she was excited about something resulted in a dead end for him. "I can't look for anything in this mess. We're going to have to empty this place out. I'll call the movers and cleaners to come and clear it later on," he stated, surveying the disarray around them. "If they find a crib in the process, we can keep it."

"Alright," said Susan still examining the portrait. Jason reached out and closed the window. "Let's go," he ordered.

"Oh, honey, the box!" Susan gazed at him with longing eyes.

Without another word of dispute, he picked up the wooden box and began walking out of the narrow path in between the clutter. Susan tagged behind him, clutching onto the two journals. A flutter of excitement crept into her thoughts. She felt privileged to be given the opportunity to read about the life of a woman who lived in her home so long ago. As they headed toward the door, she suddenly felt exhausted and dizzy and stopped to hold onto a table nearby.

"Wait, honey, I need a moment," she voiced.

Jason put the somewhat heavy box on the ground and turned toward her. "What's the matter?" he asked, approaching her and grasping onto her arm.

"I'm dizzy," she said, trying to catch her breath and maintain her composure.

He escorted her to a chair nearby and helped her sit. Susan sat clasping the two journals to her chest. At that instant, they heard an eerie sound from the ceiling. Jason directed his gaze upward to see the chandelier swaying back and forth.

"What in the world?" he uttered in bewilderment.

Susan glanced up as well. Suddenly cold sweat began dripping from her forehead, and she felt as she was passing out. "What's happening to me?" she asked.

"Hold on, Susan!" cried Jason as he attempted to grab onto her. He felt disoriented as well. Instinctively realizing that they were being watched, he turned toward the window. His eyes caught a glimpse of a black figure standing there. "Who is that? Am I hallucinating?" he asked, looking at his wife. His head was spinning.

"What?" exclaimed Susan, attempting to look in the direction her husband was immersed in.

"There's someone there by the window," he said.

The figure, however, had vanished when Susan looked. "Where, honey?" she quavered. "I can't see anything. I'm still dizzy."

"Something wearing black. It was there a second ago. What was that?"

Susan became petrified and began to panic. "Where is it? Don't let it get near me!" she cried in fear.

"Don't worry, honey. I'm here. Let's get out of here for now. Can you stand up?" he asked attempting to help her out of the chair.

"I'll try," she said and endeavored to get up. "Please take the box. I need to see those journals. Maybe this woman can help us," she said slowly, moving forward.

Jason somehow managed to get the box and maneuver himself behind his wife. They finally approached the door and paused to breathe. "What was that? It was wearing some kind of a black cloak," uttered Jason gasping.

"How did that thing get there?" asked Susan, who was shaken up.

"It's moving around."

"Is that what you saw outside and in the bedroom?"

"Yes, and now in the attic. I don't know what it is, but I'm sure going to find out."

Jason walked behind her with the box in his hands.

29

Susan and Jason made it to their bedroom with the journals. He placed the box on the ground beside the bed and turned toward his wife. "Are you okay?"

"I guess," she sighed, collapsing on the bed and taking a few deep breaths.

"What just happened up there?" he asked, sitting by her and holding on to his head.

"I told you before. I've seen that thing. It scares the daylights out of me and wears me out."

"Well, then you can't stay here," he declared. "I don't want you to get sick because of it."

"Where do you want me to go? This is my home," she insisted.

"You can stay with your mother until I figure out how to get that thing out of the house. Let me call Detective Johnson tomorrow."

A spark of protest flashed across her face. "No. I'm not going to have some *thing* drive me away from my own home," she declared in indignation. "I'll get to the bottom of all of this."

"How? It has some powerful venom," he added.

"Maybe there's some kind of an explanation in those journals," she uttered, directing her gaze at the two journals she had placed on the side of the bed. Susan got up and slowly edged toward the window and peered outside. The tranquility of the setting sun appeased her troubled thoughts, and suddenly, she recalled what her mother had said. She resolved to protect her villa and drive out whatever was haunting it. "I'll find an answer," she sighed.

"Honey, I feel better if someone was here with you. Norton evidently is of no use. Who knows if he's the reason for all of this?" he protested, approaching her and putting his arms around her.

"Don't worry. If I really need someone here, I'll call Mom. She can scare anything off just by her mere presence. Oh, by the way, I have to call her and tell her the good news."

They received a cold shoulder from Norton at dinner time. He was disinclined to speak more than two words to either one of them. After locking up the house, Susan and Jason came back up to the bedroom.

"What's the matter with that old man?" he asked furiously.

"I don't know. Maybe he's mad that we went up to the attic," replied Susan.

"Who cares? It's our home," he retorted in anger.

"Honey, I know. But we need to be very tactical with him. If he is causing all of this, then we're going to have to be even more cautious," she uttered.

"I will not be threatened by some old man who lives in my house and relies on my generosity," he snapped in indignation. "I should've listened to you when we first moved in," he sighed.

"What did I say then?" she asked with an inquisitive expression.

"Well, I remember how you reacted when I told you about him. You were upset that a caretaker was here. Maybe I should've asked him to move out that same day."

"No need to bring up the past," she assured. "Don't worry, darling. Whatever the problem is, we can solve it."

A few minutes later, they both got into bed. It had been a long and grueling day. Jason was exhausted, and before long, he was fast asleep. Susan kissed him on the forehead. A flux of thoughts and emotions seized her mind as she sat on the bed musing. The angry apparition put her in panic. Taking a deep breath, however, she came to the realization that whatever that was haunting their home had to be dealt with head on. Taking the journal to her lap, she opened to the first page and began reading.

> *April 17th, 1867*
>
> *I am so happy! I married the love of my life today, and he has brought me to this beautiful home in the mountains. It is like a dream from which I never want to awake. He entices me with everything he does—his sweet kisses, his gentle yet strong embrace, his affectionate words, and most of all the manner in which he surprises me—my handsome Arthur. Do I deserve you and all of this bounty that comes with you? A humble and simple woman such as myself who came from nothing and who had nothing. Now I am the mistress of this magnificent home with all its beauty and splendor. We are so happy together. He meets my every need and showers me with gifts besides. Oh, how I want to give him all the children in the world, to make him happy, just as he has made me. He calls me his delight. I love him so!*

The entry ushered a sense of joy in Susan and a warm feeling came over her. She thought about her life and how it resembled that of Eleanor in many ways. Jason was the love of her life and had given her everything she had desired. She tried to stay awake to read a few more entries. Jason was sound asleep and she felt safe beside him. Flipping the next page, she continued reading.

May 20ᵗʰ, 1867

I haven't written for a while. That's because I've been so busy furnishing our new home. Arthur has ordered the most expensive furniture for me. It comes all the way from France and arrived on a ship last week. Workers have been bringing furniture into the house for nearly three days now. I have been going up and down the stairs, making sure that everything is in its proper place. Knowing how much I love to read, Arthur has surprised me with all the books I can possibly read. The study is packed and more besides in the attic. Oh, that Arthur! I miss him so much, and his absence pains me so. He's been so busy in the oil rig up in the border. I haven't seen him for two weeks now. He sent word that he'll be coming back tomorrow. The house will be perfect! I've missed him so much. My heart is aching for him. My arms are aching to hold him. I want to kiss his sweet lips the moment I see him. My Arthur, what a prince he is, so handsome and debonair. He'll be proud of the way I have kept our home. I take long walks in the yard in the evenings. The ocean sparkles and the breeze is gentle. Everything about this place reminds me of him and his love for me. He said he loves me now and for all eternity. I am so happy.

A few moments later, Susan was dozing off. She tried her best to keep her eyes open to get to the next entry as it was almost midnight. The house was quiet except for the sound of crickets outside coming from the open window.

May 22nd, 1867

    My beloved Arthur is back home with me. He brought me a dozen red roses. They are my favorite. I asked the gardener to grow the same type in front of the house. My Arthur works so hard. I cooked his favorite meal— shepherd's pie for dinner. We sat together in the yard and gazed at the ocean until the sun went down. He told me all about his new oil well, the drilling, the workers, and all the ups and downs of being in charge. I just like to listen to him. I love the way his mouth moves when he speaks. After watching the sunset, we went to our bedroom and made sweet love. When he kisses me he sweeps me off my feet. When he touches me, I melt like cold icicles on a hot summer day. I cannot stand being away from him even for a moment. Can a woman love a man so? My desire for him grows stronger with each passing moment.

    But tomorrow, my love has to leave me again. He just got word that there's commotion with the workers up North. He says he'll be gone for a while. I cannot stand this. Does he not know that I need him too? Why does he have to work so far away? I want to go with him, but he says it's not safe for a woman to be up there near an oil rig. I told him I didn't care about that as long as I was with him. He insists that I must stay home like the good wife that I am. When he leaves, who will fill the emptiness of my heart and soul? Who will make love to me when my desire erupts for him? I am in tears tonight. Oh, but if I could bind him with chains I would.

Susan realized that she was dozing off in between words. She closed the journal, placed it inside the drawer of the side table next to her bed, and tucked herself underneath the sheets.

Then switching off the lamp, she closed her eyes. She pictured Eleanor's life, a woman so much in love. Would she feel the same way if Jason left her for weeks at an end? Placing a hand on her pregnant stomach, she began thinking pleasantly about the child growing inside. Then she turned toward Jason, cuddled beside his warm body, and fell asleep.

30

The morning had set in. Susan stretched and turned toward her husband's bedside to discover that he wasn't there. There was a note on the pillow, however.

Good morning, beautiful! I had to go to the hospital. Didn't want to wake you and the baby. Please be careful. I will call the detective today. Don't be surprised if he visits you. I will see you at night.
Love,
Jason

Susan kissed the note and placed it under her pillow. Getting up shortly afterward, she walked into the restroom to freshen up and change. As she approached the sink, she felt the first pangs of morning sickness and immediately got the urge to throw up. "Ugh!" she uttered after washing her mouth. Suddenly, she could hear her phone ring. Walking back to the room she answered it. It was her mother.

"Hello, darling!"

"Hi, Mom," she said with a slight cough. "I was going to call you today."

"Are you alright?"

"Oh, it's this awful morning sickness, Mom. I can't stand it," she uttered in indignation.

"Morning sickness?" A pause followed. "Are you pregnant?" she asked with a flux of excitement.

"Yes, Mom, I am," said Susan, beaming.

"Oh, darling, congratulations!" voiced her mother. "I knew it. I am so happy for you. Finally, I'm going to be a grandma. Now, darling, you must take care of yourself. No strenuous work, alright?" she asserted.

"Yes, Mom. I hear you. I'll try," she assured. "Listen, Mom. I've got to go eat something. I'm starved."

"Oh, of course, darling. You're eating for two now. So watch what you put inside that stomach of yours. I love you."

"Love you too, Mom. Bye," she said and hung up.

After taking a soothing bath, Susan got dressed and came down to the living room. Her stomach was still a bit queasy. She headed toward the coffee pot. Pouring some in her mug, she took the first sip. Suddenly the words "shepherd's pie" came to her mind. She had recalled reading it in the journal. "So Eleanor's husband liked shepherd's pie," she uttered to herself. "How does Norton know that?"

As she walked out of the kitchen, she almost bumped into Norton, who was dressed for the day with his usual black suit and apron.

"Good morning, madam," he said.

"Hello, Norton," she responded.

"Would you like me to make some breakfast for you?" he asked politely.

"No, thank you. Maybe in a little while," she uttered, heading toward the stairs.

"Alright, then, madam. I need to attend to the cleaning chores," he said.

Norton turned around and headed toward the rear door. She was instinctively going to ask him what he cleans outside so much but refrained as she didn't want to get into an argument early morning.

Turning around, she went up the stairs with her coffee in hand. Walking into the bedroom, she shut the door. She placed the mug on the side table and took the journal out of the drawer. Then comfortably sitting back on the bed, she covered her legs with the sheets. Opening the journal to the place where she had left off the night before, she began reading.

> *June 23rd, 1867*
>
> *I haven't felt like writing. I miss my Arthur. He's been gone for weeks and I'm all alone in this big house. On top of that, I keep getting this strange sensation at the pit of my stomach. What is wrong with me? I'm not sick, yet I feel as if something is amiss. I desire for my love to come back to me. Why does he have to be so far away? The next time he comes home, I will surely endeavor to stop him from going away again. Yesterday, I ventured out to the furthest inch of my property. It leads to the mountains and is so beautiful and calm. The trees sing a song to me as I walk past them as if they too feel my despondency. The flowers are in bloom. I picked as many as I could and filled a vase with them when I came back home. My heart was still empty. There is no word from him. Where could he be? What could he be doing so far away from me? Does he not miss my presence? He said that he loves me, and his love for me is like the ocean that I see each day when I step out of my home. How can one survive without the other half of his heart and soul? What type of scandal is this? I am beside myself with anguish. Oh, if I only had a child to cherish and fill up these silent rooms with laughter.*

As Susan read this entry, her heart sank for this woman. She gazed up at the ceiling and pondered. Suddenly, she felt Eleanor's emotions and tears came rolling down her cheeks.

June 27th, 1867

My Arthur came back this morning. He looked tired and his spirits were faint. When I asked him what had transpired, he said that he had lost an oil rig to his competitor. I could see the anger in his eyes as he detailed the horrid events to me. I attempted to console him, but he refused my advances. When I tried to kiss his lips, he turned away from me. What has happened?

I think I am with child. If that is the case, then my wildest dreams have come true. How can I tell my Arthur this when he is in such sour spirits? My stomach is queer, and I cannot hold anything down. There is a woman named Bessie who cooks for us now. Bessie is middle aged and is very kind. She and the caretaker run the affairs of my home. But I make the shepherd's pie. I will not share my recipe with her, for it will be me and only me who will make this dish for my Arthur.

I wanted to be held by him tonight. He turned away from me though. I couldn't tell him that I was with child. How can I share my joy when he is in such despair? Is losing a rig so devastating? After all, things in this world are so temporary. What must I do to get back my beloved Arthur? He is lost in his thoughts and doesn't want to be bothered by anything else. This journal is my only friend at present. I share all my thoughts on these pages. I feel like I have been abandoned by the very one who swore to love me through thick or thin. After all, when he suffers, I suffer as well. He is a part of me and I am hopefully a part of him.

Susan wiped her tears as she read the entry. "Ah, the poor woman," she uttered to herself as she continued. She took a sip of her coffee. "What a coincidence. I'm pregnant when she was pregnant over a hundred years ago." A feeling of warmth enveloped her.

June 30th, 1867

My Arthur had to leave again this morning. He barely kissed my lips as he left. Such anger and rage in his eyes. What is wrong with him? I am not sure when I'll see him again.

Bessie cooked eggs for me. I couldn't hold it down. She knew I was with child even before I uttered anything. She offered me a home remedy for it, bed rest and soup. I enjoy her company. I don't want to share too much with her. After all, I cannot treat her as my equal. That caretaker is a different breed altogether. Norton is his name. He has the demeanor of a pigheaded individual and a temper to match, says Bessie. He seems to begrudge my existence. I want to get rid of him, but Arthur insists he stays as one must have a man in the house while he is away. I am the woman of this house and he better do what I say regardless if Arthur is here or not.

On to more pleasant thoughts now. I feel my child growing within me. It is a wonderful feeling to know that one can bring forth life to this world. I hope it's not one but two young ones, as they would bring twice as much joy to this home. Bessie was right. I didn't regurgitate all day. She brought my meals to bed and encouraged me to walk nevertheless.

Susan turned to look at the time. It was close to eleven in the morning. She didn't realize how quickly time was flying. Eleanor's thoughts felt real and tangible to her. As she read her words she identified with her and felt as if she was living her life at that time. Suddenly, there was a knock on the door. Startled, she sprang out of bed. Hiding the journal under the pillow, she walked up to the door. Opening it she saw Norton standing at the threshold.

"Pardon me, madam, but there is a Detective Johnson downstairs to see you," he uttered nonchalantly. Susan remembered Jason's note.

"Thank you. I will be right down," she said and closed the door. She hurriedly went to the vanity table, took out her hairbrush from one of the drawers, and brushed her hair a bit. Then she put on some lipstick. Walking out of the room, she closed the door behind her. Norton was nowhere to be seen.

Walking into the living room, Susan noticed the detective leisurely pacing back and forth. He had a long-sleeved gray jacket over his full dress suit.

"Hello, Detective," she uttered warmly.

"Good morning, Mrs. Smith. How are you?" he asked, smiling at her.

"Fine, thank you. "Please sit down," she urged him. "I understand my husband called you?" she asked, sitting across him.

"Yes, he did, early this morning. The moment I walked into the office, the phone rang and there he was on the other end," he uttered jovially.

"Listen, Detective, can we talk outside?" asked Susan after cautiously looking around.

"Sure, ma'am, whatever you'd like," he complied.

Susan got up and headed toward the front door. The detective walked with her and opened the door for her. The cherub fountain was as elegant as ever.

"That's some structure you've got there. The best part of the house!" he remarked pointing at the fountain.

"Oh, thank you. I know. I love it too," she added.

"Whoever built it had good taste," he uttered. The detective's car was parked on the driveway. They walked past it all the way to the edge of the yard and halted. "So I spoke to your guests and asked about your friend Zoe's whereabouts during the party. Each one of them corroborated your story."

"Alright," said Susan. "So what's happening with her case?"

"Well, we don't have much information to go by except for the photos. Unless we find out who this woman is, I'm afraid we've got ourselves a cold case," he uttered gravely.

"What?" exclaimed Susan in frustration.

"Unfortunately, since the search party cannot come up with any additional findings about who that is, we're facing a dead end." Susan heaved a sign of disappointment yet endeavored to maintain her composure. "I'm sorry, ma'am, but until we get further evidence, we cannot convict anyone. Anyway, let's leave that matter aside for a moment. Dr. Smith tells me that there's some kind of presence in the house."

"Yes. I feel awkward bringing this up, considering the reactions I've received from your police department regarding such matters in the past," she stated bluntly.

"I apologize for all that confusion and raucous, but I'm here now and I'd like to know what's going on. Please keep in mind, Mrs. Smith, I'm concerned about your safety," he assured.

"Thank you. It's good to know that. Well, I've seen it several times before. It's some kind of black apparition or a wraith. I can't even begin to describe it, but it suddenly manifests and is gone the next minute. When it does appear, things move and I feel weak," she said.

The detective listened to her intently. "What are the things that move?"

"The chandeliers mostly," she sighed. "Look, Detective, I know how this sounds to you. I don't want to make a fool of myself in front of anyone, but this is real. My husband saw it too when we were up in that attic," she insisted, pointing to the tower.

"Alright. I believe you. It's just I'm not used to dealing with the paranormal. I'm more comfortable with cases that have to do with tangible things. I don't even know how to proceed on something like this," he stated, pondering.

"My husband is very concerned. And now that I'm expecting, he's even more worried."

"Well, congratulations, ma'am!" exclaimed the detective with a slight smile on his face. "I will do all that's within my power to protect you and your child," he assured her. "Now, I've been wanting to ask you, why you insisted on speaking with me outside?"

"It's because of Norton. I don't want him to listen in on our conversation."

"I see. Is he in some way responsible for what's happening in your home, because if there is even an inkling that he's involved, I will take him downtown and keep him in the jail cell there," he declared resolutely.

"I'm not sure, Detective," responded Susan. "That's what I'm trying to figure out. You see, while we were up in the attic I found a box of old journals. They belonged to the original owner of the home, that's to say, the wife of the owner. Her name was Eleanor Mortimer."

The moment Detective Johnson heard the name, his eyes lit up. "I've heard of her. Yes, the Mortimers. They owned this place."

"How did you know?" asked Susan quizzically.

"I've read about the history of this place. There are articles from old newspapers. Boy, that Mortimer was a one of a kind man," he replied in a sarcastic tone.

"I see. Well, I'm reading through her journals to find some kind of explanation for all of this. In the meantime, I was wondering if you can get me any information about the history of this place. Maybe we can piece the puzzle together," suggested Susan with a twinkle of enthusiasm in her eyes.

"Sure, ma'am. I'll see what I can do. But at present, do you want me to keep an officer here for your protection?" he inquired.

"Let me think about that," replied Susan. "I'm not in any imminent danger at the moment."

"Are you certain?"

"Yes," she assured.

"I'll take a look around the place before I leave though," he said. "Please call me at any time if there's a problem. Understand?"

"Yes, I will. And thank you for coming," she said, heading toward the house.

Susan came in and closed the door behind her. Leaning against it, she gazed at the elegant furniture and everything else in front of her.

"This is all from France, and it's over a hundred years old," she uttered to herself with a bit of fascination.

31

It was past lunchtime, and Susan abruptly felt the urge to eat out. She got into a pair of blue jeans and a long-sleeved knit top. She clipped her hair back, put on some fresh makeup, grabbed the journal from under her pillow, and took her purse from her closet. Taking a tote that hung from behind the door, she thrust the journal and the purse inside. Suspecting the possibility that Norton might come into her room to snoop around while she was gone, she dragged the box of journals to her closet and pushed it all the way inside. Then she covered it with blankets and old clothes to make the hiding place look inconspicuous. Closing the closet door, she stepped out. As she came down the stairs, the smell of freshly cooked stew inundated her. Norton was making lunch. Repulsed by the odor, she quickly walked out.

Susan looked forward to getting out of the house. She was excited to drive her new car as well. The afternoon was cool and, thus, was a perfect day to enjoy the weather outside. She wanted to pay another visit to the restaurant that she took her mother to, have lunch there, and read a few journal entries over a nice cup of hot coffee. The sudden craving she felt for freshly made chicken soup was overwhelming. "Wonder if they serve it there."

The drive in town was relaxing. Since it was a Saturday, people were out and about, walking on the streets, shopping in stores, or purely socializing inside and outside restaurants. The ocean glistened in the sun. As she passed by, she could see beachgoers enjoying the sand or catching the waves. Breathing the fresh cool air brought her a sense of exhilaration. She felt the urge to call a couple of her friends to join her for lunch yet held back because she desired to read the journal after lunch without any interruptions.

Susan pulled the car into the restaurant parking lot. To her surprise, only a few vehicles could be seen. "What? They don't have business on a Saturday?"

She parked the car, got out with her tote, locked the doors, and headed toward the restaurant. Walking in, she noticed a few people scattered here and there, enjoying meals and pleasantries. The restaurant itself was cozy and inviting. The lighting was dim, which made the interior cool. The aroma of freshly baked bread enticed her and made her craving even more intense. A moment later, the waitress walked up and welcomed her. Susan requested to be seated at the far corner in the front area, facing the window. The waitress walked her to the table and handed her the menu. Without looking, Susan requested a bowl of chicken soup and bread. The waitress was happy to comply.

"And to drink, ma'am?"

"I would like a hot cup of coffee," she replied.

"Right away," uttered the waitress, taking the menu. "Your order will be ready shortly," she assured and walked away.

Susan hung her bag on the chair and sat down. Peering out through the window, she could see her red car right across. As she gazed outside, she was suddenly lost in thought, wondering about the next diary entry. Taking it out of the bag, she flipped the page and began reading.

July 3rd, 1867
  My love came back home today. He was in better spirits than he was the last time I saw him. I made a

special dinner for him. Lamb stew with bread and wine. He was a bit sullen, but I assumed that it was due to exhaustion after the long trip back home. I waited for the perfect moment to tell him that he was about to be a father. After dinner, we went outside to the backyard and took a stroll in the garden. The ocean was quiet. The cool breeze was comforting. As Arthur lit his pipe, I told him that I was with child. I expected him to be overcome with joy and to tell me how proud he was of me. But to my heart's discontent, he showed absolutely no excitement or enthusiasm. His nonchalance crushed my spirit. I thought that's what he wanted, to be a father to many children. What was the purpose of having a big home, if not to fill its emptiness with the life and laughter of little ones? He walked inside without saying anything to me. My heart was broken. Did I do something wrong?

Tears come rolling from my cheeks as I sit upon my bed writing these words in the middle of the night. My bed, where I am all alone tonight. He decided to sleep next door. Why is this happening to me? We were married only a few months ago. Does he not love me? Doesn't he want our child?

"Excuse me, madam," came a voice from the side. Susan was taken by surprise for she was deeply engrossed in the entry. The waitress was standing with the food.

"Oh, pardon me," uttered Susan putting the journal aside. The waitress placed the soup and freshly baked garlic bread on the table. The aroma of the meal roused her senses and her appetite.

"I'll be back with your coffee," she assured walking away.

Susan took the spoon and began sipping the soup. It was heavenly. The bread was warm and crusty. A few moments later, the waitress returned with the coffee. She placed the pot and a cup in front of her.

"Please let me know if you need anything else." Susan shook her head in compliance. "Enjoy your meal," she said.

Susan savored every bit of the soup and bread. The hot coffee was also a welcoming addition. Within minutes of eating everything, she desired a second serving. Calling the waitress back to the table she asked for a refill of the soup and more bread. While she was waiting, Susan continued to read.

July 7th, 1867

When I woke up in the morning, Arthur was gone. He had left no note or any kind of explanation as to his whereabouts. I plainly assumed that he had to go back to work to solve all the problems up there. Either way, not even a kiss goodbye or an inkling as to when he will be returning. What am I supposed to do? What am I supposed to think? I'm all alone in this big house with two servants and my precious little child on the way.

Bessie had made me breakfast. I didn't have the appetite, but I ate anyway for the sake of my baby. Arthur had managed to isolate me from my family. Nobody wants to speak to me. I wish I had my beloved mother near me. She would help me to find a way out of this predicament that I'm in. But fate took her from this world a year ago. She warned me that this would happen with Arthur. I guess she knew him more than I did. That's probably why she refused to let me go. I regret marrying him. I should have listened to my beloved mother and walked away when

I had the chance. He has broken my heart. What will become of me and my child?

July 8ᵗʰ, 1867

I had an awful nightmare last night. I awoke screaming. Nobody came to my rescue though. It was dark and quiet all around me, as if I was surrounded by the dead. I dreamt that Arthur was running away from me. I was going after him. But the closer I got to him, the further he went from me. Is this the end of my life with him? My prince is no more. In his place are emptiness and despondency. I got out of bed and went downstairs in the dark. I came out of the house to the blackness of the night. I just want to disappear. This big house is like a tomb. Am I to live eternally here with a broken heart?

"Here you go, ma'am," said the waitress as she placed the second serving of soup on the table. Susan took a deep breath and placed the journal on the side. Then she began eating. As she gazed outside, she thought about Eleanor and the utter misery she was in. She could never imagine being abandoned in such a manner, especially with a baby on the way. Her phone rang. Taking it out of the bag, she saw Jason's number.

"Hello, darling," she answered.

"Hello, honey. How are you?"

"I'm having lunch at the restaurant," she responded. "I'm so hungry, I had to get two orders of soup."

"You went out to town?"

"Yes. I wanted to get away from the house," she said, sipping her coffee.

"That's great, honey. Did Detective Johnson come this morning?"

"Yes, he did. I told him everything. He said he'll help however way he can."

"That's good. Listen. Drive back safely, alright?"

"Okay, darling. Don't worry. As soon as I'm done I'm going back home. I'll call you when I do," she assured him.

"I'll see you in the night," he said before hanging up the phone.

Susan was happy to hear Jason's voice. His constant care and concern toward her were anchors in her life. She felt fortunate to be surrounded by his love. Continuing her meal, she gazed out the window. More people were parking their cars outside the parking lot and heading toward the restaurant. The dinner rush was starting. Susan, however, didn't feel the impulse to leave just yet. Calling the waitress, she asked for another refill of fresh coffee as the pot was getting cold.

"Of course, ma'am," uttered the waitress. "Is there anything else I could get for you?"

"No, thank you. You can take the soup bowl," she said chowing down the last spoonful of soup. "Oh, by the way, I was wondering if I can stay here for a while longer. I have some reading to do," she said.

"Sure, ma'am."

"Thank you for your hospitality," said Susan gratefully.

As the waitress walked away, she continued reading.

July, 15ᵗʰ, 1867
I couldn't keep anything down today. This baby is causing such a commotion. Bessie was so concerned and fetched the town doctor to the house. Dr. John Vanderbeik was his name. He is a very handsome, tall gentleman who has a few years of delivering babies, I hear.

He examined me and said that he's concerned about my weight. Apparently, I had lost some. He asked me what the cause of this was. I couldn't tell him what I was enduring with Arthur. It would be shameful to share my marital problems with a stranger that I met for the first time. Yet his kind eyes and mannerisms were comforting. I told him that I couldn't sleep at night and that I had recurring nightmares. He asked me about Arthur. I told him that he was away for long periods. That was all I had the heart to divulge. How could I tell this man that my so-called husband didn't seem to want his child? He took out a notepad from his medical case and wrote out a prescription for wholesome food and bed rest and told me that he would come to visit me every two weeks. That was nice. At least somebody besides Bessie cared about me and my baby.

I am up in the middle of the night thinking about Arthur, where he might be or what he might be doing. Does he even care that I'm carrying his child? Oh, I wish I could find him so I could throttle him with my bare hands.

Bessie made some vegetable broth for me. The good doctor had given her instructions on how to make it. She told me later. He had also advised her to make a few other recipes to settle my stomach. I ate everything, and I haven't thrown up yet.

Susan kept skimming pages of the journal. In the proceeding entries, Eleanor's anger and vexation toward her husband become more pronounced and real. His long absence led her to question his lack of love or regard for her. She, however, expressed her love for her unborn child and her desire to protect him. Therefore, taking the doctor's advice with regards to the pregnancy was her priority. Eleanor described how her queasiness subsided little by little after eating the meals that Bessie made in accordance with the doctor's directive. She was looking forward to the good doctor's visit again.

Gazing at the window, she realized that evening was setting in. The dinner rush was in full swing. As guests were pouring into the restaurant, Susan realized that she had to either give up her table or stay for dinner. Not wanting to drive alone at night, she put the journal in her tote, stood up, and walked to the front. The waitress who served her was at the counter, greeting those who were arriving. Susan thanked her and stepped out of the restaurant.

The fall ocean air was penetratingly chilly. She took out the coat from inside her bag, put it on, and buttoned it up. Street lights were already turning on here and there.

Getting into the car, she placed her bag on the passenger seat next to her. Then turning on the ignition, she pulled out of the parking lot and got onto the street. The traffic was moderate. As she drove on, her thoughts returned to Eleanor and the journal. She began to sympathize with her. Never had she realized that there were people in this world who endured such trials. Knowing that this woman lived in her home over a century ago made her plight all the more real.

32

It was dark by the time Susan made the turn up to her property. She still had to drive quite a way along the lonely road to her villa. The chill in the air became more pronounced as she continued the drive up. The mountainous terrain on either side was a bit more daunting at night compared to the daytime. She thought of Jason who made this trip home each night and never minded it a bit. Suddenly, the chill in the air became much more severe, and her body began to shiver.

The ocean air can't be this cold, she thought to herself. She suddenly heard whispers in the air as if someone was attempting to communicate to her. Feeling perplexed, she peered in different directions to determine if anyone was watching her. Only boulders and swaying trees were visible. Terror crept into her mind, and she began to speed up. Finally reaching the gate, she hurriedly entered the driveway and drove into the garage. Susan felt an inexplicable yet sinister presence around her, which put her into a panic. Getting out of the car with the tote on her shoulder, she looked around. The trees in the front of the yard swayed back and forth, and she continued to hear whispers.

"Who is there?" she shouted. "Come out whoever you are," she demanded. "I'm not afraid of you!"

The trees continued to move to and fro as if in anger. The whispers persisted in the darkness. She couldn't make sense of them, but anger seemed to emanate from them. Suddenly, she was almost blinded by a set of headlights approaching her. Moving to the side, she noticed that it was Jason. He abruptly stopped the car and looked at his wife through the shutter.

"Honey, did you just get home?"

"Yes," Susan responded. "Oh, thank goodness it's you," she uttered in relief.

"Well, I'm glad someone's happy I'm home!" he exclaimed, pulling into the garage. He parked and stepped out. Going toward his wife, he grabbed her from behind, and kissed her. Susan was caught off guard and reacted defensively. "Are you alright?" asked Jason in alarm.

"Yes, I guess," she replied, taking a deep breath and embracing him.

"What's the matter? You're as prickly as a porcupine."

"I don't know. Maybe I'm losing it altogether. Did you hear anything strange when you were driving up here?"

"Strange? Like what?" he asked quizzically.

"I mean like a voice of some kind?" she continued.

"No, honey, not really," he replied, taking the tote off her shoulder. "What's going on? You're shivering."

"I heard something, and I suddenly felt cold," she replied.

"Honey, you're pregnant. You shouldn't be out on a night like this. Come on. Let's go inside," he said, taking her hand.

They entered the dark living room. "He hasn't even turned on the lights," complained Jason as he switched on the chandelier. "I've had the most exhausting day," he sighed and began climbing the stairs. Susan followed. As they went up, they saw Norton coming down.

"Good evening, sir," he said looking at Jason.

"Good evening," responded Jason nonchalantly.

"Good evening, madam," he said, directing his eyes toward Susan.

"Hello, Norton. Why is the living room dark?" she asked, halting for a moment.

Norton gazed at her apologetically. "I'm sorry, madam but I guess I didn't realize that you were out of the house. I thought maybe you were in the room resting," he replied.

"No. I went out to lunch."

"Dinner is in the kitchen," he uttered and continued going down.

"Thank you," said Susan and followed her husband who had already disappeared. Entering the room, she took a deep breath and sat on the bed. Jason was in the bathroom, showering. He had laid her tote on the bed. She took the journal out and put it inside the side table drawer. Then she stretched on the bed for a few minutes with her eyes closed. Jason came out quietly, sat beside her, and kissed her. Susan placed her arms around his neck and kissed him in return.

"Are you feeling better?" he asked, looking into her eyes.

"Fine," she replied.

"Come on. I'm starved. Let's have dinner and talk about your day," he said, grabbing her arm.

They came into the kitchen. The aroma of tomato sauce was all around. A huge pot perched on the stove. Jason took a plate, walked up to it, and opened the lid.

"It's spaghetti and meatballs," he said, looking at Susan who grabbed a plate as well. A bowl of fresh salad lay on the side counter. He served some onto his plate and helped his wife as well. "If you weren't pregnant, I would've brought a bottle of wine," he remarked.

"You should have anyway," said Susan, sitting at the table beside him.

"I don't want to drink without you, honey," he replied, taking a bite of the meatball.

Although she began eating, Susan couldn't shake off her uneasiness. "I'm reading the journal," she uttered in between bites.

"Oh good! Did you find anything useful?'

"Keep your voice down, darling," she cautioned her husband. "Well, Eleanor is pregnant and she's not very happy.

"Why?"

"I think her husband has abandoned her. He doesn't want the baby."

"What kind of a man wouldn't want his own child?" he asked in irritation.

"I don't want to jump into a conclusion but I think he might have had an affair," she continued. "I feel so bad for her. I can't imagine going through what she went through. If you leave me for any reason, you won't have your legs to walk with, Dr. Smith," she said sternly.

"That's a bit harsh!" uttered Jason.

"I mean it!" declared Susan, glaring at him.

Jason placed his fork on the side of his plate, took Susan's hands, and looked into her eyes. "Honey, what happened to Eleanor over a century ago isn't going to happen to you. You know why?"

"Why?" she asked.

"Because I really, and I mean really, love you and our baby. I will always be there for the two of you and the many more children that we'll have in the future," he affirmed.

"Thank you," she said contentedly. "Anyway, I'm still on the first book. I'll keep you posted as I go along. How was your day?"

"Tiring as usual. I had two surgeries back to back. I didn't even have time to eat," he said.

"Honey, how can you operate on someone on an empty stomach?" asked Susan with a mark of concern on her face.

"Well, after a while you get used to it. Believe me, when you're holding someone's life in your hands, food is the last thing in your mind," he replied, stuffing his mouth.

33

After dinner, they went up to the bedroom. It was dark and quiet. Susan turned on the side lamp, got into bed, and took the journal out. She flipped to the next entry. Before she could begin reading, Jason edged toward her, took the journal away, and began kissing her. Unable to resist her desire for him, Susan began kissing her husband in return. As he was making love to her, Susan felt a chill go through her body. Although she was aroused by him, her mind wasn't at ease. She sensed someone was watching them. A gust of cold air suddenly entered into the room through the side window. The curtains fluttered, and Susan was overcome with a sinister feeling. She, however, curbed her uneasiness to give in to her husband's affections.

"Are you okay?" asked Jason.

"I just feel cold."

"I'll warm you up," he uttered, embracing her and kissing her neck.

Susan felt safe surrounded by her husband's affection but was startled when she heard whispers coming through the window as if carried in by the air.

"Did you hear that?" she quavered while abruptly glancing at the window.

"Hear what?" asked Jason while continuing to kiss her neck.

"The sound coming from the window," she replied, agitated.

"No, honey. It's just the wind," uttered Jason, who brusquely stopped to glance at her.

He put her mind at ease and continued to clutch her toward him. Before long, Jason had fallen asleep. Susan was still uneasy. She got down from bed, walked toward the window, and closed it. Then getting back to bed, she took the journal and began skimming through the entries in search of the next.

August 1st, 1867

Arthur's whereabouts are unknown to me. I haven't heard from him for weeks. I wonder if he's going to come back, that wretched man! How could I have ever loved such a brute? If I would have known that he was going to abandon me and my baby, I would have never married him.

I take long walks in the garden and breathe out the anger that's inside of me. It is like a poison, and I don't want it to poison my baby. Dr. Vanderbeik is supposed to come today to check up on me. I'm looking forward to seeing him again. He will be so proud of me. I've been eating as he had directed. Bessie is preparing all my meals and the morning sickness has improved. I can't wait to see him.

Night, August 1st

As expected Dr. Vanterbeik came to see me in the afternoon. He was dressed in a black suit. I love his dark eyes. I'm afraid to look at them because he moves me so. I don't want to fall in love with him. He felt my stomach. When he touched me, a feeling of warmth overcame me. His gentle mannerisms set my mind at ease. He was quite content that my health was improving. I told him that this was his doing.

We took a walk together in the yard and talked a while. I told him that Arthur had abandoned me. He was upset to hear that I was suffering so. I asked him about his life. He's a bachelor and quite the catch for any woman, I might add. As we were walking along, I tripped and he caught me. I only wish he could have held me longer, but he's a gentleman, and I do not want to impose my troubles and needs on him. He said he would come to see me again in a couple of weeks. I am looking forward to it.

Susan perused through the following entries to find anything useful or significant. Eleanor described how her baby was growing, and with every gently flutter she felt in her womb, she was falling more and more in love with the child. She continued to maintain her fears of an uncertain future. Yet John would ease these thoughts as he declared his love for her. Despite her reservations, a relationship seemed to be blossoming between them.

September 2ⁿᵈ, 1867

Oh, I can't begin to describe how I feel about John. I want him in my arms every minute. He presented me with a dozen red roses and declared his love for me today. He says I am beautiful. What should I do? Am I still married to that brute Arthur? After all, he has clearly abandoned me. No word for months now. Can I declare myself free from him so I can be with John? His sensual kiss penetrated my soul today. His tender touch takes me to a place far from any misery. When I told him I used to play on the swing as a little girl, he even put a swing out in the backyard for me, so I could sit and enjoy the cool ocean breeze. Although he didn't say so in words, I think he aims to marry me. Can he fight Arthur if he comes back?

Susan placed the journal down and mused on the words for a moment. She realized that the swing in the backyard had been there for over a century. Suddenly feeling light-headed, she closed her eyes and rested her head against the headboard of the bed. A few moments later, she felt as if she was in a dream. She got out of bed, put her housecoat and slippers on, and went down the stairs. The house was dark. She continued to walk to the kitchen as if propelled by an unknown force. She walked steadily through the dark all the way to the back door, which opened on its own. Coming out, she stood still facing the night. The sea breeze was blowing her hair. Susan was in a trance and did not move. Suddenly, the apparition in the white dress appeared in front of her. She was seated on the swing, glaring at Susan, who suddenly awoke as if nudged abruptly from a deep sleep. Seeing the apparition in white fixing her angry stare at her, she endeavored to let out a cry. No voice came from her mouth. It was as if every muscle in her being was paralyzed. The apparition stood up. Her long black hair was shining and her dark eerie eyes continuing to shoot a venomous glance at her. Opening her mouth, the woman let out a cry of grief that Susan felt at the core of her being. It was a suffering that she had never felt before, as if a sword was pierced into her very essence. At that instant, the apparition vanished, and Susan regained her mobility. She cried in terror and fell to the ground. A few minutes later, Jason came rushing to the yard and called on to her. Susan, however, was too weak to move.

"Honey! Susan!" he cried. "Wake up!"

She attempted to regain her composure. "What?" she asked in confusion.

"Are you okay? What happened?" he asked, attempting to help her up.

Susan held onto him and stood up. Jason scrutinized the premises to determine if anyone was around. The yard was dark and silent. As his eyes turned upward, he saw Norton abruptly move away from the window. A faint light was visible from his room. Jason walked her inside. They passed the kitchen and into the living room. He switched the chandelier on. Susan covered her eyes as the light was too bright. He helped her onto the sofa.

"What happened? Why did you go outside in the dark, honey?" he asked. Jason was upset.

Susan stumbled with her words. "I don't know. I thought I was dreaming," she replied holding onto her head.

"Were you sleepwalking?" he asked.

"I don't know." Then suddenly it dawned on her. "It's her!" she exclaimed, standing up.

"Who?" asked Jason, agitated.

"Eleanor Mortimer. She's the woman in the white gown, the one we saw in the property that night. She was in the garden just now, sitting on the swing." Fear gripped her once again. "Did you see her?"

"Darling, calm down. I didn't see her," uttered Jason, attempting to placate her. "But I did see the old man looking down from his room. He probably saw the whole thing. Why did you go out in the middle of the night?"

"I don't know. It was like a nightmare. When I woke up, I was on the floor. I felt as if my heart was going to break," she cried, wiping the tears from her eyes.

"What does that mean?" he asked holding her.

"She was in so much pain, Jason," she continued.

"Honey, you're shaking!" he said, feeling her body. He took the throw that was on the sofa and covered her.

"I can't explain it, but she's very angry and broken inside. I felt it."

"I think you need to stop reading those journals immediately," ordered Jason.

"No no. I need to find out what happened to her. That's the only way to help her," she insisted.

"You're putting yourself and the baby in the line of fire. That woman or spirit or whatever you call it killed Zoe and her baby, remember? Who knows where this is going to end up? I don't want you leaving the house in the middle of the night," he asserted.

"But I didn't even know that I was going anywhere," protested Susan.

"Exactly my point! I don't believe in this kind of thing, but I sense a whole heap of trouble," he uttered in anger. He looked at the wall clock. "It's two o'clock in the morning. Come on. Let's get to bed. I've got a long day tomorrow," he said, helping her up.

Jason tucked his wife under the covers and climbed onto the bed beside her. "Are you feeling okay?" he asked.

"Yes, darling. I'm sorry I worried you," she said, gazing at him apologetically.

"That's alright. What are husbands for if they don't wake up in the middle of the night to rescue their wives now and then?" he sighed closing his eyes.

"Very funny," retorted Susan and kissed him. A few moments later, both of them were fast asleep.

34

The next morning, Susan woke up early and made breakfast for Jason. She was in the kitchen, cooking a ham and cheese omelet and fried potatoes, when Norton came in. He was dressed for the day as usual.

"Good morning, madam," he uttered.

"Good morning," replied Susan nonchalantly, turning away.

"How did you sleep last night, madam?" he asked in a sarcastic tone.

Susan turned toward him and fumed with anger. "I'm sure you know the answer to that!" she snapped.

"I don't know what you mean by that, madam," he protested.

"Of course, you do. In fact, you know everything that's going on in this place. Well, I assure you that, soon, I'll find out too. If I discover that you have anything to do with anything, I will turn you into the police," she asserted in anger.

"Is that a threat, madam?" asked Norton with glaring eyes.

"Call it what you want. But this is my home, and quite frankly, I think you have overstayed your welcome," she snapped.

"If that's the case, I will leave immediately," he stated and went out.

Susan took a deep breath and pondered for a moment. When the coffee was ready, she took two cups and poured some for herself and Jason, who happened to walk in.

"What's wrong?" he asked, approaching her.

"I saw Norton storm up the stairs just now." Jason was ready for work and looked strikingly handsome in a long-sleeved light blue shirt, a checkered tie to match, and long dark pants. Susan gazed at him longingly.

"Well, I finally told him off. He said he's going to leave," she uttered in exasperation.

"Honey, calm down! I know you're upset. Just don't think about things too much, alright?" he said, taking the coffee and kissing her.

"Do you think he'll leave?" asked Susan, turning toward him.

"Does it matter to you?" he asked in return.

"Not really, but now I feel bad," she said regretfully. "I'll talk to him later."

"I saw him looking down at you last night," he sighed. "I don't want to fight with him over that right now because I need to go to work with a clear head. I have a very complicated surgery I have to oversee today."

"I'm sorry, darling. I don't want to upset you with all this Norton business. I don't know what to do," she uttered somberly.

"Just leave him be for now, darling. We'll deal with him later. Even if he leaves, so what?" Jason served himself some breakfast. "This smells delicious," he remarked. Jason sat at the table and looked at her. "Are you alright?"

Susan took a deep breath and gazed at him. "I don't want to think about it. All I can say at the moment is, as long as you're with me, I'll be fine."

"That's right," assured Jason.

"You look very handsome, by the way," she blurted.

"Thank you," replied Jason, shooting her a smile.

As they were finishing up breakfast, Norton walked into the kitchen with a stern look on his face. He placed what seemed to be a traveling bag on the side counter. Susan and Jason turned around and gazed at him.

"I'll be leaving you," he stated. "But before I do, I want to apologize to both of you. I may not have been totally honest about matters concerning this house," he rasped.

Jason stood up with his plate in hand and walked toward the sink. "Kindly elaborate," he stated peering at Norton.

"The fact of the matter is, there's history here, and I would like to preserve it at any cost," he insisted.

Susan took a deep breath and stood up to protest. "I need to know what type of history this is, so I can feel safe," she asserted when suddenly the doorbell rang.

"I'll get it," uttered Jason, stepping out.

"I assure you, madam, I have no intention of harming anyone. Sometimes the past is best kept where it is, in the past."

"Go back to your room, Norton," she ordered. "I'm giving you a second chance," she uttered, washing her plate.

"Very well if you insist," he said, picking up his bag.

Jason walked into the kitchen with Detective Johnson by his side. Norton shot him a hostile look and walked back upstairs with his bag.

"Good morning, Mrs. Smith," said the detective.

"Hello, Detective," said Susan with a smile on her face. "Would you like some breakfast?" she asked.

"Please call me Eric," he insisted. "Well, I would love some if it's not too much trouble," he said.

"It's no trouble at all. Please, have a seat," said Susan. Both men sat by the table and glanced at each other. "So what brings you here, Eric?" asked Jason.

"I dropped by the other day when you called me on the phone. Mrs. Smith shared some concerns about an apparition she had seen," he replied with a spark of concern in his eyes. "Well, I've found some information that I'd like to share with both of you."

Susan set a plate with the remaining omelet and fried potatoes in front of the detective. She then brought a fork and a cup of coffee.

"Thank you, ma'am," responded the detective with a grateful expression. "Come to think of it, I had forgotten about breakfast altogether. I came to the office so early in the morning and saw that my desk was swamped with paperwork. I've been working on organizing them ever since," he added.

"So what did you find?" asked Susan.

The detective took a bite of the omelet and complimented her on its taste. Then he pulled out an envelope from the inside of his coat pocket and placed it on the table. "Is it safe to talk here?" he asked.

Susan walked toward the staircase and looked up. Seeing that Norton was nowhere to be seen, she went back to the kitchen. "Yes, it is," she replied.

Jason opened the envelope and took the contents out. They were old newspaper clippings. "What are these?" he asked.

"These are the particulars that I told Mrs. Smith about the other day. I had to go to great lengths to find these newspaper articles," he stated, taking a sip of his coffee.

Susan approached Jason and peered over his shoulder. Jason handed her one of the articles. The paper was browned up and tattered in the corners. The article was from the newspaper *The City Reporter* and was dated February 18, 1887. It stated,

John Mortimer Dies Suddenly in
Unexplainable Circumstances

The son of Arthur Mortimer was found dead
yesterday in his villa up in the mountains. The
police discovered his body at the home. He had
been stabbed several times in the back. Was this
death an accident or murder? The city police are
intently studying the circumstances surrounding
this case. John Mortimer has had a very troubling
childhood, especially since the violent death of his
late mother Eleanor Mortimer, who died suddenly
when he was one year old . . .

The article went on to detail certain aspects of the
investigation and the names of the police officers in charge. A
picture of John Mortimer was on the side. Susan scrutinized it
closely and realized that this picture somewhat resembled the
dark apparition she had seen.

"Could this be him?" she asked Jason, pointing at the picture.

Jason peered at it and pondered. "I'm not sure, honey. I
only saw that thing from far," he replied. Jason then handed
the second article to his wife. It was dated July 18, 1869, and
showed,

Eleanor Mortimer Found Dead in Her Mountain Villa
Police discovered the body of Eleanor Mortimer
yesterday afternoon in her home up in the
mountains. According to investigators, she was
strangled to death. Police are closely studying
the circumstances surrounding her violent
demise. Sources reveal that she had a bitter
relationship with her husband, Arthur Mortimer,

the well-known oil tycoon. It is unsure if he is responsible for her death. Police are currently questioning him and the caretaker of the house Norton Abram. Neither one of them are cooperating however.

A picture of Eleanor Mortimer was at the bottom of the article. Susan felt a chill go through her body.

"This is her!" she insisted pointing to the picture. "This is the woman in white and the one in the portrait up in the attic." She looked at Jason and the detective with affirmation. "Wait a minute!" she uttered abruptly. "The article mentioned Norton. Is he a relative of the one here?"

"That's probably his grandfather," speculated the detective.

"So did they ever find out who killed them, Eric?" asked Jason.

"No, it's a cold case. It's the biggest cold case of our city," he replied. "Since this was the most prominent family in town back then, you could just imagine the attention that surrounded these events. People were talking about it for months and years afterward."

"If John Mortimer was the heir who died, then Norton lied to us from the beginning," remarked Susan.

"What do you mean?" asked Jason.

"Honey, do you remember him telling us that the only heir died of illness?"

"Yes, I do. On our first day here," replied Jason.

"He was murdered," she uttered. "Can you reopen the case?" she asked, turning toward the detective.

"If there's new evidence, I can," he replied.

"What does the police department have in their keeping as evidence so far?" continued Susan.

"Well, I haven't checked into that. These events happened over a century ago. I don't even know if anything they gathered would even last that long," replied the detective. "I will check the storage. Maybe I can find the case file."

"See what you can dig out. All I can say is that she and her son never left the premises. Whatever happened to them was so awful, they cannot rest in peace," commented Susan.

"Well, honey, it doesn't matter what it was. You need to stay clear of all this. If something happens to you, I'll never forgive myself," said Jason gravely.

"Jason, Zoe is dead, and her case is going cold. Eric told me that there's no hard evidence to convict anyone. Well, maybe it's because we're dealing with the paranormal. We have to get to the bottom of this before it's too late," she uttered in great concern.

"As I said before, my offer about stationing an officer here still stands," interjected the detective.

"I'd like that," said Jason taking a deep breath. "This is just too much for us. I'm not home most of the time, and Susan's all alone. I'd feel a lot better if someone were here to look over her shoulder a bit. I don't mind paying the guy extra until some resolution is reached," continued Jason.

"The person I'm thinking about has been in the force for about five years now. He can fight people, but spirits are a whole other ball game. We're not trained to take them on," remarked the detective as he finished his food. "Thank you so much for breakfast, ma'am."

"You're welcome," acknowledged Susan.

Seeing that the detective was done eating, Jason stood up. "Let's walk into the den," he urged him. "I feel a lot better if we keep this conversation a bit discreet," he added.

"Of course," concurred the detective, standing up and pushing his chair in.

The three of them exited the kitchen and entered the den, which was a large room adjacent to the main dining room. It was cozy inside with a sofa at the center and a coffee table next to it. Susan closed the door shut and approached her husband and the detective, who were pulling in the window curtains. After they finished, they walked up to the sofa and sat down.

"What do we do with Norton?" asked Susan, sitting beside her husband. "And is Abram his last name?"

"Probably," replied the detective. He thought for a moment. "It is very likely he knows all about these matters. It may not be easy to get him to admit to any crimes committed by his ancestors or even Arthur Mortimer. As caretakers, they regard loyalty their utmost priority. Steer clear of him for the time being and try not to anger the old man either because he might cause you harm. We're not sure what he's capable of at this point. As I say, keep your enemies closer," he cautioned them.

Jason gazed at his wife and nodded his head in agreement.

"I want the case reopened though," insisted Susan.

"What for, honey?" inquired Jason. "There's no new evidence."

"Maybe if we solved the cases, they can finally be at peace," she responded, gazing at him. "And I have to do this for Zoe," she declared with resolve.

"If I do reopen the case, I need to conduct a thorough search of the premises," declared the detective.

"That's fine," stated Susan.

"I will come with my team in a couple of days. In the meantime, I'm going to send an officer here."

"Where will he be stationed?" asked Jason.

"He can take turns being outdoors and indoors. The only requirement is for him to be fed three meals a day and maybe get some accommodation. He will be working around the clock though," affirmed the detective.

"That's great! I'll see to it that he's comfortable," conceded Susan in an enthused tone. "Another question, Eric," uttered Susan abruptly. "Where were the bodies buried?"

"According to records, they were buried in the cemetery downtown," replied the detective. "I've got to get going," he said, looking at his watch.

Jason handed the envelope with the articles back to the detective and walked with him to the door. As he opened it, he immediately noticed Norton pass by with a frown on his face. Jason ignored him, accompanied the detective out to the front, and waved goodbye to him. Susan met Jason as he came back inside. She embraced him and kissed him.

"Are you going to stay home today?" she asked.

"Dressed like this?" he said in a jovial tone.

"Well, it was worth a shot," she sighed, wiping his shirt.

"No, honey, I have to leave for the hospital right now to check on some research matters and oversee the surgery I told you about," he uttered. Holding onto each other, they walked up the stairs. "Are you going to be alright while I'm gone?" he asked.

"Yes. But if worse comes to worst, I'll come and stay with you in the hospital," suggested Susan with a slight grin on her face.

35

It was past noon by the time Jason left the villa for work. Susan saw him off with a passionate kiss. She promised to be careful. Jason took comfort in the notion that an officer would be sent to guard the premises before sundown.

Susan came into the house, locked the door, and went up the stairs to her room. Her desire to visit the cemetery in search of the Mortimer graves was overwhelming. She went into the bathroom, took off her night robe and nightgown, and stepped into the shower. Feeling her growing baby bump brought a surge of joy to her heart. After taking a soothing bath, she came back into the room and opened the closet and got dressed for the day. Then she took the journal out of the drawer. Realizing that she was almost at the end of it, she carefully took the next one from the box that she had hidden away in the closet. Then taking the tote that hung behind the door, she thrusted the journals into it. She put on her shoes and walked out of the room. Entering into the kitchen, she opened the refrigerator to get a bottle of water. Norton was out in the backyard, watering the plants. She didn't feel the urge to tell him that she would be out for most of the day visiting Zoe's grave and those of the two Mortimers.

Susan went into the garage and pulled out her car. She made a turn around the fountain and drove out of the yard.

She felt a bit guilty because she had not informed Jason about her intentions and plans for the day.

"He won't mind. Besides, I'm going to take a stroll down the beach today. Walking is good when you're pregnant," she uttered to herself as she admired the passing mountainous terrain. She decided to get a bouquet of flowers for Zoe. As she drove along the town's main road, she kept an eye out for a flower shop. Eventually locating one, she parked in front of the store. Bouquets of various flowers were neatly arranged inside. Walking to the counter, she asked for gladiolas, which were Zoe's favorite. The saleswoman wrapped up five pink gladiolas in white tissue and ribbon and handed them to her. She was quite old, yet very well dressed.

"Here you go" she uttered gently.

"Thank you," said Susan and paid for the flowers.

"Aren't they beautiful?" remarked the lady.

"Yes," replied Susan.

"Are they for anyone special?" she asked with quizzical eyes.

"For a friend," replied Susan.

"Well, I hope your friend enjoys them. They are grown with great love and care," commented the lady.

"Thank you," said Susan before exiting the store. Getting back into the car, she carefully placed the flowers on the front seat and headed toward the cemetery. The last time she was there was during Zoe's funeral, and she had a vague recollection of the directions. As she drove along, she kept an eye out for a certain turn that needed to be taken. She remembered that a large coffee shop was at the turn junction. A few minutes later, she could see this shop ahead. Carefully approaching the junction, she made the turn and drove up a few miles. Mountains and bare land could be seen ahead. Several homes were scattered hither and thither on the sides. Before long, the cemetery appeared on the side. The humungous gate was open, and she drove in. There was a small parking lot for visitors in one section. Parking the car, she got out with the tote on her shoulders and the flowers in her hand.

Susan took a deep breath and peered in all directions. Not a soul could be seen. It was windy and the sky was somewhat overcast. An unexplained sullenness took over her, as she headed toward Zoe's grave.

As she walked along the grassy path, she passed numerous headstones and crosses on either side. Many had weathered edges and looked as somber as the surroundings. Some of the graves that she passed had dried up flowers placed in front or next to them. She gazed over her shoulder now and then to see if anyone was behind her. Silence echoed as she headed on in search of her friend's final resting place. Finally, it appeared in front of her. The headstone of her beloved friend read, "Zoe Bellamy, beloved wife, daughter, and friend, 1955–1991." Andrew had managed to get a picture of her engraved underneath the writing. In it, she was smiling.

Susan gazed at her friend and let out a sigh. She placed the flowers by the grave and sat down. "I can't believe you are gone," she sighed. Her eyes were brimming over with tears. "I miss you, Zoe. I wish you were here. I need you now more than ever. There are so many things I have to tell you. I know who did this to you. Believe me, I'm facing the same sinister enemy. The only problem is I don't know how to stop it, and I'm afraid. I think about you all the time. Oh, did I tell you that I was pregnant? I'm going on my second month now. Time flies, ha? I'm so sorry you didn't get the chance to be a mom. You would have made an excellent one."

Susan paused for a moment and looked around. She inhaled the tranquility of the mountains that surrounded her. Several trees could be seen scattered further off, and their branches swayed in response to the mild wind. "Well, at least you're close to me," she uttered directing her eyes back at Zoe's picture. She suddenly heard a sound from the side. Startled, she turned around and saw Andrew standing behind her. "Andrew!" she exclaimed, getting up on her feet. "You scared me!"

"Hello, Susan," he said. He had a surly expression on his face. Susan immediately walked up to him and gave him an embrace. "It's nice to see you," she uttered with a gentle smile.

His appearance had changed since the last time she had seen him. In place of the man with the well-maintained physique that she was familiar with stood a gaunt figure. He wore a gray coat and blue jeans and had a queer mustache and something of a beard. Susan touched his face. "When was the last time you shaved?" she asked in concern.

Tears began flooding his eyes. "Not since I lost my wife and baby," he sighed.

"Andrew, you have to take care of yourself. You've lost so much weight within the month," she exclaimed.

"What does it matter? My Zoe is gone," he uttered, wiping his tears with a kerchief that he pulled out of his coat pocket. Susan gave him another embrace.

"I'm sorry, Andrew," she said gravely. "But she'll never leave you or me ever! She loves us too much."

"What am I supposed to do without her? I have been robbed of my happiness. I feel that just yesterday we were married and now she's gone. Where is the justice in that? She was my whole life and I was excited to be a father to our child," he sighed, raising up his head dolefully and gazing at the mountains. "Did you know that she was getting the baby's room ready?" he sighed. "I can't even bear to go in there or sleep on our bed. I feel like selling the whole place and getting lost. I don't know what to do. I feel so broken inside. How do you get past something like this?" he asked turning towards her.

"Live your life. Make her proud," replied Susan with firm resolve. "You'll be happy again."

"It's easy for you to say," he snapped in anger. "You've still got Jason. I have nobody," he said dismally.

"That's not true!" she asserted. "You have your family and you have us. I don't have the answers to everything. But all I can say is that Zoe wouldn't want you to mope and be miserable like this. She'd want you to live your life again."

"Well, how do I do that when I miss her each day like crazy?" demanded Andrew.

"Do what she would have wanted you to do. Do the best you can each day in her memory, and she'll always be with you."

Andrew took a deep breath and walked over to the grave. He glanced at the flowers that Susan had placed on the ground next to it. "Those are beautiful," he remarked.

"I know. Gladiolas were her favorite," uttered Susan.

"Don't I know it? I used to buy her those now and then. Maybe I should've done it more often," he sighed. He neared toward the headstone and placed a kiss on Zoe's image. "I'll try my best to make you proud, darling," he declared. Susan approached him and held onto his arm. A moment later, Andrew turned toward her and shot her an apologetic gaze. "I'm sorry for being so down in the dumps and being so rude. I didn't even ask how you were."

"That's alright," she sighed.

"So you're pregnant."

"How did you know that?"

"I heard you a few minutes ago when you were talking to her," he replied.

Susan smiled. "How much of that monologue did you hear?"

"Enough, I guess," he responded.

"Yes, I am pregnant."

"Congratulations! Zoe would've been so happy for you," he uttered with a spark of joy in his face.

"Thank you, Andrew. I know," she continued sullenly.

"Zoe would've been almost four months pregnant today," he said somberly and looked down.

"I'm sorry, Andrew."

"You'll make a great mom! Zoe told me how you and Jason have been trying for a while."

"Yes, we have." Susan peered longingly at the mountains.

"What's the matter? You don't seem to be very happy about it," he remarked.

"It's complicated," she replied.

"What's the complication?" asked Andrew with a curious look. "Is everything alright?"

"You know, you're a bit like Zoe. I guess she's rubbed off on you. She could always read in between the lines when it concerned me. I'm pretty good at putting up a front sometimes. But I could never hide anything from her. She would always figure out when something was wrong."

"Well, what's wrong, Susan?" continued Andrew looking gravely at her.

"I'm afraid, Andrew. I'm afraid for me and the baby. I try to hide it from Jason because I don't want him to worry and lose his mind over all that's happening. He has to perform lifesaving surgeries every day, and he needs to have the proper mind-set for that. He can't be worrying about the patients and me. So I try to be brave in front of him." Andrew listened to her intently. She began strolling past Zoe's grave.

He trailed behind her. "What are you afraid of?" he asked.

"The same thing that took Zoe," she replied turning around. "It's in my home."

"Is it real?" His countenance changed, and he seemed to become more perturbed.

"Yes. She is real. I saw her twice. Her anger is paralyzing. I passed out the last time," said Susan. "Did the police show you the pictures from Zoe's camera?"

"Yes," he replied. "But I didn't believe it at first. The police gave me a bunch of mumbo jumbo and the coroner's report said that my Zoe had a heart attack out in your property. Who was that woman in the picture? Is she the one who caused it?" His expression became increasingly troubled.

"Yes. That's Eleanor Mortimer. She was the wife of Arthur Mortimer, the previous owner of my villa. She roams around the property, and she's deadly. Zoe was probably caught off guard by her and became terrified."

"How do you fight something like that?" asked Andrew.

"I don't know. I found some of her journals in the attic, and I'm going through them to see if I can figure out why she's still here."

"What can I do to help?" he asked.

"Well, I want to find the graves. A detective is working on the case. But then again, these are angry spirits, and I don't know how much of a help he can be."

"What do you mean spirits? Just exactly how many are we talking about?"

"There are two, Eleanor and her son John."

"So you've seen both?"

"Yes. Jason and I have seen them."

"Why do you want to find the graves?"

"I don't know. Maybe to find some clue that could help me."

"Does Jason know you're here?"

"No. He'll blow his top if he knew I'm looking for them," said Susan. "Please don't tell him," she asked earnestly.

"Okay, I won't. But if you're so adamant at finding them, I'll help you," suggested Andrew.

"Thanks," replied Susan in relief.

"So where do we begin?" he inquired looking around.

"They're very old gravestones. One died in 1869, and the other almost twenty years later," she said.

The cold chill was getting more pronounced, as the afternoon hours began to fly past them. Susan and Andrew walked in different directions in search of the headstones in question. As time elapsed, she grew more impatient. Hundreds of graves were scattered all over, and the likelihood of discovering two graves that were over a century old was becoming grim. It was getting late, and she was hungry.

"I think I found it," came an abrupt voice from afar.

Susan turned and saw that Andrew was in one of the farthest corners of the cemetery and peering closely at a headstone. She paced toward him as quickly as she could. Approaching him, she glanced at the headstone as well. It was that of Eleanor Mortimer. The top portion of the stone was missing and the remaining part was dirty and worn out. Yet her name was intact. The grass had grown beneath it. "That's it?" asked Susan scrutinizing the gravesite.

"Yes, I guess so," replied Andrew.

Susan checked the surrounding headstones in search of John Mortimer. It was nowhere in the vicinity however.

"I don't see anything unusual," uttered Andrew, examining the half-broken stone.

"I guess not," sighed Susan. "Her son isn't buried next to her."

The grave appeared tattered and beaten up as a result of over a century of wear and tear. As she glanced at it, the image of Eleanor Mortimer instantly came to her mind, and she abruptly stepped away.

"He could be anywhere," remarked Andrew, as he perused the surrounding. "What's wrong?" he asked, turning toward her.

"Just the thought of her creeps me out," she responded.

"Come on. Let's go then," urged Andrew. "This type of thing may not be good for someone who's pregnant."

"Alright." As they headed toward the gate, Andrew looked at her in bewilderment. "Why not just leave the house?" he asked. "If you're afraid of this thing, just move out. You need to protect your child."

"I don't know," she sighed. "Don't I have a right to fight for my own home?"

"Listen, Susan. You can contend with flesh and blood. But this type of spiritual force can't be dealt with that way. If it were a person who took my Zoe away from me, I would've killed him by now. That's what's frustrating about this whole thing. Who do I take my revenge on?" snapped Andrew in indignation. His voice edged with contempt.

"Can I ask you something?" inquired Susan.

"Sure," he replied.

"Are you angry with me?" she asked.

"For what?"

"Do you blame me for Zoe's death?" she blurted out.

Andrew was taken aback and halted immediately. He took a deep breath and gazed at her gravely. "No, Susan, I don't blame you. I never did. If anyone is to blame, it should be me. Instead of being with her, I got drunk that night. But it's time I moved past that and forgave myself," he declared.

Susan embraced him. "It wasn't your fault either," she insisted. "She was taken from both of us. We have to move on no matter how difficult it is," she uttered somberly.

The sky was getting darker by the minute, as they finally approached the parking lot. To their surprise, they were the only two visitors at the cemetery. "This is a very lonely place," remarked Susan.

"Some days there are more visitors than others," sighed Andrew. Are you going home?" he asked as he neared his car.

"I was going to grab some lunch and maybe take a walk along the beach."

"Alright then. Have a nice rest of the day. Just be careful alright. I don't want anything happening to you too," he uttered, getting into his car.

"Yes, I will. Thank you, Andrew. You take care," she said and got in.

Andrew drove out of the parking lot. Susan took a deep breath and pondered for a moment. "I'll come again to visit you, Zoe," she uttered, and a few moments later, exited the cemetery.

36

Susan was famished and began driving around town in search of a place to grab a quick bite. Her cravings were getting the best of her. Eventually, she spotted a sandwich bar up ahead and sped up to it in hopes of being the first in line to order whatever was on the menu. She parked the car in front of the shop, hastily walked in, and ordered the largest burger with the most meat. She also ordered a large chocolate milkshake on the side. Grabbing her lunch, she raced back to the car, hopped inside, and began eating ravenously. The burger was delicious and so was the milkshake. Feeling much better, she headed toward the general direction of the beach. Approaching its vicinity, she pulled the car over and parked it on the side of the road. Then getting out, she cautiously ambled down the rocky interface in between all the way down to the sandy shore. It was three o'clock in the afternoon and beachgoers thronged the surroundings. Susan took off her shoes and strolled along in search of a quiet niche to sit and read the journals. The waves surged up and down and the sound that emanated from them was pacifying. The gentle breeze caressed her face. A few brave surfers were out taking their chances with the rising tides. Children were swimming, as parents who sat nearby kept watchful eyes on them. Finally finding what seemed to be a quiet corner by the rocks, she sat down and gazed out into the vast expanse of the ocean. Her thoughts drifted out as she attempted to process the events of the day when suddenly her phone rang. It was her mother.

"Hello, Mom," she said with a spark of delight in her countenance.

"Hello, darling. How are you?"

"Fine. I'm relaxing here at the beach," she replied gazing in the general direction of the villa. Unable to see it from where she sat, she turned her eyes back to the ocean.

"Oh, that's the sound I'm hearing," responded her mother. "How are you feeling?"

"I'm okay. I just had lunch," replied Susan.

"Are you taking care of yourself?"

"Yes, Mom. I'm trying my best," she assured.

"How is the morning sickness?"

"It's not as severe."

"I had the same problem when I was expecting you. I threw up every day for a couple of months straight."

"Sorry about that," she responded sarcastically. "I hope this baby won't put me through something like that. I won't be able to make it."

"You'll be fine. Alright, darling. Call me if you need anything. Tell Jason I said hello."

"Sure, Mom. Come for a visit soon," she urged her.

"Okay, darling. I just wanted to see how you were. I'll talk to you later," she said and hung up the phone.

Susan placed the phone in her bag and took out the journal. She opened to the next entry.

December 18th, 1867

    I am up in the attic, as I cannot go down to face the brute who showed up at the door after four months. I couldn't believe my eyes as I saw him bring another woman to my house. How dare he! So this is what he has been doing behind my back all this time? The long absences are now justified. When I asked him who this woman was, he berated me in front of the unwelcomed company and demanded that I ask no more questions of him; that he has the right to do as he desires. Here I am married to him and carrying his child, but he has the faintest regard for me. This woman from some netherworld comes into my home and acts as if she owns it with her lavish gowns and frippery. How dare she! How dare they! This is my home. I shall get even with both of them.

I cannot go downstairs to my bedroom for this is an abomination. It is too much for my child to bear. Oh, if only John knew what I am enduring right now. If only I could get word to him to come here. Arthur could never stand up to him. The evil man!
Bessie brings my food up to me. I have a bed, table, and chair here. There is a round window through which fresh air can come in, and there are books to read. How long will they stay? What am I to do? I am trapped in this house, and the child in my belly screaming for justice. There they are, at this very moment, holding hands and laughing. What lies has he told her? Is she unable to see beyond his loathsome exterior to uncover the wolf that is hidden inside, lying in wait to pounce at the right moment on a helpless woman? Does she not know he's a married man? What folly is this?

Susan took a deep breath after reading the entry. She felt Eleanor's heartbreak and her pain of abandonment. As she peered out to the ocean, she spotted a young couple enjoying the surging waves. The woman let out a roar of laughter, as her significant other endeavored to lift her over the oncoming waves. A dash of joy slithered into her mind as she observed them. Then she drew her attention back to the next entry.

December 28ᵗʰ, 1867

I felt a flutter and a gentle kick this morning. I feel my beloved child growing day by day. My spirit wells up with joy when I sense his movements. The brute has left the house with his woman. I am back in my room resting, as John had advised. It is after Christmas and my spirits are damp. No visitors or celebrations. Just Bessie, Norton, and me. Norton cannot be trusted. I wish I can ask him to leave. He is Arthur's second hand and does exactly what he says. I don't know what he tells Arthur about me, but I feel the urge to be wary around him.

John came to see me this morning, and I told him about my baby's movements. He said that was a healthy sign that he is growing. We took a long walk. I told him about Arthur and the woman he brought up to my home. He said he can take me away from the house if I wanted him to. But I am afraid. What if Arthur finds me? He is sure to hurt me and him. He is a rich man and has loyal men all over this small town. John is a young man. I don't want his life to be destroyed because of me.

We walked up to the mountains. I asked him about his other patients. He said that he has this whole day reserved just for me. I was flattered! He gave me a present, a belated Christmas present he said. It was a silver mirror and hairbrush. I will cherish it always. Up by the mountains, just me and him, I feel as if I'm in a different world, far away from this hurt and anger. The tall trees have bird nests. John pointed one out to me, the mother bird tending to its young. As I glanced at it, he clasped me close to his chest and kissed me. I have never felt such a sudden exhilaration in my spirit. I want to be lost in this kiss forever. His firm hands holding my body close to him, I felt helpless. Is this real or is it just a figment of my imagination? As I turned around, he grabbed me close to him and began caressing my bosom. I felt as if I would melt in his arms. He began making love to me. How could I resist him? My emotions took the best of me, as I surrendered to him. I am in love with John.

As we walked back to the villa, John held my hand. I haven't felt such love . . . not even with Arthur. John told me to take care of myself, that he would come back to see me as swiftly as he could. When we approached the garden, Norton was tending the roses. He glanced at John and me. I fear he sensed something, as we passed by. John had to leave. I didn't dare kiss him for the old man was watching my every move. John understood.

I placed the mirror and brush inside my bedroom cabinet drawer. They have my name, "Eleanor," engraved in them. I shall never part with them for they are symbols of John's love for me. They are precious . . . more precious than anything I own.

This was the last entry. Susan closed the journal and gazed toward the ocean. She could see the sun beginning to set. All of a sudden, she realized that Eleanor was writing about the silver mirror and brush that she found in her bedroom vanity table. They were still there. A shiver ran down her spine, as she mused upon the emotions and feelings attached to those objects. She placed the first journal by her side and took the second one out. She decided to read one or two more entries before leaving.

The breeze was becoming a bit intense. Voices and laughter of people in the vicinity could still be heard. Susan began reading.

January 15th*, 1868*

   I am in my room with the door locked to keep that monster away. He appeared early morning with his woman. This time, it was a different one. I had nothing to say, and quite frankly, I do not desire to know anything that Arthur says or does. He approached me and asked me about John. He demanded that I tell him if I was in love with him. His temper was at its boiling point, and I feared that he would hit me. I had no choice but to say I didn't love anyone except the child that I was carrying. How dare he dictate terms to me when he is the model of infidelity and evil! I am most certain that wretched old man relayed my business with John to Arthur. I asked Bessie if she told that brute anything. She vehemently denied and claimed that she would never betray my confidence in such a manner. I believe her.

   He's eating, drinking, and making merry with the tramp he has brought into my home. Wonder what he did with the other one he dragged in here last month? I imagine he has another home somewhere, and I am most certain Norton knows about it. What should I do? I'm not cut out for murder. My mother raised me better than to kill a husband no matter how horrific he might be.

   I have nothing to eat tonight. Bessie is too busy serving Arthur and his company. She isn't allowed to come up. The poor thing has to see such an appalling sight. I don't want to go down, for if I do, I'm afraid he might hurt me in his drunken revelry. Oh, my John, how I wish you were here with me tonight.

The sun was setting and a light drizzle began. Many of the beachgoers had already left. Susan closed the journal and put both inside her tote. She decided to head home before dark. As she stood up, the gray clouds suddenly gave way to a squall. She hastily began making her way up to the car. Upon coming to it, she quickly released the hood of the convertible to cover its interior from the rain. Getting inside, she cautiously pulled out to the road and headed home.

37

The rain and the fact that it was a Friday evening created more traffic on the road than usual. Susan didn't realize how quickly time had elapsed. It was almost six o'clock by the time she made the turn from the main highway onto the road up to her villa. The overcast sky gave rise to darkness that she was not used to seeing in and around her property. Suddenly, the rain began to pound on the windshield, and she had difficulty distinguishing the path up ahead. Water was being thrashed onto the mountainous terrain on either side as well. A terrible uneasiness suddenly overtook her, as she nervously gazed around. As she peered to the side of the road, she suddenly saw the woman in white appear in the darkness like a flash of lightning and disappear within an instant. Her face was white and her black eyes were glaring at Susan during that split second.

Susan was overcome with fear and she began to speed up on the road ahead when suddenly the apparition appeared in front of the car. Susan screamed and slammed on the brakes as hard as she could. The car came to a sudden halt, and she hit her head on the steering wheel which knocked her senseless for a few minutes. Opening her eyes, she looked around in a daze and realized what had occurred. She turned on the ignition but the car wouldn't start.

"Oh no! Come on, start!" she cried, trying the ignition again. The car, however, wasn't starting. Shaking in fear, she raised her head and looked through the rearview mirror. Eleanor's ghost was seated at the back, her eyes glaring at her, and her mouth opening as if to devour her. Susan let out a scream, jumped out of the car, and began running up the road. The rain was still pouring down heavily. She could feel Eleanor's presence, as if she was being watched when suddenly a car honked from behind. When she turned around, the headlights almost blinded her.

A man parked his car behind hers and stepped out with a flash light and pointed at her. Soaking wet and partially covering her eyes with her hands, she ran toward him. "Please help me," she cried.

"Are you alright, ma'am?" he asked.

"No. My car stopped, and I have to get home on foot. It's just that I saw something, and I'm afraid," she uttered.

"I'm Officer Sam Bosworth of the downtown police, and I can take you home. The only thing is we're going to have to get around your car because it's blocking the way."

Susan walked up to him and saw that he was wearing several badges. He was soaked wet too. "Are you patrolling my property, Officer?" she asked in relief.

"Did you say this is your property?" he asked with a spark of surprise in his eyes. "Are you Susan Smith?"

"Yes."

"I was on my way to your house. I'm the officer assigned to patrol. The detective told me to get up here. Looks like I came right on time, ma'am," he commented with a smile on his face.

"Well, I don't know how to thank you," said Susan. He opened the door of his police car for Susan to get in. "Wait!" she said abruptly, remembering that her bag was in the convertible.

She hastily went toward the car, opened the front door, and got her bag. Closing the door, she made haste toward the police car. Officer Bosworth was making a call to the station, requesting a tow truck to get to the road in order to bring her car home.

"Alright, please be my guest," he said, opening the door for her.

"Thank you," she said. Susan noticed that the officer was quite tall and well built. She couldn't distinguish his facial features clearly, but he had a mustache. They got inside and the officer began steering his car around the convertible. The mountainous incline stood on the opposite side and he tried his best not to scratch either vehicle.

"This is a very close call," he remarked, as he finally managed to get his car back on the road in front of the convertible. "The tow truck is on its way," he uttered, looking at Susan. "You're bleeding from your forehead!" he exclaimed.

"Yes. I hit my head on the steering wheel," said Susan, wiping the blood with her sleeve. "I'll tend to it when I go home. My husband is a doctor."

The officer shook his head in approval. "Are you alright?" he asked with concern.

"Yes, I'm fine. Just a little shaken up," she said, flustered.

"So you said you saw something?"

"Yes."

"What was it?"

"It's complicated," uttered Susan, feeling a bit awkward.

"I've been in the force for five years now, ma'am, and believe me when I tell you, I've seen it all. So whatever it is that you saw isn't going to surprise me a bit," he insisted.

Susan took a deep breath. "It's a spirit," she blurted. "My home is haunted by two angry spirits."

The officer glanced at her and paused for a moment. "I guess I was wrong! I haven't seen it all," he said sarcastically.

"Well, it's true!" uttered Susan in a bit of indignation.

"I'm sorry, ma'am. I didn't mean any disrespect. I'm sure whatever it is we can sort it out," he assured.

Susan, however, was still in shock and kept her eyes peeled all the way to the house. Officer Bosworth drove up to the driveway and parked the car in front of the cherub fountain. The rain was still going on. Susan peered into the garage to see if Jason's car was inside. To her relief, he hadn't come home.

"This is some mansion, ma'am!" he remarked.

"Thank you, Officer," said Susan.

"Now there's no need for formalities. Please call me Sam," urged the policeman.

"Sure. Come inside. You can get settled in," urged Susan and got out of the vehicle. "Where should I park?" he asked.

"You can pull into the garage," she replied, pointing toward it. The garden light poles were sufficient for her to see her path ahead, as she hastily made her way to the front door. Susan used the key to open the door. The lights were turned on inside and it was warm.

A few moments later, the officer walked in with a bag. When he noticed the exquisite interior, he was speechless.

"You know, ma'am, I mean no offense by saying this. But the men in my department are very boisterous. If I want them to shut up, I'd show them this living room. The whole row of boys would be speechless," he remarked, as he surveyed the room from top to bottom.

"That's quite the compliment," responded Susan. "Thank you. You can have any room on the third floor," said Susan. "Please follow me."

The officer picked up his bag and trailed behind Susan, all the while admiring his surroundings. Susan noticed that Sam had blue eyes and blond hair. From the looks of it, he was in his late twenties or early thirties. As they were climbing up the stairs, Norton was on his way down. He gazed at her with a show of surprise.

"Madam, you're soaking! And you're hurt!"

"Yes, I got caught in the rain and bumped my head by accident," she uttered.

"Should I get some medicine for that?"

"No, that's quite alright. I have some peroxide in the room. It's just a minor cut. By the way, I'd like you to meet Officer Sam Bosworth from the police department. He'll be staying with us for a while."

Norton's countenance changed immediately, and Susan could sense that he was a bit uncomfortable. "It's nice to meet you," he uttered in a tone of apathy.

"Same here. Norton was it?" uttered the officer.

She walked him over to one of the bedrooms with a bath. "Please let me know if you need anything. The bathroom is right in there and fresh towels and other necessities are already at your disposal. I'm going to go down and check on dinner. My husband will also be coming shortly," she responded.

"Wonderful!" said Sam. "Can't wait to meet him. Oh, by the way, ma'am, I will be starting my shift at night, right after dinner."

"Great! See you in a bit," said Susan and headed toward the stairs.

Susan came to her bedroom and closed the door behind her. Turning on the light, she walked over to her bed and sat for a moment, attempting to process what had occurred. She was still shaken up. Then she removed her wet clothes, placed them in a nearby laundry basket, and put on her pajamas and house robe. She went into the bathroom and began washing her face. The cut was still bleeding. Taking some peroxide from the cupboard under the sink, she dabbed a bit on the cut with a piece of tissue. The bleeding was not as intense as it was before. Then she went back to the room, took the two journals out, and placed them in the bed stand table drawer. Walking up to the vanity table, she pulled out the bottom drawer. Inside were the silver mirror and hairbrush. Hesitantly, she took them out to examine them. The silver had extravagant carvings. Each had the name "Eleanor" engraved on the back. Two or three long dark strands of hair were trapped in the brush, which she hadn't noticed the first time she had seen them. A chill went through her spine again when, suddenly, the bedroom door opened, and Jason stood at the threshold. Susan was alarmed that she dropped the brush on the floor.

"Honey! What happened?" he asked, walking in. "I just saw the convertible being towed to the yard." He began scrutinizing her. "What happened to you?" he asked again, placing his hand on the wound on her forehead.

Susan picked up the brush and put it back in the drawer. "Oh, nothing. I just got caught in the rain," she replied, trying not to alarm him.

"The rain?" he asked in confusion. "Where did you go?"

"Well, I went to visit Zoe's grave this afternoon. I took some gladiolas. Andrew was there, and we had a long talk about everything. He's going through a rough time, and I was able to help him out a bit. Then I went for a walk on the beach when it suddenly began pouring. By the time I got here, it was dark already. Anyway, the car stopped on the way up."

"You're hurt! How did that happen?" he asked, holding her tight.

"Well, I kind of hit my head on the steering," she replied, trying her best to be calm about things.

"I don't understand," he remarked, attempting to make sense of the situation.

"I saw something on the road, and I suddenly hit the brakes," she uttered. "Afterward, I tried to start the car again, but it wouldn't. I'm fine though" she assured. "Oh, by the way, Officer Bosworth arrived right on time to help me out. He's the one who called the tow truck."

Jason took a deep breath, sat on the bed, and pulled her close. He placed his hand on her stomach. "Is the baby alright? My stethoscope is in the car."

"Yes, darling, he's fine," she said, caressing his head.

"Why didn't you tell me you were going out today?" he asked.

"It was just in the spur of the moment. I wanted to see Zoe," she asserted. "And do I have to tell you every time I decide to leave the house? Besides, I didn't want to bother you at work."

"Just leave a message for me. I need to know where you are," he urged.

"Why?" she asked as rebellion welled up in her. "I need to get out sometimes too, you know!"

"I know, honey, but you're pregnant," he uttered.

"Yes, you keep reminding me every day," she retorted and walked toward the window.

"Look. We'll table this discussion for later when you've calmed down," he stated, approaching her and holding her from behind. "Did you get soaked in the rain?" he asked, touching her hair.

Susan was about to lose her temper, but she bridled her tongue. Then she snapped at him and stormed out of the room.

<u>38</u>

Two big pots were on the kitchen stove. One had spaghetti and the other had meatballs. Susan took three plates and laid them on the table.

"Would you like me to help you, madam?" came a voice from behind.

Turning around, she saw Norton approaching from the side. "Sure, if you'd like," she replied indifferently.

Norton took the pots one at a time to the table and served the food onto the plates. Then he grabbed some silverware and placed them on the side. Jason appeared a moment later with Sam.

"Please have a seat, Sam. Make yourself at home," said Susan with a smile.

Norton shot an indignant gaze at Sam and Jason and exited the kitchen.

"Was it something I said?" asked Sam, a bit baffled.

"Oh, don't worry about him," said Jason. "He's quite temperamental. The more you hang around here, the more you'll get used to it."

Sam sat at the table. He had changed into a new uniform and looked very pleasant. Jason sat beside him and gazed at his wife.

"Mighty nice food, ma'am," he commented and began digging in.

Jason started to eat as well. Susan sat across him with a glass of milk. She took her fork and tasted the meatball. Sam glanced at the both of them as an awkward silence ensued.

"So Mrs. Smith tells me that you are a doctor," he uttered gazing at Jason.

"Yes. I am a cardiologist," he replied. "So, Officer, may I call you Sam as well?"

"Of course," he replied jovially.

"So how does this work with your being situated here?" asked Jason curiously.

"Well, the detective tells me that you folks have a bit of a problem on the premises. Some kind of an intruder appearing? Is that right?"

"In a manner of speaking, yes," replied Jason. Susan was unforthcoming as she was still upset with her husband.

"So what I will do is begin with the night shift. I shall guard the outside premises and get some shut-eye in the morning. Then I'll start again late afternoon or evening. You know, ordinarily, there would be two officers sent, one for the day and the other for the night, so we could take turns. But we're short on staff, so it's only going to be me."

"That's great!" blurted Susan finally, breaking out of her silence.

"Can you kindly tell me what it is that I'm guarding you against?" he inquired, shooting a curious glance at the two of them.

"If you don't mind, Sam, we want to speak to you about this in confidence after dinner," uttered Susan.

"Of course," he replied, chewing on his meatballs.

After dinner was over, Susan asked Jason and Sam to follow her to the study. She opened the door and turned on the light switch. The chandelier that loomed from the ceiling radiated its brilliant light to every corner of the lavish room. Once the three of them entered, Jason closed and locked the door from the inside. The officer was dumbfounded.

"Wow! I've never seen such an office!" he exclaimed.

"Thank you," responded Jason. The curtains were drawn in. "Would you like to have a seat?"

"Of course," replied Sam and walked over to the leather sofa by the bookshelf. Susan sat next to him, and Jason pulled out a chair and sat in front of his wife.

"Now that we're alone, would you like to explain the situation?" asked Jason, looking at her.

"Yes, I would. So like I mentioned to you on the way here, we're talking about angry spirits. I can't quite explain it, but I feel unsafe. Knowing that someone like you is patrolling would put my mind at ease."

"So if you don't mind me asking, do these spirits, as you say, take human form or turn into anything tangible?"

"I don't know," replied Susan.

"The reason why I ask is, my gun and expert fighting skills if I say so myself, are only going to work against flesh and blood. I don't have the training to fight something that is not of this world. But I'll do what I can to protect you, folks," he assured.

"Thank you," said Jason.

"What of Norton? Is he a danger to you?" continued Sam.

There was silence as Susan mused for a moment. "I'm not sure," she responded.

"What do you mean?" asked Sam, with a quizzical expression.

"What she means is we're not certain if he has anything to do with it. He's not upfront with us," responded Jason gravely. "If you ask me, he knows about everything and is hiding it all."

"Has he hurt you folks in any way?"

"No, but his behavior is erratic. And there's Penny," commented Susan.

"Who's that?" asked Sam.

"She was my cat. I found her stabbed a while back. We don't know who did it. And I'm sure you know about Zoe, my best friend," said Susan gravely.

"I don't know if you folks remember, but yes, I was here when they discovered the body," said Sam. He stood up and paced back and forth for a moment pondering. Then turning around, he came and sat back down. "Alright. I will keep an extra eye on the man."

"Thank you," said Jason gratefully. "I leave for work at different hours because I'm on call all the time. So I need you to watch out for her, especially since we're expecting our first child."

"Well, congratulations!" he exclaimed. "I will do my best," he assured.

"What about you, Sam? Do you have kids?" asked Susan.

"No, ma'am. I'm not married," he replied. "Hope to someday though. That is if I find my match."

39

As they went to bed that night, Officer Sam stood guard outside. Norton gave him the cold shoulder and was seething with disapproval because he did not like this stranger moving into the room next to his.

"What are you going to do about my car?" asked Susan as her husband was climbing into bed.

"I'll call the auto shop tomorrow and have a mechanic come over to check it out. I'm exhausted. I had to perform a surgery that I hadn't planned for the day. The man had complications and went on sudden cardiac arrest. If I hadn't operated on him, he would've died."

As he laid his head on the pillow, Susan planted a kiss on his cheek. "I'm sorry, I got mad at you," she sighed.

Jason gazed at her. "I'm sorry too. It's just I'm so worried about you and all that's happening."

"I feel better now that Sam's outside," she said with a spark of relief.

Susan turned off the lamp and cuddled near Jason. A few minutes later, she could hear him sound asleep. Cautiously moving away and sitting up on the bed, she turned the lamp back on. Then taking the journal from the drawer, she flipped the page to where she left off. Susan couldn't get the image of Eleanor's face out of her mind. Knowing that Jason was next to her and Sam was outside made her feel secure. She glanced through some of the entries that followed. Eleanor kept talking about Arthur, his mistress, and their stay in the villa. She was locked up in the bedroom in fear and brooding in anger.

> *January 25ᵗʰ, 1868*
>
> *I had to walk to the outskirts of my property to meet up with my love, John. That Norton watches me like a hawk and reports on my every move to the brute. At least I know that I'm not being watched out here. It's a long walk to our rendezvous point and my baby doesn't seem to like it. He's been kicking more than normal. John met me there, and the moment he saw me, he made haste toward me and kissed me. I told him I missed him. He said the same to me. John checked on the baby's heartbeat and said he or she was growing well. We sat under a tree and talked for hours. He had to park his car out by the road and make the long walk up here to be with me. He said he didn't mind, as long as he got the opportunity to see me. I indulged in his presence yet warned him to be careful because the brute suspects our relationship. He agreed and assured me that nothing would keep him away from me. "What about my child?" I asked him. John wants to be a father to him, as Arthur despises anyone but himself. I was elated to hear that, yet I have to be wary of the evil that's in my home. I have to protect my child from it and attempt to keep John away from it as well. If anything happened to him, I wouldn't know what to do.*

Susan skimmed a few entries and made her way to the middle of the second journal in search of anything substantial. Arthur's visits made Eleanor more and more apprehensive. She detailed how he treated her cruelly because he didn't want the child. Instead, he engaged in several other extramarital affairs, coming and going with various women and engaging in sexual conduct with them in the different rooms at the villa. She disclosed her fears in the diary. Arthur did not take kindly to her protests. In a drunken rage, he instead raped her to the point where she almost lost the baby. Eleanor continued to lock herself in the bedroom for fear of being abused. Bessy brought her food and drink during these months and was her only other contact. She finds bruises on Bessie's face and body as well. When asked, Bessie divulged that Arthur ill-treated her if he didn't find the cooking to his satisfaction. Susan discerned that Eleanor was locked up in their bedroom over a century ago and that she quite possibly slept on their bed. All of a sudden, an ominous feeling came over her. Eleanor had endured this suffering and probably written her journal entries on the bed. The house had witnessed injustice done to such an innocent woman.

As Susan continued to glance through the entries, she stumbled upon one that was quite distressing.

March 20th, 1868

The baby is due any day. I have difficulty moving. I'm afraid of being alone when the time comes. What am I to do? The brute and his woman are still in my home. They go to different rooms at different times to enjoy each other's company. I can hear them in the night. I'm not allowed to come out even for a meal. I can't get word to John to come here in case I need him. Bessie is forbidden to leave the villa. She is afraid of the brute as well. Norton keeps an eye on her and reports on her activities to the brute. What have I done to deserve this? How can I bear such heartbreak each day, each moment?

I tiptoed to the kitchen to get a drink of water in the middle of the night. I hoped to not run into anyone but quietly take a drink and get back to my room. The brute was there. He was drinking profusely. When he saw me, he came to me. Although I attempted to run, I wasn't fast enough. He grabbed hold of me and threw me to the floor. I cried in pain. He shouted at me in anger, saying that he regretted ever marrying me and he certainly didn't want the child. I somehow managed to stand on my feet and get back to my room. I locked the door behind me and got into bed. The side of my stomach was in pain. I was rubbing my belly all night and speaking out the good intentions that I have for my precious little child. I hope he heard me. I cannot sleep a wink, so I'm writing in my journal. It helps to put down my sorrow on these pages. It's a release. Besides my beloved John, this book has been my only companion. My tears have drenched these pages.

March 21ˢᵗ, 1868

I woke up in the morning with a terrible pain in my stomach and cried for Bessie to come up. I stood up with the greatest difficulty and opened the door for her. As she came in, she saw me bleeding. There was a pool of blood on the bed and the floor. I was horrified! I moved the bloody sheets and got back into bed. Bessie told me that Arthur and his tramp had left the premises. I told her to quickly go to town and fetch John. She did as I asked. The wait was pure torture, as Bessie had to walk to John's office in town. I knew that the baby was coming.

I don't know how long she was gone, as I was going in and out of sleep. I somehow managed to keep writing in these pages as I wanted to stay awake in case the brute showed up. Finally, John came. I didn't even realize that he was there or what was happening. But when I woke up, he was holding the baby in his arms, and I was in terrible pain. He told me that he had to operate on me as the babies were in an awkward position on my belly. What did he mean babies? Bessie was by my side, and she had tears in her eyes. "Where was the other one?" I asked John. For the longest time, he didn't want to tell me anything. He told me later, that this was because I had lost a lot of blood and I was in pain. One of my babies had died in the womb apparently due to the fall the night before. My heart was broken. I had given birth to two baby boys and one of them was dead. That murderer killed my baby! John gave me the one he was holding. Bessie helped me sit up on the bed. When I held him in my arms, I instantly fell in love with him. I looked at John with tears in my eyes. He smiled at me gently. Instantly, I knew who I would name my son after. His name will be John. I wish I could change his last name to that of my beloved . . . even my own name for that matter . . . but there's some paper somewhere with a judge's signature which states that it has to be otherwise. My baby is so tiny and a precious thing to behold. John sat by me for the longest time. Bessie brought me some broth that evening, which helped me get my strength back. What of the baby I lost? Bessie took him out. She later told me she buried him in the yard. The poor precious gem! It's as if half of my heart is buried with him.

John stayed by my side the whole day. He gave Bessie some instructions on how to tend to the baby, as I was still healing from the surgery. My baby looked so peaceful. He has the most beautiful hazel eyes I have ever seen. He doesn't cry but gazes at me. I love him . . . more than life itself . . .

As Susan read the entries, she stepped into Eleanor's life and felt the pain she went through and the joy of holding her surviving child. She recalled seeing Eleanor's apparition for the first time with a newborn baby in her arms. Susan began to wonder if the child she held was the one who died. A flux of thoughts and emotions began to plague her. Feeling a bit worn out, she placed the journal back in the drawer. Then switching off the lamp, she turned toward Jason, cuddled him from behind, and fell asleep.

<u>40</u>

Officer Sam was patrolling the premises in the middle of the night. The rain had ceased and the air was cool and still. He had his pistol and baton on the side. Knowing that it was a chilly night, he wore his policeman's jacket. He walked both the front and back yards armed with his flashlight, never ceasing to admire the extravagant architecture and façade of the villa. The ocean was still except for the occasional waves that welled up.

Walking to the edge of the backyard, he stopped for a moment to inhale the crisp ocean air into his lungs. The distant horizon reflected the moonlight, which appeared as a million crystals floating on the surface of the water. He could see the surrounding mountains and the cloudless black sky looming before him. There was no noticeable sea breeze however.

As Sam admired the scenery, he suddenly heard a strange sound from behind. Turning around, he noted the swing. It was swaying back and forth, gently at first but progressively faster, as if being pushed by some invisible force. He became startled. The chain swinging was getting louder. He aimed the flashlight directly at the swing, which was oscillating violently at this point.

"Who's there?" he called out in alarm. "Show yourself!" he demanded.

Looking around he perceived nothing out of the ordinary. Suddenly, a chill went through his spine and he became increasingly disconcerted. "Calm down!" he urged himself. "I'm a trained officer of the law, and I've got a gun." His eyes vigilantly searched the premises. Gazing up, he spotted Norton's dark shadow from the third-floor room. The light was on. A moment later, Norton moved away from the window. Sam became wary and instinctively pulled out his gun from the holster and looked around with the flashlight. The swing had stopped moving. As he went closer to examine it, the black apparition suddenly appeared in front of him. Its hooded face was looking down at the ground and its mere presence brought on a terrifying feeling within him. Sam attempted to pull the trigger. It became locked, however. The ghost raised its head and glared at him with its dark eyes. Its human face was gray and yet stricken with anger and suffering.

"Who are you?" Sam asked shaking to his core. "What do you want here?"

It opened its mouth as if to utter something horrific. Instantly, Sam felt a momentary paralysis in his body and was unable to move. The ghost kept its mouth open and whispers of anger could be heard all around. Sam fell to the ground as if struck by a bolt of lightning. A few seconds later, the apparition disappeared.

41

Susan awoke early morning with a queer feeling in her stomach again. She sprang from the bed and rushed to the bathroom and began throwing up. Hearing the noise, Jason rose up and went into the bathroom to check on her. He stood at her side and tapped on her back.

"You alright?" he asked, still half asleep.

"No," she replied washing her mouth. "Oh! I feel awful!" she uttered as another wave of nausea overtook her. "When is this morning sickness going to be over?" she asked in frustration.

"It depends on the person," he replied. She looked at herself in the mirror and began taking a few deep breaths. "That helps too," commented Jason. "Just relax," he said, as he coached her with the breathing. He took her toothbrush, squeezed some toothpaste onto it, and handed it to her. "Try to distract yourself, honey. That helps with nausea."

"What do you mean?" asked Susan, gazing at him with the toothbrush in her mouth.

"Well, what I mean is focus on something else other than throwing up. It'll help you control the urge and the nausea," he replied.

"Okay, Doctor. I'll try," she retorted, attempting to read the instructions on the tube of toothpaste that was on the side. A few moments later, she turned toward him in agreement. "Yep, you're right," she uttered.

"Good," said Jason kissing her on the shoulder.

Jason stepped into the shower a few moments later. Susan looked at him through the mirror. She couldn't stop admiring her husband's physique."

I'll shower after you leave," she said.

"I'd rather have you join me," he voiced from inside.

"Maybe tomorrow," responded Susan with a chuckle. "I've got to go check on Sam and get breakfast for the two of you."

She hastily made the bed, changed her clothes, and headed down the stairs. The house was quiet. She walked toward the front door. Opening it, she stepped outside. It was a bright morning and the air was cool and crisp. She breathed it in and a sense of satisfaction engulfed her. The rain had left a damp driveway and the grass was greener than normal.

"Sam!" she called out, surveying the yard. Silence echoed. Stepping out to the driveway, she continued to scan the premises. "Officer Bosworth, where are you?" she called out again. She edged toward the backyard, endeavoring to avoid the puddles. Nearing the tree with the swing, she suddenly beheld Sam lying prostrate on the ground.

"Sam!" she gasped, rushing toward him. "Sam, wake up!" she gasped, tapping on him. "Oh, my goodness! What happened?" she cried in panic. His eyes and mouth were open. Susan placed her ear on his chest. "Oh, gosh, he's not breathing!" she exclaimed in fear.

Standing up, she ran toward the kitchen all the while calling for Jason. Racing through, she hastily made her way up the stairs to the bedroom. "Jason!" she cried. "Something's happened to Sam. He's not breathing!"

Jason came out of the bathroom with a towel tied around his waist. "What? What's wrong?"

"It's Sam. He's not breathing!" she cried, getting her phone and dialing the police. "Where is he?" cried Jason in agitation.

"In the backyard by the swing," replied Susan. Jason immediately put some clothes on and rushed out of the room in a flash. Susan kept holding the line to the police department.

"Oh, pick up! Pick up!" A moment later, someone answered. She explained the situation and demanded that they get an ambulance to the premises immediately. Then she rushed downstairs. Coming out to the yard, she could see Jason attempting to resuscitate Sam.

"Is he breathing?" Jason shook his head and continued to press down on his chest, counting all the while. Then he blew into his mouth and repeated the pattern. A few moments later, he stopped. With a sigh, he gazed down. "What?" gasped Susan as tears began cascading down her cheeks.

"He's dead," replied Jason solemnly. "From the looks of it, he's been gone for some time. His body is very cold," he commented. "Did you call the police?"

"Yes," replied Susan, wiping her tears. Jason came up to her and embraced her. "What happened to him?" she asked in fear.

"I don't know, honey," he replied gravely. "But I think he may have seen something." An eerie chill came over her. "Do you think it was her?" she asked.

"I'm not sure. But this is getting too dangerous," he commented. "We're going to have to leave the house," he sighed.

Susan knelt beside Sam and touched his hand. It felt cold, and his fingernails had begun to turn blue. "He must've died in the night then," she remarked, wiping her tears. She noticed the flashlight and pistol on the ground near him.

"Don't touch anything!" ordered Jason. "The police are going to ask all sorts of questions." Susan stood up and moved away.

"I've seen enough death to last a lifetime," she commented and walked to the edge of the yard. The tide was up, and she could see surfers attempting to outsmart the waves. Her fears and uncertainties surged with them. The peaceful surrounding of the ocean was a contrast to what she was feeling on the inside.

"We have to leave today, honey," uttered Jason. "This is not good for you or the baby."

"Where do we go?" she asked, somberly wiping her tears.

"We'll check into the town hotel for the time being and then decide what to do from there," he suggested.

"What about the hospital?" she asked.

"I'll call in and explain what happened. You're my priority," he said, taking out his phone and dialing the number.

The police arrived at the villa a short while later. The officers promptly red-tagged the scene. An ambulance also arrived, and the paramedics checked for vital signs on Sam's body. As none were found, he was covered in black cloth and hauled inside the ambulance. The gun and flashlight were collected as evidence. The detective came up to Jason and Susan.

"There's no sign of a struggle. Can you tell me if you saw anything?" he asked, attempting to maintain his professionalism amid the troubling circumstance.

"No. We were asleep," insisted Jason. "My wife discovered him this morning when she went out looking for him."

"Sam was very strong. So if there was no struggle, then it must've been something that he wasn't able to fight," said the detective.

"What happens now?" asked Susan, getting increasingly distressed.

"We have to examine his body further to determine the cause of death," he responded.

"I don't know what to say. He was doing the night patrol out here," added Jason.

"Where is the old man?" asked the detective, surveying the area.

"I don't know," replied Susan. "I didn't see him this morning."

"I have to question him," he asserted.

"Let's go inside," said Jason, as he directed the detective into the kitchen.

Susan was still in disbelief. "What is happening?" she sighed, gazing up.

Two of the officers were still examining the ground for footprints or any other important clues they could find. The only prints that they saw were those of Sam's shoes in the mud and on the cement.

"So who killed him?" one of them asked. The other shook his head with a grave expression.

"I can't believe he's gone his first night on patrol in this place," remarked the first.

Susan knew that Eleanor was somehow responsible for this second death as well. As horrifying thoughts crept into her mind, she attempted to get a hold of herself by sitting on the swing and taking a few deep breaths, unaware of the fact that the black figure had taken Sam's life.

42

Jason and the detective went to the third floor. Norton's room was closed. The detective immediately began banging on the door. "Open up! It's the police," he hollered. There was no response, however.

"Norton!" bellowed Jason. "Open the door!" There was silence. "Just break it down," suggested Jason.

"Alright, if you don't mind," concurred the detective. "Stand back!" He slammed his foot on the door. Jason joined in as well with a few kicks. After some effort, the door dropped to the ground with a loud thud and the two men stepped inside. Seated at the center of the king-sized bed was Norton. He was fully dressed in his regular black suit and was glaring at them as if he were greatly angered. The room appeared dark and melancholy, as the walls were a deep grayish color. The curtains were drawn in.

"Norton!" shouted Jason. "Didn't you hear me?"

Norton, however, continued to glare at him. The room had a peculiar odor, a bit nauseating, one might add. "What is that smell?" asked the detective, looking around. He was immediately drawn to the enormous portrait that hung on the left wall. Approaching it, he glanced at the face. "Who is this?" he asked turning toward Norton. He refused to answer. "Can you not hear me, man?" demanded the detective again.

"I think it's the original owner of this house, Arthur Mortimer," replied Jason.

"Oh, really? And what's this?" he asked, touching the urn right beneath it. "Is this what I think it is?"

"I don't know. This is the first time I've been in this room. Susan got a peek a while back though. She seems to think that it is the man in the portrait."

"You mean to tell me that the man was never really buried?" asked the baffled detective.

"I'm not sure, but I think it's time to get rid of all remnants of that family," asserted Jason in indignation. He grabbed the urn and went out of the room. Placing it on the side of the hallway, he walked back in and yanked the portrait off the wall. The heavy painting came off with the wall hinges and all. "It's about time I put an end to this nonsense!" he continued to rave.

"Stop that!" howled Norton. "How dare you do this to my master?"

Jason and the detective ignored Norton's admonishment. Jason hauled the picture out of the room and threw it into the hallway.

"Where is that smell coming from?" asked the detective, surveying every corner of the room.

"I don't know what he's been doing in here," ranted Jason in anger. He headed toward the window and opened it to let some fresh air inside.

"Norton!" uttered the detective approaching the bed. "Where were you last night?" Norton, however, didn't answer but rigidly looked away. "Alright," he sighed, directing his gaze at Jason. "I have to arrest him under suspicion of murder." He took the handcuffs that were hanging from his side and moved toward Norton. As he grabbed his arm, Norton suddenly snapped and was overcome with a fit of fury. He began raving angry expressions.

"How dare you enter my home?" he demanded, glaring at Jason. His voice had changed. It was raspier and vicious. Jason didn't bother to respond. As the detective endeavored to cuff him, Norton struggled violently. "Get your hands off of me! You don't know who or what you're dealing with here," he bellowed in exasperation. "This is the master's home, and you, trespassers, will pay with your lives!"

Jason instinctively went to the detective's aid and held Norton down.

"Yeah well, your master is dead, and it's about time you accepted it," retorted Jason nonchalantly.

Despite his struggles, the detective finally got the cuffs on. Pulling Norton from the bed, both men pushed him out of the room. As they were going down the stairs, two of the officers were headed up. "Take him to the car. He needs to be questioned," said the detective.

"Right away, sir," said one of them and grabbed Norton from the side.

He continued to rave and rant in anger. "I will call on the master to take you out next," he uttered. "This is his house, and you have no claims to it," he bellowed.

Susan was seen coming up as well. "Honey! Stay there," ordered Jason as he hastily made his way toward her. Susan halted and watched Norton being led out through the living room.

"What happened?" she asked as Jason and the detective approached her.

"He doesn't want to answer questions," replied Jason. "Can you ask one of your officers to take that portrait and urn out of my house?" he requested.

"Yes," replied the detective and walked out.

A moment later, he came in followed by another policeman who headed upstairs. "Those items will be taken to the station for examination. If they are of no use, we'll dispose of them with your permission of course."

"Please, get rid of them," urged Jason. "You have my permission."

"I need to speak with both of you," insisted the detective.

They went to the living room. Susan walked up to the front door that was left ajar. She could see the officers directing Norton into the police car. Two other police cars were parked behind the one that Norton got into. A few moments later, the officers drove off with him. Turning around, she detected another policeman headed toward the door dragging the portrait with one hand and carrying the black urn with the other. Susan moved to the side so that he could go out. Then she closed the door with a heavy heart and approached Jason and the detective. She sat by her husband and looked gravely at the detective, who was seated across from them.

"I'm glad that's taken out," she sighed. "What a lot of baggage that is!"

"I don't quite know what to make of this awful thing," uttered the detective after pondering a bit. "All I can say is that we lost an excellent officer who had a big heart."

Susan began sobbing.

"I'm so sorry," added Jason glumly. "I'm not sure where we stand in all of this. I don't want the police to have any doubts or misunderstandings concerning my statement with regards to where my wife and I were when this occurred. We were fast asleep and had no idea that he was dead in the yard," assured Jason.

"I know. Don't worry. Considering what happened to your friend Zoe, I am fully aware of the circumstances. At least I think I am," he said.

Jason held on to Susan, who was breaking down. "Don't cry, honey. It's not good for the baby," he said.

She gazed at the detective somberly. "What are we going to do, Eric?"

"Do you have any idea what might've happened to Sam?" asked the detective.

"I think it was Eleanor," replied Susan, who felt rather awkward uttering the name. "She's dangerous and she's trying to tell us something."

"What is that?" asked the detective gazing curiously at her.

"She's angry, and maybe she doesn't want us here," she replied. "I've read through a couple of her journals. The woman has suffered in this house. She was abused by her husband and she lost a child. Maybe she's never gotten over it."

"I don't know much about spirits, ma'am, but what you're saying gives me the creeps. How can you prove all this?"

"I don't know. All I can say is that I've seen and felt her presence. She's angry. Her son's around here too. As I said to you before, Jason and I both saw him in the attic. I've seen him in the yard and in my bedroom. He's pretty venomous," she added.

Jason gazed at her with a perplexed expression. "Honey, I thought you abandoned those journals."

"No. I must confess I've been delving into them. I need to find the root cause of all of this misfortune," she sighed.

"But you're pregnant! Your emotions and feelings affect the baby!" he snapped in anger.

"I'm sorry, honey, but I had to," she insisted.

"Alright," declared the detective. "Since this is officially a crime scene, the two of you have to leave the premises at least temporarily until all of this is sorted out.

"I'll call a hotel, and we can move by the afternoon," suggested Jason.

Susan glanced at the floor in dismay. "What can we do to get rid of them?"

"I don't know the answer to that," replied the detective. "We're not trained to deal with supernatural entities. There are people qualified for that."

"Who?" asked Jason. "Do you know anyone who we can talk to?"

"Well, there is this one woman who might be able to help. She comes to the station on occasion and helps out with cases that are difficult to solve. I mean ones like this," he replied. "Her name is Edna, and she lives on the east side of town. It is a two-story old white-colored house. You can't miss it. She doesn't have a telephone. So you're going to have to see her in person."

"Thank you. We'll do that. What about Norton?" asked Jason. "What's going to happen to him?"

"We'll have to detain him until he answers our questions. From the way he was acting, he knows exactly what's going on. Are you two going to be alright? Do you want any help with moving?"

"No. We'll just pack a few things for the time being. I need to get Susan out of here as soon as possible," said Jason glancing at her.

"Alright then. I have to get going. I'll keep you posted on Norton's situation. Please give me a call about Edna," he said, walking up to the front door.

Jason went out with him and saw him off to his car. Susan peered out to the side yard through the window. The police were still there tagging the house.

43

It was late afternoon when Susan and Jason came to the garage with a few suitcases in hand. They had decided to take Jason's car and leave the convertible behind for the time being as it would not start. Jason loaded their luggage in the trunk and helped his wife to the passenger seat. Susan was deep in thought and didn't speak much. In addition to her clothes and some other personal belongings, she had put two journals in one of the suitcases. She had managed to steal them away from the box in her closet while Jason was elsewhere in the house.

"Did you call the hospital about your leave?" she asked as he got into the car and began reversing.

"Yes," he replied. "I took a short leave of absence. Others in the department will cover for me for the time being. I explained the situation to them."

"Okay," replied Susan grimly.

The police had left the scene a short while ago, and the yard was still as a tomb except for the occasional chirping of birds. Susan gazed at the villa one last time, as they drove around the cherub fountain. She felt as if her once lovely home had become a death trap for anyone who stepped into it. Imprisoned within and beyond its walls were two generations of suffering and death. This evil had somehow managed to creep into their lives and the lives of those who they cared about.

"Where are we going?" she asked.

"Well, first of all, we need to get some lunch and then check into a nearby hotel," replied Jason, as they began driving down the road. For a while, neither one of them spoke. "Are you alright, honey?" he asked after a while.

"I don't know what to do," she uttered in sadness and frustration. "Will we ever be able to go back to the house?"

"Not until those evil things are driven out," asserted Jason.

"Maybe we should speak to the woman that Eric brought up. Can we go after lunch? It doesn't hurt to find out what she has to say," she suggested.

"I don't know. Maybe we should just abandon the whole place and put it up for sale," he uttered, pondering.

"Oh no! Please, honey, let's first see if we can somehow get them to leave before making any decisions," entreated Susan. Despite the peril she was facing in the villa, deep down, she still wanted to help Eleanor find her peace somehow. She felt a strange sense of empathy toward her and the suffering she endured.

"Alright. If she can't help us, then I'm going to speak to the realtor," he declared with resolve. Susan agreed. "And what was the name Eric said?"

"Edna."

After having lunch at a restaurant in town, they headed to the closest hotel. It was a small yet cozy place overlooking the surrounding mountains. As they pulled up to the front, a bellman dressed in a red suit walked to the car and offered his assistance. Jason unlocked the trunk for the man. He took the suitcases out and began loading them up to a cart. Another man who was wearing the same attire came out and opened the door for Susan. Then he offered to park the car. Tossing the keys to him, Jason walked inside with his wife. The lobby was warm and quiet. Its light-colored walls issued a welcome feel. Several arm chairs were neatly set on the sides with tables next to them. A few guests were seated, reading what looked like newspapers and magazines. As they neared the front desk, the manager greeted them with a smile. He wore a black suit and bowtie and looked very professional.

"Good afternoon, sir," he said.

"Good afternoon," uttered Jason. "Are you the manager?"

"Yes, sir. How may I help you?" he asked kindly.

"We would like to have a room," replied Jason.

"Of course, sir. And for how long?" he asked taking out his logbook.

"For a week," he replied.

"And your name, sir?"

"Dr. Jason Smith and my wife Susan."

The man marked down the information on his book and turned to the cubby behind him. He pulled out a key and walked back up to the counter. "This is your key and the room number is marked on it. Your room is on the third floor. Is this to your satisfaction?"

"Yes. Thank you very much. Do you want me to pay you in advance?"

"No, sir. When you leave. And would you like meals brought up to the room?" he continued.

"Yes. That would be great!" said Jason.

"Wonderful. So if you climb up the stairs to the third floor your room will be all the way at the end on the left side," he stated. "Or, you can take the elevator on the right," he uttered pointing to it.

"Let's take the stairs," said Susan.

Jason and Susan went up the steps to the third floor as the manager had directed. The narrow hallway was dark. Susan could see the light creeping in from the one small window that stood at the end of the hall. They came up to the room and opened the door. Susan walked in. The room was small and the walls were a light brown shade. A queen-sized bed with green sheets lay at the center with a table and a chair on the side. A wooden closet was on the opposite wall and the restroom door stood next to it. The room had one window. Susan headed toward it and opened the panels. Fresh air came in, and she somberly let out a deep breath. The rugged peaks silently loomed ahead of her and the silence around her goaded her in.

"It'll do for a while," remarked Jason, glancing around in all directions. A moment later, the doorbell rang. Jason opened it to find a bellman standing at the threshold.

"Your luggage, sir," he uttered.

"Yes. Please bring it in," ordered Jason. The bellman walked in and placed the bags on the floor by the bed. Jason handed him a tip and accompanied him out. Susan sat on the bed and appeared to be despondent.

"I can't rest," she said. "My mind is not at peace."

"Alright. Let's go see her," sighed Jason. Susan immediately sprang up and headed toward the door. "Wow! That's what it took to get her going," he uttered to himself, shooting a smile at her.

"What was that?" asked Susan.

"Nothing, dear," he replied.

They came down to the lobby. "My car please," he said to the manager.

"Yes, of course, sir" he obliged and handed the keys to the bellman standing beside him who was immediately on the run.

Jason and Susan walked out. A moment later, the car was brought to the front. The bellman got out, opened the door to

Susan, and graciously moved away. "So did Eric say the east side of town?" he asked.

"Yes. Which way is that?" inquired Susan, perusing the surroundings. "Maybe we should ask someone."

"No, I think I can figure out where east is, honey," remarked Jason as he pulled out of the hotel parking lot. He made a sharp right turn and headed straight. Afternoon traffic was bad. "We have to drive all the way to the end of town, right?" asked Susan.

"That's what he said," replied Jason.

As they drove on, the road became narrower and the traffic subsided. The mountains, however, continued to grace either side, and the terrain was studded with houses here and there. As they approached what seemed to be the outskirts, an old two-story house came into view at the far end.

"That has to be it," said Susan peering at the approaching house. They drove up to it and parked the car by what seemed to be a dirt driveway. There was no other house in sight for what seemed to be miles in all directions. Getting out of the car, Susan and Jason cautiously climbed up the stairs that led to a front porch. The house appeared to be quite old. The white paint in the wood panels was breaking down in every direction, possibly due to years of wear and tear. A chair stood on the side of the porch with several cushions on it. The windows were closed and curtains were drawn in. They stepped up to the door, which was also quite ancient-looking, and knocked. A few moments later, it opened, and an old woman stood at the threshold.

44

"Can I help you?" asked the woman. She was short and thin with long gray hair. Her wrinkled up face, however, was adorned with a gentle smile. She wore a long off white dress.

"We're looking for Edna," replied Susan.

"I'm Edna," she uttered. "What can I do for you?"

"I am Susan Smith, and this is my husband Jason. We need to speak with you. May we come in?"

The woman pondered for a moment and opened the door wider and urged them to enter. "Of course. Where are my manners?" she said. "Come in."

After Susan and Jason walked inside, she closed the door from behind. Susan looked around. The house was dark, except for a couple of lamps that were lit—one was on the large dining table at the far end and the other on the mantle up ahead. A few cushioned chairs stood on the side of what seemed to be the living room. After being in the villa for months, Susan had to get accustomed to a small place such as this.

"From what I'm sensing, you come from a big fancy house. Am I right?" asked the woman. Susan was caught off guard and felt a bit awkward. She didn't know how to respond. "That's alright. I've lived in this house for almost half a century now. It's not much, but it's home," she remarked. "Please, sit down," she urged, pointing to a sofa at the right of the fireplace.

"Thank you," said Susan, moving toward it. Jason followed her. They sat down and looked at Edna. A wooden coffee table stood in front of them. A vase filled with fresh daisies was placed on it.

"Let me get a bit of light in here," she uttered as she walked toward the front window. After pulling the curtains to the sides, she edged toward one of the cushioned chairs, dragged it toward her company, and sat in front of them. "Now, what can I help you with?"

Susan looked at her and smiled. "We have a problem, and we were wondering if you could help us?"

"I will if I can," she replied kindly. "What is the problem?"

"Detective Eric Johnson says that you have some understanding with regards to spiritual matters."

"Some understanding. That's right," concurred Edna.

"Well, our home"—Susan paused for a moment attempting to gather the proper words to express herself—"is haunted by these angry spirits. The situation is so dire that we had to temporarily move out until a resolution is reached," she sighed.

"I see," said Edna. "When you say dire, what are you referring to?"

"They have caused two deaths already, my best friend Zoe and the police officer, Sam, who was on patrol last night. The police have red-tagged the house until further notice."

"Where is this house?" she asked curiously. Her wrinkles were very conspicuous in the lamplight.

"It is up in the mountains. We bought the place a few months ago," responded Susan.

Edna mused for a moment. "Are you referring to the villa that was abandoned for over a century?"

"Yes," said Jason.

"You know, I've never really seen the place, but I've heard some about it. The people in town say it's a beautiful house. But I've also heard of the dark past surrounding it," she added gravely. "But before I move on any further, I feel congratulations are in order."

A bit of surprise flashed across Susan's eyes. "For what?" she asked.

"I see that you're expecting a child. What a great gift!" she exclaimed blissfully.

"Oh, thank you," responded Susan. Jason held her hand. "I had forgotten," she said sullenly.

Edna edged closer to Susan, held her hand, and looked into her eyes. "I sense great turmoil inside you. This, however, is not good for your unborn baby. What parents think and feel affect them and helps shape their lives in the future," she said in her raspy yet gentle voice.

"I know," responded Susan.

"The woman you fear possesses your home in spirit. She has never forgiven the man who caused her so much pain and agony. I sense there is another kin of some kind. This second entity, however, is controlled by one who still lives," she uttered, clutching onto Susan's hand.

"How did you know that?" asked Susan in alarm.

"It's a gift," she replied.

"The person you're referring to is Norton," interjected Jason. Edna glanced at him inquisitively. "He is, or was, the caretaker of the villa," he continued.

"What can we do to save our home?" asked Susan in desperation.

Edna released Susan's hands and lapsed back to her chair. She pondered for a moment and glanced at them. "I cannot make any assumptions yet, and I don't want to without going to the house and getting a feel for what you're up against. I've dealt with my share of spirits during my lifetime. Some just linger and are not out to cause any harm. Others, though, like the ones you've faced, are consumed by rage and anger and therefore are quite potent."

"How?" asked Susan.

"You already know the answer to that. I sense you've learned about her in some manner. She died in a fit of rage and thus has never found her peace," replied Edna.

"Can you come with us to the villa?" asked Susan earnestly.

"Yes. We can go tomorrow morning. My only requirement is that you give me a ride. These old legs are not as strong anymore for all the walking that I have to do. I used to be quite adroit during my younger days. Now, not so much," she added with a smile. "Oh, where are my manners? We've been talking for so long that I forgot to even offer you some refreshments. How about some tea and freshly baked cookies?" she asked.

Susan turned to Jason and shook her head in agreement. "Yes, thank you. That'll be nice," she uttered.

"Wonderful!" said Edna standing up and heading inside.

"What do you think?" asked Susan, looking at Jason.

He stood up and headed toward the window. "If she can help us, that'll be great!" he responded, peering out into the silent and desolate road.

A few minutes later, Edna came with a silver tray. She placed it on the wooden table by the couch. A fancy-looking ceramic teapot, three cups, and saucers lay on it. A small plate with cookies was on the side as well. "Please, help yourself, dears," she urged them.

Susan poured some tea for herself and Jason. Taking a cookie, she smelled it. Instantly, her cravings returned, and she realized how famished she was. Taking a bite, she immediately began to savor it. "This is good!" she remarked.

"My family recipe for oatmeal cookies," responded Edna, sitting down. Jason was also graciously enjoying his share.

"Do you live alone?" asked Susan.

"Yes. Ever since my Charlie died last year, it's just me in this big house," she sighed.

"Do you have any children?" asked Susan boldly.

"Unfortunately, no. I never had any little ones," she responded, pouring herself some tea.

"This is a very quiet area," commented Jason.

"Yes. I love silence. It helps me to think," she said. "How is Eric by the way?"

"Busy with the trouble we're facing," replied Jason.

"He comes here now and then to check up on me," uttered Edna with a fondness. "I've helped the police in some difficult cases. I always tell them to keep an open mind about things. It makes finding answers a whole lot easier. I can predict things, but I may not always be right. One of the lessons that I had to learn in my line of work was to accept my own imperfections. I try my best to help though," she added.

Susan sensed the peace that emanated through her words. "Back to the problem at hand," interjected Susan. "What can we do to get rid of these angry visitors in my home?"

"I wouldn't call it your home yet, dear," she responded. "It's her home. Until she and her kin leave, it will never be a proper place for you to raise your family. The answer to your question, however, is it depends on how potent the spirit is. If it cannot be persuaded to leave, then you're going to have to do what's best for you."

"And what is that?" asked Susan.

"You must leave her territory. There really is no resolution during such a scenario," replied Edna. Susan took a deep breath and stood up. "I'm sorry to disappoint you, but sometimes you just have to leave things be."

The evening was setting in. Susan and Jason got ready to leave Edna's home and thanked her profusely for her pleasant company. "We will come tomorrow morning," assured Jason taking leave.

"Will see you then," responded Edna as she waved goodbye.

Susan got into the car. "Where to now?" she asked, looking at Jason.

"Back to the hotel," he replied turning on the ignition.

45

Detective Johnson came into his office at the downtown police department in the afternoon. He had just left the villa about half an hour ago and stopped over at a sandwich bar to pick up some lunch. As he came in, the two officers who had arrested Norton approached him.

"He's in the interrogation room, sir. The captain is waiting on you," said one of them.

"Thanks," uttered the detective and headed in that direction.

The office was busy. Clerks were at desks answering phone calls. Officers of different ranks were pacing up and down in haste, attempting to get work done. Detective Johnson walked into a narrow hallway where a man in a black suit was standing by a door. He wore his policeman's badge on the side. The man was tall and his belly was sticking out. He had a thick mustache and a friendly face.

"There you are," he uttered seeing the detective. "Had lunch already?"

"Yep," he replied. "So what have we got here?" he asked, looking through the window of the interrogation room. Norton was pacing back and forth as if flustered and perplexed. He was blathering to himself.

"I didn't want to talk to him before you came. He's very peculiar," remarked the captain.

"Don't I know it?" added the detective. "Come on, Captain. Let's take him on together."

The detective opened the door and both men walked in. Norton, though, paced back and forth nonchalantly. The detective glanced at him.

"Sit down, Norton!" he ordered. Norton immediately turned around to look at him. "I said sit down!" he demanded.

Without a fuss, Norton walked to the chair, pulled it out, and sat. He placed his elbows on the table that was in front of him. The captain remained by the door. The detective gazed at him. Norton, however, intentionally looked elsewhere in anger. "You have the right to an attorney," advised the detective.

"I have no need for one," snapped Norton. "Let me go back to my home," he rasped angrily.

"Not until you answer my questions, old man," said the detective. "Did you know that Sam was a great guy? Not only was he a celebrated law officer for the five years that he served with us, but he was also a wonderful and caring individual. Why would you want to harm someone like that?"

Norton immediately looked up at him in vexation. "I didn't harm him!" he declared.

"Then who did?" demanded the detective, placing his hands on the table and staring into his face. Norton began to mumble resentfully.

"Why are you doing this to me?" he asked as he began to brim over with tears.

"Because I need to know the truth!" demanded the detective loudly.

"The master's son did it," snapped Norton.

"Who is the master's son?" asked the detective. He glanced at the captain as well.

"John Mortimer is his name," replied Norton. "Oh, what am I doing? I'm betraying him," uttered Norton to himself in frustration and worry.

"Betraying whom?" demanded the detective. Norton didn't reply. "Answer me!" he bellowed.

Norton shuddered at this and began shaking. He suddenly started to sob. "I'm betraying the master," he quavered in between sobs.

"I will ask you one more time to answer me, or else you'll be charged with murdering a police officer," asserted the detective. "Now who is John Mortimer and what does he have to do with all of this?"

Norton began to break down under the pressure and decided to reply. "He is the son of Arthur, my master."

"You mean to tell me that a dead man killed Sam?" asked the detective while pacing back and forth.

"He isn't dead," shouted Norton.

"That's absurd! There's an article about him, explaining that he was stabbed in the back and murdered decades ago."

"You stupid people!" snapped Norton. "You only know what you can see through your shallow eyes. Even then you'll never figure out the truth," he remarked sarcastically.

"Well, why don't you enlighten me then, old man?" asked the detective in anger. "How is that possible?"

"The master's son is angry. Like his mother, he doesn't approve of visitors. But he won't come until he's called," said Norton with an eerie smile on his face.

"Who called him?" demanded the detective.

"I did. He has to protect his domain," replied Norton nonchalantly. "So I am not technically responsible for the death of your officer. He was an intruder."

The detective took and deep breath and turned toward the captain, who shook his head in discontent. Then he sat in front of Norton and looked deep into his eyes. "Listen, Norton. You're old now. Don't you think it's about time you let go of the Mortimers and found some peace for yourself? How long are you going to be under their influence? Do the right thing for once. It doesn't matter what happened in the past or what you've done for them. Do the right thing now. Please, for your sake. If you speak the truth and help us out, I guarantee you'll get immunity." A pause ensued.

Norton took a deep breath and looked up at the detective. "I don't want immunity. I don't deserve it," he uttered gravely. "What do you want to know?"

"Everything!" replied the detective. "Go back to the beginning and tell me what happened." Norton mused for a moment and sighed. The strict code of loyalty that he upheld for so long seemed to be chipping away under pressure. "I will not give you another chance, Norton!" bellowed the detective when Norton finally caved in.

"Alright! Alright! I'll tell you," he quavered, wiping his tears.

"Go on then," ordered the detective glaring at him.

"Everything that I'm going to tell you right now comes from my father, Norton Abrams the Second. I didn't know my grandfather that well because he had died before I was born. Arthur Mortimer was my grandfather's master. In addition to taking care of the house, he did the master's every bidding. Arthur was a wealthy man. He could have anything he wanted. Although he married Madam Eleanor, he soon grew to regret that decision. I don't know why. It was said he had many mistresses, and Eleanor was angry about that as any sensible wife would be. When Arthur found out that Eleanor was expecting a child, he became furious because he didn't want an heir. He thought it would be a burden to his frolicsome lifestyle. My grandfather said that Arthur abused Eleanor quite frequently. She had to hide from him for fear of her unborn child. Eleanor was very close to the doctor who treated her during her pregnancy. I don't blame her," he sighed. "He delivered both the children, but one of them had already died in her womb. Eleanor never forgave Arthur for that. I was told that Arthur had that poor doctor murdered as well. He wanted to isolate the madam from anyone who loved her. I think, after some time, she realized that her lover was gone. She cradled John, her only surviving son. He was all she had and cherished in this world. Arthur hated the boy though. Later on, my father told me that, in a fit of anger and drunken rage, Arthur killed Eleanor. My grandfather had to raise the child, however, because now he was quite like an orphan.

"Arthur used to beat John mercilessly. The child grew in fear an animosity toward his father. He knew in his heart that his mother's death was Arthur's fault. My grandfather's loyalty to Arthur, however, was stronger than any affection he might have had for John." Norton looked down gravely. The detective placed a glass of water in front of him. Norton took it and began drinking.

"Why didn't they arrest Arthur for Eleanor's murder?" asked the detective.

Norton placed the empty glass down and glanced at him. "If Arthur wanted someone gone, it was done. Nobody around him, neither my grandfather nor any of his other women would ever speak up against him. They were too afraid of what the man was capable of."

"Who killed John?" inquired the captain walking up to the table.

"My father did," signed Norton. "He was a mere boy when he did it."

"Why?" asked the detective.

"Because Arthur demanded that of him. And to prove his loyalty to Arthur, my father stabbed him in the back while he was sleeping in the night."

The detective and captain looked at each other in dismay. "Did your father say this to you?" asked the captain walking up to him.

"Yes," replied Norton somberly.

"Where is he?" asked the captain.

"Dead!" snapped Norton, looking at the two men.

"Why wasn't he arrested for the crime?" continued the detective.

"Because Arthur wouldn't allow it. He bought off the policemen who came to investigate the crime scene. He probably offered them his blood money, and suddenly, the case became cold."

"Is this a fact or are you just speculating, old man?" asked the captain in anger.

"Oh, you would be upset. Wouldn't you?" retorted Norton sarcastically. "After all, these are your predecessors, right?"

"That's enough!" demanded the captain in anger.

"That goes to show that you've all got blood on your hands," insisted Norton, glaring at the captain.

"Alright!" interjected the detective in an appeasing tone. "So how did Zoe Bellamy and Sam Bosworth get in the middle of all of this?"

"Eleanor walks the premises. She's angry. I guess Mrs. Bellamy was in the wrong place at the wrong time. Your officer was an unwelcomed guest. Arthur told me to call on his son to get the work done. So I did. I saw him that night. There was nothing I could have done," he uttered.

"There's always something you can do, Norton," insisted the detective. "It's called the right thing!"

"Tell that to my grandfather and father," snapped Norton, standing up.

"Why do you have to listen to Arthur?" asked the captain. "He's been dead for over a century."

"That's what you think," replied Norton eerily.

"What do you mean?" asked the detective.

"They never leave. It doesn't matter how many centuries have past. He's there, and he talks to me."

"Have you ever thought of making the choice to, now let me put this delicately, not listen?" he shouted.

Norton shuddered. "I don't know. I live under his roof. My father obeyed him, so I have to follow suit," he replied with a flash of regret.

"No, you don't. It is never too late to do what's right," said the detective. "Break the cycle. Do it for yourself and others."

"Who's in the urn?" asked the captain.

"You know the answer to that," replied Norton. "Arthur Mortimer, that villain! My father never put him to rest."

"Well then, we will," resolved the detective. "What can we do to help Dr. and Mrs. Smith?" asked the detective.

"Nothing can be done for them. It is not their home. If they want to save themselves, please tell them to move as far away from that place as possible."

"Alright," said the detective. "I have one last question for you, Norton. Where was your mother in all of this?"

"I never knew her. My father only spoke badly of her and said she was a good-for- nothing tramp. So I was raised by him.

I heard of my grandmother. Bessie was her name. She died shortly after Madam Eleanor's passing," sighed Norton.

"Thank you for being honest with us. I want to keep you here for the night, just in case we need your help for anything else. There is a comfortable bed and some food waiting for you in the cell. You're not a prisoner here, Norton. I assure you. We will release you in the morning. I guarantee that."

Norton did as he was instructed without any resistance. "Nothing is a guarantee," he sighed. As he stepped out of the interrogation room, the detective could see that his facial expression had changed and he was calmer.

"Thank you, Norton," he said, tapping him on his shoulder.

<u>46</u>

It was getting dark. As Jason and Susan came to the hotel, the bellman walked toward them. Jason stopped the car and handed him the keys. They got down and headed inside. The lobby was bright with lights all around. Guests were seated in sofas, talking and relaxing. Jason and Susan approached the front desk and the manager greeted them.

"We would like to retire for the evening," he said politely. "Can dinner be brought up to the room?"

"Yes, sir," replied the manager. "What would you prefer?"

"Today's special," he replied.

"Right away," said the manager.

Susan and Jason took the elevator to the third floor. The hallway was illuminated. They walked all the way to the end and opened the room door. Susan turned the light switch and entered. She closed the window and drew the curtains in.

"I'm tired," said Jason. "I'm going to take a bath and get to bed," he said, removing his shirt. "How're you feeling?"

"Okay, I guess," she replied, sitting on the bed. Jason lifted her bags and placed them next to her. "Here. I don't want you lifting anything."

"Thanks, honey," she uttered and began rummaging for her nightgown.

"Put something out for me too, will you?" requested Jason as he walked into the bathroom.

The moment he did, she quickly dug inside the suitcase, took a journal out, and placed it under her pillow. She then removed her clothes and put on her nightgown and robe. Her baby bump had slightly gotten bigger. "Hello, baby," she uttered rubbing her belly gently. "Mommy's going to feed you now and get to bed, alright?"

The bellman rolled in a table with dinner a short while later. Susan thanked him and saw him off with a little tip. Dinner was steak, potatoes, vegetables, accompanied by chocolate cake as dessert. The steam emanating from the hot food made her mouth water. She, however, faithfully waited for Jason to come out of the bathroom to begin eating. All of a sudden, she could hear Jason's phone ring. Walking hastily toward the bed, she grabbed the phone, opened the mouthpiece, and answered.

"Hello," she uttered. "Mom, is that you?"

"Yes, darling. I've been trying to call you all day. Finally, I had to call Jason. What's going on?" Susan sat on the bed and took a deep breath. "Darling, what's happening? Why didn't you answer me?"

"I'm sorry, Mom, but I must've left my phone in the house," she replied, realizing that she had forgotten it.

"Are you alright?"

"Well, Mom, I'm fine. But we had to leave the house for a while. I think I left my phone there."

"What happened? I'm worried about you. You sound tired," she uttered with concern in her voice.

"It's complicated. The house isn't safe. Until whatever's going on is resolved, Jason and I are staying in a hotel in town." Susan didn't want to get into too much detail about Officer Sam and his death. She knew that her mother would brood over it.

"Honey, tell me what happened. Do you want me to come there?"

"No, Mom. Trust me, I'm fine. The baby's fine too. Jason is with me. You can visit when the house is back in order," she stated.

"Oh. Alright, darling. Don't scare me like that. If something happens, you must tell me. It's not right to worry your mother."

"I know, Mom. I'm sorry. It'll never happen again," she assured.

"Did you have dinner, darling?"

"We were just about to," she replied.

"Alright then. I'll let you go. Make sure you're eating right," she said. "I love you."

"I love you too, Mom. I'll call you later," said Susan.

Her mother hung up the line. Susan placed the phone on the bed and took a deep breath. Jason came out a few minutes later.

"Someone called?" he asked.

"Yes. Mom did. She has been trying to call me. Since I didn't pick up, she was worried and called your number."

"Where's your phone?" he asked, wiping his hair.

"I forgot it in our bedroom."

"No matter. I'm with you for the next few days," he uttered, walking toward the dinner table. "Come on, let's dig in," he said rolling the table toward the bed. Pulling out a chair, he sat in front of her. They both began dinner. "Are you going to call Eric and tell him what happened with Edna?" asked Susan.

"I'm sure he'll call tomorrow. I'm too tired now, honey," he replied, savoring the beef. "This is pretty good for hotel food," he remarked.

"I know. I'm starving," commented Susan, as she too enjoyed the beef.

After dinner was over, they called the front desk to pick up the table. Once everything was taken care of, they got into bed. The events and pressures of the day had taken a toll on both of them. Jason began snoring almost immediately. Reluctant to turn off the lampshade by the bed, Susan sat and pondered. Aware that Jason was sound asleep, she took the journal from under the pillow. She covered herself comfortably with the sheets, sat with her back against the headboard, and flipped the pages. Finding the entry she had last read, she continued.

> *April 24th, 1868*
>
> *I don't have time to write. My precious little John keeps me busy. He is growing so fast. He is the most beautiful baby in the whole wide world, and he brings me so much joy. I don't know what I would do without him. I watch him sleep at night. I keep my bedroom door locked and lie awake most of the night. I'm afraid that if I fall asleep, my baby will disappear. Arthur is not at home. But I fear he would return at any time. I have to hide my baby from him. He's a heartless monster who cares nothing for my precious little John.*
>
> *Bessie has been helping me a lot. She cooks and cleans. I am so grateful to her. John will be coming soon to check on me. I haven't heard from him for a few days now. It is not like him not to drop by for a visit. I'll wait for him patiently. At least I have my precious bundle of joy here to keep me company.*
>
> *May 10th, 1868*
>
> *I haven't heard from John for almost three weeks now. I am so worried. What's happening? Where is he? Have my worst fears come to pass? Has the monster gotten to*

him? Oh, that Norton . . . that evil man! It's all his fault! He must've told the monster about John and me. Where are you, John? I'm dying on the inside. I need you. My baby needs you. Please come.

My precious baby is sleeping on the bed with me. He is so peaceful. I wish I had his peace. He is my only joy. I have to protect him somehow. If it means keeping a knife under my pillow, so be it. I will destroy anyone who comes near him.

Susan placed the journal on her lap and gazed at the wall directly across her. She suspected that Arthur might have harmed John in some manner. As she contemplated, her mind wandered, and she began thinking about the day's happenings and her villa. Her exhaustion took over her shortly. Placing the journal under the bed, she tucked herself inside the covers and fell asleep. She began tossing and turning in the middle of the night. In her dream, she was walking outside in the backyard of the villa. Night had set in. The ocean was still and so was everything around her. Not a single leaf rustled, nor was a single sound heard. As she strolled along, she was suddenly prompted to venture out deep into the property. Although her desire to turn back was overwhelming, some force propelled her legs to walk in the opposite direction. As she continued past the trees and shrubs, it became darker, and fear began to brew inside her. She was telling herself to turn back, but her legs kept moving forward. Suddenly, Eleanor appeared in front of her as if out of thin air. She was dressed in her white gown, her long black hair fell over her shoulders, and her dark eyes glared at her. Eleanor gestured her to follow. Without reserve, Susan conceded and walked behind her. Eleanor was barefooted. Her entire being seemed to be glistening in an eerie fashion. They passed through the brush and continued in the rocky terrain until they approached what looked like a dead end. Susan didn't recall seeing such a place anywhere around the villa. Eleanor, however, stopped at the edge and beckoned her to come closer. Susan obliged and approached her. She glanced at Eleanor, who turned her head and pointed to the edge. Susan looked down and saw that this was a cliff and blackness stretched all around. Before she could turn, she felt and arm pushing her. She screamed, but no sound echoed from her mouth. She could see Eleanor's face, which had an expression of satisfaction.

"Why?" cried Susan. "Why are you doing this? What have I done to you?" she cried out in agony. She could hear Eleanor answering her.

"Because he did this to me. He took my child from me, and he hurt me," she cried and howled in an eerie voice.

"You must let go," Susan shouted as she fell into the vast blackness.

Suddenly she woke up shouting out those words. "You must let go!"

Jason woke up abruptly as well and turned toward her. "What's the matter?" he asked holding her. Susan was sweating profusely.

"It was a terrible nightmare," she gasped. "It felt so real though."

Jason turned toward her and cuddled her in. "It's okay. I'm here," he assured. "Go to sleep now," he said.

Susan was grateful it was only a nightmare. Yet she realized why Eleanor was possessing the villa. She died in a terrible rage, and she had never forgiven Arthur.

<u>47</u>

The phone rang early morning which abruptly woke them both. Jason answered in a groggy voice. It was Detective Johnson. "Sorry to wake you. How did it go with Edna?" he asked.

"We're going to take her over to the villa this morning," replied Jason.

"I would like to meet up with you. Call me when you get there," he requested.

"Sure," agreed Jason. "What happened with Norton?"

"I'll explain in person," he uttered.

Jason hung up the phone and looked at Susan who was wide awake.

"What's going on?" she asked.

"We have to pick Edna up and go to the villa. Eric is going to meet up with us there. He said he's got something to say about Norton."

Susan got up from the bed and went to the shower. "Order some breakfast, will you?" she said going in.

After breakfast, they left the hotel and headed toward the eastern outskirts of town. A thick mist had settled in all directions, and it was difficult to see the road ahead. "It's the marine layer," she remarked. "Whatever it is, it better clear up, or we're going to have a difficult drive up the mountain road."

"Looks like it's not going to clear, honey," uttered Jason, endeavoring to discern the way up the desolate road to Edna's home.

Edna was already waiting for them. She got into the back seat of the car, and they headed back shortly. It was a very cold morning. She wore a long white dress and a thick gray coat.

"Fall gets quite chilly here," she commented. "I haven't seen a thick mist such as this in a while, though." The roads seemed to be deserted as it was an early Saturday morning. When they neared the turn to the villa, the ocean could barely be seen for the mist appeared to engulf it. Jason turned to the road that led up to the villa and began cautiously driving. Susan kept a close eye on the terrain to warn him of any roadblocks or pedestrians, who might be lingering around in the area. They finally came into the driveway and parked the car in front of the cherub fountain. Susan longingly gazed at her home and took a deep breath. She had missed its extravagance. Yet she realized that, unless Eleanor and her son were somehow driven out, the villa would never truly belong to her.

The mist had set in the yard as well. "How beautiful!" exclaimed Edna. "I have never seen anything like this!" she uttered in amazement.

Getting out, Susan asked Edna to follow her. Jason trailed behind the two women. Susan got a hold of the key from her purse and opened the front door. As they entered, Edna's eyes began surveying the elegant surroundings. "This is a lovely place," she commented looking all over. When they came into the living room, Edna began scrutinizing the furniture. "Where did the furniture come from?" she asked curiously.

"We didn't buy anything. All of it came with the house. We believe they belonged to the previous owner," replied Jason.

Edna shook her head in acknowledgment. Then she laid her hand on one of the sofas. Taking a deep breath, she turned toward Susan who stood behind her.

"What is it?" she asked.

"These have so much attached to them," replied Edna.

"What do you mean?" continued Susan seemingly perplexed.

"What I mean is they were once bought with love. They are now tainted. I feel a presence here," she uttered, peering in different directions. She looked up at the chandelier. Turning abruptly toward the dining area, she began walking hastily. Susan gave Jason a quizzical glance and rushed after her. Edna went through the kitchen, as if she was marching on familiar territory. The kitchen was dark and silent. She headed toward the back door and peered outside. "What's that?" she asked, bluntly pointing to the swing.

"That's a swing," replied Susan.

"Can you open this door?" she asked, placing her hand on the doorknob.

"Of course," replied Susan, unlatching it from the top.

The moment the door opened, cold air rushed inside, and she felt an uncanny chill running down her spine. Edna's eyes were focused on the swing however. She walked toward it and stood a few feet away. The police had taped the crime scene. They had marked the profile of Officer Sam's body on the ground. Edna didn't notice this because her attention was directed toward the swing.

"Where did this come from?" she asked gravely.

"It was there when we got here. It belonged to Eleanor. She talks about it in her diary," replied Susan.

Edna gazed at Susan with a sullen expression. "What diary?"

"Well, when we were up in the attic one day, I found a box filled with diaries. They belonged to Eleanor Mortimer. I wanted to know what happened to her, so I began reading them. At first, I was curious, but then it became a search for answers," insisted Susan.

Edna's glance made her feel awkward. "You shouldn't read them," she uttered, directing her gaze back at the swing.

"Why? I didn't think anything wrong with it."

"When you read through her thoughts, you are awakening her. Then she senses your feelings and wields more power over you."

Jason stood behind Susan and placed his arm on her shoulder. "I guess I didn't realize that," she said contritely.

Edna walked closer to the swing and touched it. She suddenly went into a trance and a vision flashed before her eyes. She could see Eleanor seated on the swing.

It was dark around her. She had a grave expression on her face. A moment later, a man appeared behind her and his hands grasped her throat. Taken by surprise, Eleanor struggled violently to free herself from his clutches. The man, however, held on to her throat with an eerie satisfaction. A few moments later, she fell to the ground. The man stood over her lifeless body with an expression of triumphant relief.

Edna began losing balance. Susan immediately held her from one side and Jason on the other.

"Edna!" she cried in fear. "Edna, what's wrong?" Susan looked at her husband in confusion. "Oh my goodness! What's happening to her?"

They moved her away from the swing and walked her to the kitchen. Approaching the table shortly after, they helped Edna sit on a chair. Susan kept calling her.

"Let me get some water," suggested Jason and made haste toward the faucet.

"What's wrong with her?"

"She just fainted."

A few moments later, Edna regained her composure and began glancing around flustered and perplexed. "Where am I?" she asked, shaken up.

"You're in my kitchen," she replied. "What happened? Are you alright?"

Jason handed her a glass of water when his phone rang. Edna took the glass and began drinking. "What happened by the swing?"

"I had a vision," she replied, handing Susan the empty glass.

"I'm going to get Eric," interjected Jason. "He's outside." Susan acknowledged him as he headed toward the front.

"What was this vision?" she asked, getting back to Edna.

"She died there. The woman you spoke of. Someone came behind her and choked her to death, the poor thing," she replied solemnly. "That's why she's still here. Her life was taken away so unjustly and so suddenly," continued Edna.

Susan remained speechless for a bit. "What about the dark figure I saw?"

"What does it look like?" asked Edna.

"It was wearing something similar to a black cloak. Whenever it appears, the chandeliers move, and I feel exhausted and pass out," explained Susan. She walked toward the stove, took the kettle, and began filling it up with water. "Would you like some tea and cookies?" she asked. Edna could sense Susan's uneasiness.

"Yes, thank you. Are you alright, dear?"

"I feel like I'm going to lose my mind with all of this," sighed Susan.

"Just relax, dear," uttered Edna, approaching her. "According to what you told me, the black apparition could be kin. Some of them have a lot more energy than others," she commented.

Susan took some cookies out of the canister and put them on a plate.

"Do you have any pets here?" asked Edna helping herself to a cookie.

"I did. My cat, Penny. She died. I still don't know who stabbed her."

"Did it die here?"

"Yes. Just a few weeks after we moved. It was awful. I found her body in the front yard by the bushes. Somebody had intentionally killed her."

"Cats can sense apparitions and their energy. Maybe someone didn't want your cat in the house and got rid of her on purpose," speculated Edna.

"I know it was Norton," declared Susan. "So what can we do about this?" she asked, looking intently at Edna.

"Well, there's one thing we can try. We need to ask them to leave. If they aren't willing, there's nothing much you can do," she replied.

At that moment, Jason walked into the kitchen with Detective Johnson and another gentleman dressed in black wearing a white collar. Susan immediately recognized the gentleman. He was the pastor of the church where Zoe's funeral was held.

"Good morning, ladies," said the detective. "I'd like you to meet Father Luke Oswald, from the downtown church."

"Good morning," said Susan. Edna looked at them and smiled.

"I asked Father Oswald to come with me. I believe he can be of some assistance to you with regard to the problems at hand. He has an understanding about the matter, so I asked him to shed some light on it for us," Detective Eric uttered. Father Oswald smiled.

"I'm quite flattered, and I hope you don't mind me intruding like this," he remarked respectfully. Susan was glad and quite grateful that this priest who was at her best friend's funeral was here to assist her. Susan noticed that Father Oswald was carrying a bag.

"It's nice to meet you again, Susan," he said, shaking her hand. "I'll try my best to help you and your husband." He acknowledged Edna as well. Father Oswald had a very friendly demeanor and a kind voice.

"Thank you so much," said Susan.

The apprehension and uncertainly she felt began to gradually subside. Knowing that she was surrounded by people who cared about her family and home brought her a bit of comfort.

Jason came up to her and embraced her. "Everything is going to be okay, honey," he assured with a smile.

"May I explore the house a bit?" asked Father Oswald. "I'd like to get a feel and maybe bless your home if you don't mind."

"Of course," said Susan. "Would you like me to come with you?" she asked.

"No, that's not necessary just yet," he responded. "I will begin with the uppermost floor," he suggested.

Jason accompanied him and directed him toward the stairs. He noticed that Father Oswald had a small bottle of water in his hands. After pointing the way, Jason came back to join the others in the kitchen.

The detective gave Edna an embrace. "It's nice to see you again," he uttered.

"Likewise," replied Edna.

"So is there anything they need to know?" he asked.

"I'm working on it. It is a process, as I'm sure you are aware," she said.

"Yes, of course. I'd like to share some news of my own in the meantime. Norton is still in the station. He will be released later today. The captain wanted to detain him for a few more hours because he had some of his own questions for the man. We're wrapping up the case," he said.

"Wrapping up?" asked Susan in astonishment. "But why?"

"Well, he told us the whole story and confessed to certain things. He insisted that he didn't kill Sam. Something else did. I don't know if I believe it myself, but he claims that the spirit of John Mortimer is responsible."

"Is that the kin?" asked Edna.

"Yes, he's Eleanor's son," replied Susan.

"So the case is closed?" asked Jason.

"Yes, as far as the captain tells me," sighed the detective.

"What about Norton? Shouldn't he be punished for his part in the crime?" asked Jason in exasperation.

"There are no grounds to hold him. The evidence suggests no foul play. If it's a matter of a spirit being, then that needs to be dealt with in its own way," insisted the detective.

"Well, are you going to assist us in that?" asked Susan.

"That's why Edna is here and why I brought Father Oswald with me. They're the experts on the topic," remarked the detective, gazing at Edna.

The kettle began to boil. Susan took a few teacups from the cupboard and placed them on the counter. Then putting in tea bags, she grabbed hold of the kettle and poured the hot water in each cup.

"Please help yourselves for some tea," she insisted. "Did Norton say anything about Penny?" she asked, directing her eyes at the detective.

"He admitted to the captain this morning that he was, in fact, the one who killed the cat," replied Eric. "He said he was doing his master's bidding, whatever that means."

Susan immediately became upset and sat down on a chair by the table. "Why would he do such an awful thing?"

"Because he was the conjuror," replied Edna.

"I'm surprised he told you anything. We only got blank stares when we asked him questions," commented Jason in indignation.

"After I told him to do the right thing, he finally cracked under pressure. I think he does feel somewhat responsible," said the detective.

"That man develop a conscience? I doubt it," uttered Jason. He walked up to Susan and placed his hand on her shoulder. "He's done enough to escalate whatever is going on around here, conjuring spirits and worshiping the dead. He's put our lives in danger, especially Susan's. Well, I don't want him in my house anymore. I will have his things put out. Ask him to find a place of his own, Eric."

"Alright. I will tell him," replied the detective, taking a bite of a cookie and sipping on the tea.

"Shouldn't he be punished for killing my cat?" asked Susan in anger.

"You can file charges against the man for that and take it up with the judge," replied the detective.

Susan looked down somberly.

"What do you think, honey? Do you want to do that?" asked Jason.

Susan pondered for a moment. "No," she sighed. "That won't bring Penny back. Just ask him to leave. I don't want to see him again."

48

Father Oswald climbed up the stairs to the fourth floor. As he did, he was praying out loud. The fourth floor was dark and sullen as usual. He opened the bottle of blessed water that he carried in hand and began shedding drops on the ground and the walls. The attic room door was open halfway. Its lose hinges somehow held the door in place however. Creeping through the opening, he took some water and shed it in the vicinity. Unwilling to go all the way in, Father Oswald headed out and began climbing down the stairs to the third floor. He walked into Norton's room, surveyed the interior, and began reciting prayers. After disseminating drops of blessed water, he came out. He did the same with the other rooms on that floor. When he came to the second floor, he was instinctively drawn to Susan and Jason's bedroom. As he entered, the chandelier immediately captured his attention. Walking toward it, he began scrutinizing it. A queer feeling took over him, as he continued to recite prayers. It suddenly began to oscillate back and forth. Startled, he took a step back and looked around the room to determine what was causing it. The windows were closed and no draft was entering. The moment he looked up again, the chandelier fell on the bed with such force that the impact caused some of the bulbs to break into pieces and fly in different directions. Father Oswald fell to the ground and hit his head on the nearby vanity table. The bottle escaped his hand, dashed to the ground, and broke into a hundred pieces. The water spilled everywhere.

A few moments later, Jason, Eric, Susan, and Edna came racing up to the bedroom.

Susan let out a shrill cry. "Oh, my goodness! Father Oswald!"

The chandelier lay at the center of the bed. Bulbs and pieces of glass were all over the ground. Some had pierced the walls. Susan and the others were dumbfounded.

"What happened?" asked Jason in disbelief. He rushed toward Father Oswald and held him. "Father Oswald! Can you hear me? Are you alright?" he uttered in panic.

Father Oswald moved and looked up. "Yes, I think so," he said, holding onto his head.

"You're bleeding," observed Susan.

The room was in disarray with pieces of broken glass all over the ground. Susan carefully opened her closet, got a hold of a towel, and placed it on his forehead where there seemed to be a minor gash. The detective surveyed the room.

"What happened, Father?" he asked.

Jason and Susan helped him stand up. "I was praying over the room, and the next thing I know, that fell," he responded, pointing to the chandelier that was on the bed.

"Shall I call the ambulance?" asked the detective.

"No, I think I'm fine," he replied, holding the towel on his forehead.

"Come down," urged Susan. "I'll put some ice on that."

Edna held onto Father Oswald from one side and Susan from the other. Jason and the detective remained behind. Detective Johnson walked up to the bed and gazed up toward the ceiling. A rather large hole was visible and cracks could be seen around it. He was perplexed.

"What do you think happened?" he asked surveying the damage.

"At this point, anything is possible," uttered Jason. "This is going to cost me a pretty penny to fix!" he sighed.

"It's getting too dangerous," uttered the detective. "Maybe we should red tag the house indefinitely."

"Can I put it up for sale?" asked Jason in frustration.

"Nobody will buy it, considering all that's happened."

"Then I'm at a total loss. I bought this place for Susan, to make her happy. But the whole thing has turned out to be a disaster. If the problem can't be resolved, then we're going to have to move permanently and begin fresh somewhere else," he said. "I've lost all the money I've invested in this place," he sighed, pacing toward the cracked window. "I will decide on this tonight," he declared, walking out of the room.

49

Susan and Edna walked Father Oswald to the living room. He sat on the couch and rested his head. "I'll get you some ice," said Susan hastily, walking toward the kitchen. Edna sat by him.

"This is more complicated than I thought. But there is no impossible case for the Lord," commented Father Oswald, as he gazed at Edna.

"That is absolutely correct," assured Edna. "Is there anything that I can get you?" she asked in a kind voice.

"No. I'll wait for the ice," he uttered. "But I would like to ask you something. I sense that you've got some knowledge about spiritual matters. Are you ready for what's next?" he asked gravely.

"Yes, Father. I'm ready. Whatever it takes to free this house, I'm on board with you," she assured.

Susan opened the refrigerator and grabbed an ice pack. Resignation and despair took over, as she pondered on the somber circumstances that surrounded her. Just then, Edna walked in. Susan turned toward her and took a deep breath.

"Will I ever be able to get back to my home?" she asked grimly.

"Only if they are driven out. Otherwise, you cannot call this your home," she replied.

"How do we do that?"

"We have to communicate with them and demand that they leave. As spirit beings, we too have authority in this domain," replied Edna.

"So how do we get started?" inquired Susan.

She loved the villa and yearned to live in peace and raise her family. The conversations that she and Jason had about filling up the rooms with the laughter of children slithered into her mind.

"I see. You're contemplating about the past," commented Edna.

"You seem to know me so well," responded Susan, as her eyes began to flood with tears. "Oh, I'm so foolish," she uttered.

"Why do you say that, dear?"

"It's just that I was so certain I could help Eleanor. I empathized with her and felt sorry for what she went through in this house."

"It's noble to feel for others. Sometimes though, our good intentions may not be received as such. Eleanor did not have the opportunity to forgive the person or persons who hurt her so badly. It is a terrible thing for one to go through such suffering at the hands of another. No one deserves that," added Edna.

"How do you know so much about her?" asked Susan perplexed. "I had to read her journals to find that out."

"I can sense her spirit and the anger that's in the house. It's been passed down from one generation to the next. That's what makes it so potent. But we will do what we have to on our part to drive out the past from this house," asserted Edna.

A moment later, Father Oswald came into the kitchen, still holding the towel onto his head. "I thought I was going to get some ice," he commented.

"Oh, I'm so sorry!" uttered Susan, as she handed him the icepack.

Jason and the detective came into the kitchen as well. "Father Oswald, are you certain I can't take you to the hospital?" asked the detective.

"I'm most certain, Eric," he assured. "Besides, we have much more important things to do here."

Edna turned toward her company. "If we work together, we have a stronger standing against them."

"Alright, what do you want us to do?" asked Susan with renewed resolve.

"I need everyone together. We can use the dining room," she uttered, shooting a gaze in that direction. "Father, are you ready?"

Father Oswald glanced at Edna and shook his head in compliance. He walked toward the kitchen table, opened his bag, and took out a rather large crucifix, and headed toward the dining room area.

Although it was a bit past noon, the morning's gloom hadn't subsided, and the house was dark. An eerie wind had taken shape and the trees swayed back and forth outside. Jason hastily closed the kitchen door shut and headed toward the dining room where the others were gathering. Susan switched the chandelier on, and the room became bright. Edna had asked her to light a candle and place it on the table. According to Edna's instructions, all congregated around the candle and sat comfortably. Father Oswald sat next to her and placed the crucifix on the table. The small gash on the side of his head was visible but had stopped bleeding. Edna asked that everyone hold hands. Susan closed her eyes and took a few deep breaths. She clasped Jason's hand.

"Keep your eyes closed and hold on to your peace no matter what happens around you," said Edna in an assertive voice. "We command Eleanor Mortimer and her kin to leave this house immediately!" ordered Edna in a commanding tone of voice.

The others joined in with her. They could also hear Father Oswald on the background, rebuking the spirit of Eleanor in the name of Jesus Christ. As they continued, the chandelier began to sway back and forth. Susan and the others could hear this, yet they joined in the rebuking.

"We command Eleanor to leave this home in the name of Jesus Christ!" shouted Susan authoritatively.

Suddenly, the candle flame went out, as if blown out by some unknown presence. A raucous sound was heard all around and objects were being lifted and thrown around in the background. The kitchen door flung open and a strong gust of wind entered the house. Susan grew increasingly apprehensive, yet she was resolved to hold her ground. She could hear everyone's chiding and rebuking above the cacophony. Instantly there was a queer silence, and she felt as if she was being levitated. Feeling an intense curiosity, she slowly opened her eyes. To her horror, Eleanor Mortimer stood at the center of the circle. She was above the table, seemingly adrift, her ghostly presence as clear as day. Her hair was as black as night, and her face emanated the anger and hatred that had been inside her for over a century. She glared at Edna in a rage of anger, and Susan could see that Edna was looking at the ghost and rebuking her. Father Oswald stood up, and he held the crucifix in front of him. He was glaring at the ghost and vehemently commanding it to leave. Eleanor opened her mouth, as if preparing to speak, yet suddenly, her head began to oscillate back and forth violently in different directions.

Edna fell to the ground and began convulsing. Susan was mortified, yet something inside her urged her to hold her ground and continue rebuking Eleanor. At that very instant, Eleanor's head stopped oscillating and turned toward her. Susan felt a cold and immobilizing chill rush through her body. She had never felt such an agonizing sensation, as if her very most being was halted. Yet she continued to look directly at Eleanor's eyes and demanded her to leave.

"Leave this house now! I command you in the name of Jesus Christ!"

At that instant, her ghostly presence vanished, as if devoured by the very air that surrounded it. Jason and detective Eric both opened their eyes and looked around. Seeing Edna convulsing, they rushed toward her. Susan was in shock and was uncertain as to what had just occurred. Father Oswald was still holding onto the crucifix.

"Is she gone?" asked Susan, looking at him.

"Yes, she has been driven out of here," he replied, taking a deep breath of relief.

"Edna!" cried Susan making haste toward her. Jason and Eric were attempting to hold onto her. "She's having seizures," uttered Jason. He got his phone out and began dialing the police and called for an ambulance.

"Edna! Can you hear me?" called Susan.

Edna, however, continued to convulse. There was nothing much they could do until she was taken to a hospital.

The ambulance and several police cars arrived a short while later. The paramedics came into the villa and took Edna on a stretcher to the hospital. Susan could see the flashing lights of the ambulance as it left the premises.

"Is she going to be alright?" she asked.

"I hope so," replied the detective. "Don't worry. I'm going to keep an eye on her."

"She doesn't have any family, does she?" inquired Susan in grave concern.

"No. We're her family," he replied.

"What now?" she asked him.

"I'm not sure. I guess we wait and see. I still advise the two of you to stay away from here for some time until Father Oswald gives the green light on the matter. I'm not entirely certain as to what happened back there."

Susan walked into the house. Father Oswald was still reciting prayers in the dining room. She headed toward the kitchen to find everything in disarray. Pots and pans were on the floor, plates were broken, and chairs askew. There were dust and dirt on the floor as well. The back door was ajar. She immediately closed it shut. Jason came up to her.

"What happened in here?" he asked in disbelief.

"I'm not sure, but I think she's gone," she uttered. "Let's see what Father Oswald has to say."

At that very moment, he entered the kitchen and approached them. "I have to pray over the house again," he uttered. "But I can tell you with certainty that the ghost isn't here anymore."

"How do you know for certain?" asked Jason.

"It's a matter of faith," assured Father Oswald. "I will come again tomorrow to further cleanse the house with prayer. I must go now," he said.

"I can drive you, Padre," said the detective.

"Thank you," uttered Father Oswald, as he surveyed the mess that was in the kitchen.

"Lock up the house for now. I will come tomorrow," assured Eric, gazing at Susan and Jason.

After the detective and Father Oswald left, Susan and Jason locked up the villa as advised. They got into the car and went around the cherub fountain. Susan shot a glance at her beautiful villa. She knew in her heart that Eleanor was gone.

"There's one thing left to do," she commented.

"What?" asked Jason.

"We need to get rid of everything in there. There's too much history attached to it," she said with renewed optimism. Jason took a deep breath.

"Refurnishing the house will take a while," he uttered.

"That's fine," she responded, as they drove out of the yard.

50

As evening set in, Norton came out of the downtown police station. The captain had just finished his interrogation into Sam's death and the strange events of the previous day. Norton had provided a detailed account of what had occurred and his role in all of it. As a result of his compliance and assistance, the police had pardoned him and sent him home. Norton had no means of transportation. He, therefore, walked to the closest bus station and stood there for a while until the next bus arrived. Getting in, he dropped a few coins into the coin drop by the driver, walked all the way back along the center aisle, and sat down. The bus was almost empty except for a couple of passengers. He gazed outside from the window as if in a daze. Many thoughts plagued him. He was relieved that the truth had finally come out and he dared to speak up.

When the bus came close to the turn leading to the villa, he stood up and rang the bell. The driver stopped, and he got down. Then he began walking up to the villa. As he trudged along the lonely mountainous road, he mused on his life. He wasn't particularly proud of the legacy that his father had passed onto him. The lies and deception had only led to the demise of the Mortimer family and also resulted in the suffering of those who had unknowingly come to own the villa. He suddenly began to feel a strong sense of guilt, as if he too were culpable for that suffering.

I don't want to do this anymore he thought. Conjuring evil had not brought him any satisfaction or peace. Holding onto the secrets and the evil of the Mortimer family was the only life he had known for so many years, and he desired to be rid of that.

Norton finally approached the villa. He walked down the driveway and stood by the cherub fountain. It remained as elegant as ever with water gushing out from the top. The garden was quiet except for the occasional rustling of leaves in the gentle breeze. He looked up at his former home. The villa seemed to glare at him in anger, as if it knew of his betrayal. Norton scowled back defensively. He felt as if Arthur Mortimer himself was grimacing through the walls and windows.

"Why did you do it?" came the question. It was as if the very air that swept by him was calling out for vengeance.

"I had to," he cried out. "I will not be a pawn for you anymore!" he asserted angrily, staring at the villa. "No! No! I have a way out! I don't have to do your bidding anymore! I owe you nothing!" he shouted, pacing back and forth on the driveway. "I will be rid of you!" he shouted.

"No!" came the voice. "You will never be rid of me! Your father was my servant, and so are you!" it cried.

Norton paced to and fro, covering his ears as if endeavoring to block the voice he heard. "We shall see!" snapped Norton in anger.

He took the keys out from his pocket, made haste toward the front door and opened it. Entering the house, all he felt was torment and desolation, as if the whole house was about to devour him. He cried out, rebuking what he felt on the inside.

"You traitor!" came a voice from around him. "You betrayed me!" it went on in anger.

"Yes, I did, and I shall do it again!" he snapped.

"You will never be rid of me!" it went on. "I am Arthur Mortimer!"

Norton immediately headed toward the kitchen. "I will show you!" he shouted. "I will show you!"

As he walked in, he noticed the chairs, pots, and pans in disarray. Ignoring that, he went toward the sink, took a couple of gallons of kerosene from underneath and some matches from the counter drawer. Then he began pouring the gasoline all over the ground. He continued pouring on to the living room and all the way to the front. Throwing the gallons outside, he took a deep breath. Then he lit the matches and threw them onto the gasoline trail. It immediately caught on fire.

"I will be rid of you, now!" he shouted.

Norton headed toward the edge of the backyard where the ocean came into clear view. He could feel the sea breeze getting stronger. Beachgoers were out and about, some resting in the sand, and some swimming out in the deep waters. Several boats could also be seen on the horizon. Norton gazed at them and desired to be in one of them. He knew deep down that this was the only way he could be free.

51

Susan and Jason had just finished dinner. They were resting in their room in the hotel. Susan went up to the window and gazed at the mountains outside. It was getting dark.

"Should we call Eric and find out if he has heard anything about Edna?" she asked, turning toward her husband, who was stretched out on the bed.

"Alright," he said, taking the phone and dialing the number.

A moment later the detective answered. "What?" uttered Jason sitting up on the bed. "Oh goodness gracious! Alright. We'll be right there," he responded and hung up.

"What's going on?" cried Susan with a perplexed expression on her face.

"We've got to go! The villa is on fire!" he blurted out, putting on his coat.

"What?" cried Susan in alarm. She grabbed her jacket and purse.

They made haste to the lobby and requested that the car be brought up to the front immediately. Jason dialed the detective's number again. He wouldn't answer. The moment they saw the car, they made haste to it, pulled out of the hotel entrance, and headed toward the villa.

When they arrived, they could see a fire brigade parked outside the driveway. Susan got out of the car in disbelief. The villa was being consumed by gigantic flames.

"Oh no! Oh my goodness! What?" she cried looking all around.

Jason approached her and held onto her tightly. Several firefighters were already out front, hosing down the flames.

"How did this happen?" she asked, as tears began to roll down her cheeks. The beautiful rose bushes that once adorned the front were now being eaten up by the flames. She turned toward Jason and began sobbing. Jason embraced her tightly.

"It's alright, darling. It's alright," he uttered.

He could see the detective in the distance. Two police officers were holding onto a man. As Jason peered closely, he saw that it was Norton. Detective Eric approached them.

"Eric!" exclaimed Jason. "What happened? Who did this?" he asked.

"Here's your culprit," he uttered, pointing to Norton, who had been handcuffed and was being held onto by two police officers on either side. Norton looked tired and dirty. Susan glared at him in anger.

"You burned my house down?" she shouted. Norton didn't reply. He gave her a blank stare. "Great!" she uttered, taking offense by his apathy and silence. "Why, Norton? Why did you do this?" she cried.

Norton looked at her and answered. "That's the only way."

"The only way for what?" asked Jason.

"The only way to get rid of him," he replied. "He will never let go of me. I've had enough!"

"Who are you talking about, man?" demanded Jason in frustration.

"Arthur!" snapped Norton. "I had to do it."

Susan turned toward Jason and began sobbing again. The detective ordered the policemen to take Norton to the station. He turned toward Jason and Susan.

"I'm sorry for your loss," he uttered gravely.

"How did you come to know?" asked Jason.

"We received several calls from people who were at the beach. Apparently, they saw the flames from down there," he replied. "They will put out the fire," he sighed, looking at the firefighters, who were spraying mountains of water onto the flames. "I'll give you a report later. Take your wife away from here," he said.

Jason took a deep breath, took one final look at the villa, and walked Susan over to the car. Susan was distraught and couldn't bear to look at her once beautiful home.

52

It had been a month since the fire. Susan and Jason had temporarily moved to an apartment home. Although the traumatic experiences of the past few months had taken an emotional toll on her, the baby was growing healthily inside her. She had also been going to the doctor regularly. Jason stood by her. Susan's mother was also due for a visit the following week.

Edna had recovered and was back at home. Susan went to see her and speak with her over tea. The loss of her home was a hard blow.

"I still don't understand why he did what he did," uttered Susan as they sat on the porch.

The weather was calm and appeasing, and the mountains loomed around them like silent spectators. Edna mused on the question for a bit. She then took a deep breath and replied, "I don't know the answer to that. Maybe he thought that was his only way out. Sometimes, letting go of the past means a complete purge, even of the things that linger on as reminders. Unfortunately, the house was his reminder."

Susan heaved a deep sigh. "I loved that house," she uttered somberly, gazing up at the mountains.

Edna looked at Susan. Her eyes studied her downcast expression. "How is the baby doing?"

"Fine, considering all I've been through. We just found out that it's a boy," she uttered with a smile.

"Congratulations!" said Edna. "That's wonderful news!" she said as a spark of joy flashed across her face. "How is Jason?"

"He's well. The hospital called him yesterday. He had to perform two surgeries back to back," uttered Susan. "I don't know how he's doing all of it."

"Our loved ones give us the strength we need to move on during hard times. He's looking forward to his growing family, so he has to put the past behind. You must too, dear," advised Edna. "Sometimes being with our loved ones is the only home we need whether it be a castle or the smallest hut."

Susan sipped on her tea and glanced at Edna. "I think I realize what you're trying to tell me," she admitted.

"I've lived in this home ever since I married my Charlie. He built it for me almost half a century ago with his own bare hands. Yes, it looks battered and beat up. But I wouldn't change one scratch on it because it reminds me of the many years of love we shared. And that's what makes this my home," declared Edna gently. "Home is in the heart, dear."

Susan left Edna's house shortly after tea. She took comfort in Edna's words as she drove. On her way home, she pulled up to the parking lot overlooking the beach. The midday sun was warm and soothing. Beachgoers were out and about, enjoying the breeze and surging waves. Taking a deep breath, she opened the front locker and took out the two journals that she had stealthily kept all this time. Then getting out of the car, she carefully trudged down the embankment to the sandy beach. She took off her shoes and put them inside her purse. The sand was warm on her toes, and a feeling of joy suddenly crept into her spirit. The laughter of children could be heard in the vicinity. The idea of her having a child soon thrilled her. She began stepping on the waves. The water was cold. She went further and further until the ocean water reached up to her waist. Gazing into the horizon, she took a deep breath.

Yes, I am blessed she said to herself. Then she threw the two journals out to the water. They floated for a moment. But the waves swallowed them shortly after, and they disappeared from her sight.

53

Detective Johnson pulled up to the parking lot of the town nursing home. It was a small yet elegant building surrounded by a grassy area. The mountains loomed behind it. As he walked along the front yard, he could see the elderly who were boarded there. Some were strolling on the grass while others roamed around in wheelchairs. One of the men recognized him right away and hurriedly approached him. He was a gaunt old man with hair as white as snow.

"Hello, Detective!" he shouted with a smile on his very wrinkled face.

"Hello, Mr. Adams, how are you doing today?"

"Oh, fine, fine. Say, if you meet up with my son, can you tell him to come and see me?" asked the man in a bit of a stuttering voice.

"Of course, Mr. Adams. I will track him down myself and tell him that," he assured.

"Say, can I help you with anything? I know this place like the back of my hands," uttered the man with a sense of pride.

"Yes, now that you mentioned it, I do need your help. Can you tell me if you've seen Norton? I brought him here a few weeks ago," said the detective, surveying the area.

Suddenly, the man's countenance changed and he became somber. "Oh, the grouch!" he snapped. "I've seen him around here. He's a loner. Doesn't even want to say hello to me. I mean, what kind of a person doesn't even want to give another a warm greeting in the morning?" he asked in exasperation.

The detective shot a smile at him. "If you can tell me where I can find him, I promise to tell him to say hello to you the next time he sees you," said the detective.

"Oh, alright," retorted the man. "He likes to hang out alone in the yard out back. You'll probably find him there," he said, pointing to the back of the building.

"Thank you so much, Mr. Adams. I owe you one," said the detective and headed in that direction.

As he approached the back, he could see tables and chairs neatly scattered on the grass. A couple of ladies were at one table, enjoying tea and pleasantries. At the far end of the yard, he saw Norton seated on a chair, looking vacantly at the mountains. The detective greeted the ladies and proceeded toward Norton.

"Hello, Norton," he said, walking up to him.

Norton turned around and looked at him. "What do you want?" he snapped nonchalantly and turned his gaze back to the mountains.

"Well, I just dropped by to see how you were doing," he replied. "The judge has ruled that you remain here until further notice. He decided that you weren't in your proper mind when you set the villa ablaze."

"Whatever!" uttered Norton, still staring at the mountains. "I know why I did it."

"Mr. Adams over there tells me that you aren't speaking to him," added the detective.

It's nobody's affair who I talk to and who I don't talk to," he snapped.

"Alright," sighed the detective. "As I said, I just dropped by to see how you were doing." Norton was silent. "Take care, Norton," he said and left.

Norton kept his eyes fixed on the mountain peaks. In his silence, he kept rebuking the feelings of guilt that still haunted him. *It isn't my fault*, he said to himself. *They made me do those things*, he uttered repeatedly as he began pacing back and forth.

CPSIA information can be obtained
at www.ICGtesting.com
Printed in the USA
BVHW031702020320
573844BV00001B/30